THE GROOM
WENT MISSING

An Agent Victoria Heslin Thriller
Book 5

JENIFER RUFF

COPYRIGHT

THE GROOM WENT MISSING

An Agent Victoria Heslin Thriller, Book 5

JENIFER RUFF

Copyright © 2022 Greyt Companion Press
ISBN ebook: 978-1-954447-18-9
ISBN paperback: 978-1-954447-17-2
ISBN hardback: 978-1-954447-19-6

Written by Jenifer Ruff
Cover design by Rainier Book Design
All the characters in this book are fictional. Any resemblance to actual people living or dead is a coincidence.

Visit the author's website for more information. www.Jenruff.com

THE GROOM WENT MISSING is the fifth book in a series of standalone mystery thrillers featuring FBI Agent Victoria Heslin. You can find a list of those books and others by Jenifer Ruff at the end of this novel.

PART 1

CHAPTER 1

With the motor idling, Richard Luna sat in darkness behind the wheel of his Tahoe, monitoring the warehouse doors, alert for any sign of trouble. His fingers tapped the small cooler beside him. A pint of double chocolate gelato melted inside it.

Richard knew this area well. It depressed him. He'd grown up on these streets. Back then, he didn't recognize it for the dump it was, and now it was worse. Crime had increased, drug deals in particular, bringing down the property values and driving out anyone who could afford to move. Dilapidated homes, shuttered stores, and abandoned warehouses riddled the area. A failure. Sort of like his acting career, which hadn't taken off the way he expected. Why did so many of his thoughts always come back to that? He made more money now than he'd ever imagined—easy money—but the sting of having failed left a permanent bruise on his ego.

His mother's words echoed in his mind. "You can always get a new agent and get back to auditioning." Little did she know it couldn't happen now. What started as a small gig here and there to pay the rent had blossomed into a career where loyalty trumped all, and no one quit. Ever. Not by choice. The waste of his looks and talent might disappoint his mother; she couldn't brag about her son being on television, but she could certainly appreciate the Celtics tickets he'd bought to take her and his nephew to tomorrow's game. Best seats in the house. Movie star seats.

Luna rubbed the hard piece of skin protruding from his cuticle and noted the time on his dashboard. Five minutes had passed. Marco and Tommy had to drop off their bags, make the exchange, and get in and out within ten minutes. Any longer, and Luna would have to check on them.

Two more minutes passed. A paranoid feeling crept up on him. A gut reaction that something wasn't right. Not a sixth sense. Rather, years of experience subconsciously telling him if a deal was going well or not; if he merely needed to watch his back or draw his gun. He'd never trusted the Ritz Brothers and something about this drop seemed off. He wouldn't put it past them to attempt a renegotiation of their cut again. They didn't comprehend their relative smallness in the grand scheme of things. They were insignificant and replaceable, and getting too big for their britches, as his great grandmother used to say whenever Luna or one of his siblings had an opinion on anything.

Shots rang out, startling Luna and echoing through the dead neighborhood. Luna drew his gun and opened the passenger window. The warehouse door flung open. Tommy burst out and zigzagged toward the Tahoe, firing over his shoulder. Blood seeped through his shirt, spreading in a dark stain around his shoulder. He yanked the front door open and lunged inside. "Go, go!"

Despite Tommy's command, Luna didn't depress the gas pedal. He steadied his weapon and watched the door, waiting for Marco. "What happened?"

"They just wrote their death sentence. That's what," Tommy shouted, slumping against the seat. "Go!"

"What about Marco?"

2

"He's not coming. They got him. Go! Go!" Tommy gritted his teeth and snarled.

"Are you sure?" Luna asked. "I'm not leaving him unless you're sure."

"He took two or three rounds." Tommy shuddered, his face racked with pain. "No way he made it. What are you waiting for?!"

The warehouse door burst open again. Luna held his fire long enough to see Marco stagger out and lurch toward the SUV. Each heavy step left a thick trail of blood on the ground.

Luna trained his weapon at the warehouse. Now that Tommy and Marco were out, Luna wouldn't hesitate to shoot if the door opened once more.

Marco collapsed against the outside of the car with a solid thud, splattering blood across the back window.

"Get in!" Tommy shouted.

Marco kept himself upright, managed to get the door open, and fell into the back of the vehicle. "I got him," he mumbled. His eyes fluttered closed, and he groaned. His gun dropped from his hand and his body went limp on the seat.

"Hang in there, Marco. We'll get you help." Luna turned away from the dark blood pooling over his upgraded black leather and sliding to the all-weather floor mats below. His blood, his skin, every fiber in his body seethed with anger as he peeled away from the warehouse. If the Ritz brothers weren't already dead, they would be soon. No one crossed Salazar's organization and survived.

CHAPTER 2

FBI Agent Victoria Heslin smiled up at her boyfriend. The suit he wore for his friend's wedding rehearsal fit his triathlon-toned body perfectly, making him irresistibly handsome. Ned was near impossible not to like. He possessed a quiet strength and a steady determination in all he did—from healing hurt puppies to completing triathlons. For someone like Victoria, who adored animals and preferred them to most people, the sweet veterinarian was an ideal catch. What more could she ask for?

Ned's blue eyes met her own before he started his speech. "Good evening, everyone. It's great to see familiar faces, and it's amazing how far our friends will travel for free cocktails." He grinned. "I'd like to say a few words about this special couple. For those who don't know me, I'm Ned Patterson, one of Scott's best friends. He's like a brother to me and I'm honored to be his best man. Scott and I met freshman year at Cornell, roomed together for two more years, and stayed close ever since. During that time, I got to know him well. He is one of the kindest, most selfless, and most focused men I know. If I ever need my appendix removed in a hurry, there is no one I trust more than Scott. He's always made good decisions. Like passing up Alpha Delta Phi's biggest party because he had a big physics test the next morning. You have to admire those choices. Though we still say you missed out, Buddy."

Victoria laughed, enjoying Ned's delivery.

"Scott didn't date much in college. He was too busy getting nearly perfect grades, keeping in shape, volunteering his time at the homeless shelter, and impressing everyone on campus by being an all-around good guy. To be honest, we all thought he would be the last one of us to settle down and get married. But when he met Bailey, he knew. Now, I'm not going to be humble here, I am hugely to thank for their good fortune. I convinced Scott to take a break from his med school studies and visit me. We were on the greenway when he first saw Bailey. She was in nursing school at the time. We'd just finished a long run and were dripping with sweat. We probably smelled, in fact, I know we did, but Scott said, 'I have to meet that woman.' And then he made the best decision of his life by summoning the courage to introduce himself. Messy hair and sweat circles be damned. Scott and Bailey discovered they were both from outside Boston, and thanks to their mutual interests in running and saving lives, they hit it off immediately."

The twinkle of mischief disappeared, and Ned's expression grew serious.

"To Bailey—thank you for making Scott an even better person than he already was, which is no small feat. The love and trust between the two of you is enough to inspire us all. So, let's raise our glasses to Scott and Bailey. May you continue to make wonderful memories together, finding joy in your before-sunrise runs, your marathon hospital shifts, and so much more. Thank you for letting us be part of your special day."

Ned lowered his pretend glass and leaned back against the hotel room's dresser. "What do you think?"

"It's perfect." Victoria clasped her hands under her chin. "I can't wait to meet Scott and Bailey."

"You're going to love them," Ned said. "And they're going to love you. Scott's entire family is great." Ned turned to the mirror and grabbed a tie from the dresser. He wrapped it around his neck and secured a knot. "You know, Scott's a lot like you. He's introverted. Also focused. Determined. Smart."

5

"You can keep going with that list. You were just starting to get to the good stuff." Moving to his side, Victoria smiled at their reflections. She wore a simple, sleeveless navy-blue sheath dress that accentuated her slim figure. She'd straightened her shoulder-length blonde hair, and now she tucked it behind one ear.

Ned beamed at her. "You look gorgeous."

"Thank you. You're looking pretty good yourself. We look a lot better than we did a few months ago."

Ned had a few scars on his face and in some places, his skin wasn't as smooth as it once had been, but most of the frostbite damage had healed nicely.

Victoria held up her hands, displaying her three missing fingertips, a constant reminder of their plane crash in Greenland and the people who hadn't survived. "We're lucky."

"Very lucky." Ned turned and gathered her in his arms. They shared a deep kiss that confirmed Victoria's hopes for a romantic and relaxing weekend and made her wish they didn't have to leave the room just then.

Slightly breathless when they separated, they gazed into each other's eyes, and Victoria felt a little weak in the knees.

"Ready to meet everyone?"

"Ready as I'll ever be." Victoria picked up her purse, heavy from the gun she always carried.

Ned's phone rang. He glanced at the screen and accepted the call. "Getting nervous, Big Red?" he asked, holding his phone against his ear, listening to whatever Scott was saying as Victoria grabbed her winter coat and gloves.

"Yeah. I'll remind you. Don't worry," Ned said, opening the door. He gestured into the hallway for Victoria to go first.

As they walked down the hotel's brightly lit corridor, with Ned's hand on the small of her back, Victoria thought about his speech. She would love to have a relationship like the one he described. No doubts. No reluctance. Wholeheartedly moving forward together. Maybe this weekend would bring her and Ned to that point. What better opportunity for romance than a weekend with a beautiful wedding, a luxurious hotel, and an interesting city to explore?

Ned finished the call and slid his phone into his coat pocket. "Scott is on his way from his condo. After the rehearsal we're coming back to the hotel for the dinner. Most people from the wedding party are staying here for the weekend, including Scott's family."

They were almost at one end of the hall near the elevator when a tall, blonde woman in her late twenties or early thirties exited a room. She carried a sweater bunched in one hand. Her shirt was inside out. A tag popped up from the tiny stitching running down the side. Tears glistened in the woman's eyes. Her face flushed with color as she briefly met Victoria's gaze. Just as quick, she looked away and hurried past them, continuing down the corridor.

Victoria turned to watch the woman disappear around the corner. No one ever knew what was going on in others' lives, the pain and secrets they kept hidden. Cases from Victoria's past came to mind. Domestic assault. Forced prostitution. "I hope she's okay," Victoria whispered.

"You're on vacation," Ned said, pressing the down arrow on the elevator. "Lighten up. She's probably fine. There isn't always a dark side to everything."

7

CHAPTER 3

Wearing booties over her shoes, Detective Lisa Suarez walked around the empty warehouse. White puffs of breath appeared from her mouth. She tried not to shiver in the freezing air. Shivering was a sign of weakness, something Lisa dared not show.

The newest officer, Missy Blake, walked beside her. The higher ups in the precinct had assigned Blake to assist Suarez. Suarez had been a great cop, and not just in her own mind, and now a determined detective. She wasn't sure yet if Blake would be more of a help or a hindrance.

Both women wore the large, unisex winter coats provided by the precinct. Blake looked petite and feminine, while Suarez looked like a big blob. Their appearance wasn't the only striking difference between them. Blake knew how to be charming in a flirty way. She was chatting with Detective Logan right now, and even though they were at a crime scene, Logan seemed to bask in her attention.

Why did Blake want to be a cop, anyway? She looked like she belonged in one of those fancy boutique stores with beautiful people and whitened smiles. Not in a dark, depressing crime scene. But Blake came from a family with a long history of wearing badges. Her grandfather, her father and her brother were all cops. Suarez's family, on the other hand, had a long history of incarceration. Taking a glass-is-half-full attitude, Suarez believed her family background allowed her to think more like a criminal and gave her an edge.

As often was the case, this crime occurred in a "bad" area of town. Lower class. One where people aren't likely to talk or even report crimes. But someone had. Detective Suarez was first to the scene because she'd been visiting her grandmother, who needed help to get into her bed these days due to her arthritis and diabetes. She lived a few blocks away on a street where low-income apartments butted up against abandoned industrial warehouses—the ones often used for exchanges involving stolen goods and drugs. Her grandmother had lived there her whole life. She was stubborn enough that she'd die there if she had her way. And for that reason, among others, Suarez was determined to make the area less of a crime zone for people like her grandmother who couldn't or wouldn't leave.

Suarez arrived at the warehouse just sixteen minutes after dispatch received the first reports of gunshots fired. Officer Blake and Detective Logan arrived shortly after with their sirens blaring. As a result of their efforts, white evidence markers pinpointed where bullet casings and bullets were scattered about. Red markers identified blood spatter and two distinct pools of blood. They had photographed everything.

Suarez covered her mouth as she coughed, which felt like a knife scraping the inside of her throat. "What we know is that at least two people left the scene injured," she said, pointing to two separate trails of blood. "He or she—probability wise, they're males—fled the building and must have entered a vehicle at the curb."

Of course, there were no security cameras in the immediate vicinity.

Detective Logan wrote something in his notebook, and said, "I'll check the area hospitals and urgent care centers."

They had to do it, but Detective Suarez knew it would be a waste of time. Whoever got shot in the warehouse wasn't going to visit a hospital.

"Let's upload the blood samples and see if we get a match," Suarez said. "Maybe we'll get lucky."

***

The police department occupied an old brick building on top of a hill. Detective Suarez had an office the size of a small closet. No windows. Just enough room for a desk with a chair in front and behind it. The space became hers after a more senior detective deemed it too claustrophobic. Suarez was used to small, unassuming spaces, and it was a giant step up from her previous desk, which was surrounded by dreary gray, chest-height partitions.

She was finishing her second coffee of the morning and reading through her emails when someone knocked.

"Detective?"

In the doorway, Blake held a file against the form-fitting sweater that hugged her perfectly shaped breasts. "What is it?"

"We got a lead on last night's shooting."

Suarez gestured for Blake to come in. Since there were no dead bodies, the shooting wasn't a priority for anyone except Suarez. She wanted to know if they were dealing with a teen gang versus warring cartels.

"I found a surveillance camera on Danbury Street," Blake said, stepping forward. "Five blocks east of the warehouse. Anyone driving there would have to take that road."

"Great. Get the footage."

"I did. I've already looked at it. Someone reported the gunshots at 10:22 p.m. I scanned the video beginning at 9:00 p.m. through 10:45, which is just minutes after you arrived."

"Did anything stand out?"

"Yes. Traffic was light. A black Chevy Tahoe passed the camera at 9:56. Driving approximately the posted speed limit. The same vehicle came back in the other direction at 10:20, driving at an excessive speed."

"Did you get the plates?"

"I can't see the plates. But I got something better." Blake beamed, looking like an advertisement for something that tastes great and has no calories. "I have a headshot of the driver. It's a little blurry, but it might be good enough for facial recognition. I've already started the process." Blake opened her file and set a 5x7 photo on the desk.

"Good job, Blake."

"Thank you, Detective Suarez. I'll let you know if we get a name."

CHAPTER 4

The church Scott and Bailey chose for their wedding was an imposing, neo-gothic cathedral with a large spire. Unfortunately, construction ropes blocked the parking lot entrances. Beyond the ropes, a backhoe loomed over a crater-like hole. Ned drove past, hunting for somewhere else to park nearby. Stately and well-maintained historic homes and brownstones lined the roads, spaced tight together. Every unoccupied space in front of them had a sign saying, *No parking without sticker. Towing strictly enforced.* On the bottom of one sign, someone had scrawled *These Bastards Mean Business* in black ink.

With the car's warm interior keeping Victoria comfortably relaxed, she didn't complain when Ned circled the mostly residential area for the third time.

"Someone gave us a heads up about the parking situation," he said. "But this is ridiculous. How do people live like this? At this rate, we're going to miss the rehearsal. I'm just going to park and risk getting towed."

"Look, someone's leaving," Victoria pointed to a Ford sedan with glowing taillights.

Ned slowed to a stop and flicked on his blinker. "We're at least three blocks away. Do you mind walking?"

"Not at all." Victoria was grateful she'd opted for comfortable dress boots rather than heels. "And we're still early, we've got plenty of time."

When the Ford left, Ned pulled their rental car next to a large oak tree between a Volvo and a Mercedes. Victoria zipped her coat and slid on her gloves before stepping out into the chilly air. With the sun low on the horizon, she and Ned linked arms and headed to the church on the sand and salt-coated sidewalk. Small mounds of dirt-crusted snow remained frozen solid in shaded spots under the trees.

When they reached the church, soft golden light glowed from the tall windows, beckoning them inside. They entered through the giant, red front doors. Inside the vestibule, two good-looking men about Ned's age, wearing sport coats, greeted him with energetic calls of "Patterson. Man!"

Ned grinned and introduced the taller of the two first. "This is Liam Wolf."

The rakish blonde had a squared jaw and a small tattoo on the side of his neck. He exuded confidence. Handsome and he knew it.

Ned's other friend had dimples in his cheeks and soulful eyes. "David Benzowicz," he said, extending his hand. Next to him stood a beautiful Latina woman.

"Hi. I'm David's wife, Maria," she said.

Ned placed his hand around Victoria's shoulder. "This amazing woman is my date, Victoria Heslin."

David's dimples deepened as he smiled at her. "Heard a lot about you."

"Yeah. Glad you came." Liam said, his tone welcoming.

The outer doors opened again, ushering in a gust of cold air. Everyone smiled at the gorgeous, glowing woman who entered. She had to be the bride. Thick brown hair with golden

13

highlights fell in perfect waves, framing her face. Her sun-kissed skin resulted from a trip to a tropical location or a natural-looking spray tan. She returned the smiles and walked straight to Ned.

"Wonderful to see you." She hugged him, then beamed at Victoria. "I'm Bailey. You must be Victoria. I'm so glad you came with Ned."

"It's really nice to be celebrating with you," Victoria said. It was easy to see why anyone would fall for Bailey. She had a kind and confident way about her. She probably had a wonderful bedside manner with her patients.

Bailey turned to a middle-aged man whose rounded face and big brown eyes resembled her own. "This is my father."

"Nice to meet you. I'm Bill Ballard. And forgive me if I don't get everyone's names straight today. Are you from around here?"

"We came from Virginia," Ned answered.

"Victoria is an FBI agent," Bailey told her father.

Their conversation got interrupted when an attractive middle-aged couple entered the vestibule with a striking woman who looked to be in her early thirties.

"Those are Scott's parents," Ned said. "Dr. Redmond, though I'm sure he'll have you call him Vince, and Stephanie Redmond. And that's his sister, Jules."

Scott's father had a full head of gray hair, a round face, a thick neck, and a bulbous nose. Victoria wondered if Scott had inherited that same nose.

Scott's mother was a taller than average woman and looked elegant in a form-fitting navy dress. Dark ruby red lipstick colored her full lips. Her smooth, unwrinkled skin made her appear much younger than her husband.

Their daughter, Scott's sister, wore her red hair back in a loose bun. She removed her coat, revealing a silk caftan with a

14

floral pattern over an anorexic-looking body. With a tight, thin smile, she continued to stare at Victoria through smoky eyes for longer than what Victoria could attribute to polite curiosity.

Ned dipped his head. "Hey, Jules."

"Long time no see," Scott's sister answered in a deep, raspy voice.

Ned edged closer to Victoria until they were touching from shoulder to wrist. "I heard you're doing well, Jules," he said. "Bought your own killer place in Aspen."

"I did," Jules answered. "I was traveling there often. The galleries have been so busy. Anyway, it's pretty fantastic."

"If it's half as nice as your uncle's place then you got lucky."

"I think it's nicer, but don't tell him that. And luck has nothing to do with it. You should come see it sometime."

Victoria didn't miss the flirtation in Jules's invite but didn't let it bother her. Some people were just like that. What Victoria couldn't wrap her head around was Jules on skis. She would probably look fantastic, like a sexy ski-bunny, but one fall might snap her bird-like bones.

"Where's your brother?" Ned asked Jules. "He told me he was picking up your family at the hotel."

"He's parking the car," Jules answered. "He'll be here in a minute."

"He just messaged me he's having trouble finding a parking spot," Bailey said.

A young woman with two French braids stepped forward, shaking her head and rolling her eyes upward. "Yes, the parking situation is a problem. I hope you all got my note about it so you knew before you arrived. I'm Kayla. The wedding planner. From Planning Your Big Event. Hello everyone. Just so you know, parking *will not* be an issue for the wedding tomorrow, so don't

15

worry about that. We have limos scheduled to take you from the hotel."

"Why are we all standing around out here in the foyer shivering?" Mrs. Redmond asked. Heavy bracelets slid down her wrist as she lifted her arm in a sweeping gesture toward the inner sanctuary. "Let's move inside."

Inside the main part of the church, Ned helped Victoria remove her coat as she admired the stained-glass windows and the elaborately carved beams on the arched ceiling.

Three women stood talking near the altar. Two were in their late twenties or early thirties and wore business casual style dresses. Victoria instantly recognized the taller of them as the same woman who entered the hotel corridor crying and wearing her shirt inside out. Apparently, she was also a wedding guest. Again, Victoria wondered what had upset the woman.

The third in the group appeared a few years younger than the others. Or perhaps it was her attire—a baggy, off-the-shoulder sweatshirt and strategically ripped jeans—that made her seem so. She left the altar and walked down the aisle toward the newcomers.

"Bridget, did your suitcase show up yet?" Mr. Ballard asked her.

"Hey, Dad. Nope. They're supposed to bring it to my hotel as soon as they locate it. Guess I should have stuffed the dress in my carryon so this couldn't happen. But I mean, seriously, how does an airline lose one random suitcase? Like, where did it even go?" She threw up her hands and scrunched up one side of her mouth.

"Don't worry about it," Bailey said. "If that's the worst thing that happens, I have no complaints. Besides, the maid of honor can wear something different from the other bridesmaids. I have a black dress that will look great on you. I brought it to the hotel. And you always look gorgeous in anything."

16

THE GROOM WENT MISSING

Bailey impressed Victoria. She was the farthest thing from a nightmare drama-queen bride. She seemed as genuine and gracious as she was lovely.

Bridget gave her sister a giant bear hug. "You are the best. I won't screw up anything else. I promise. At least I'll try not to." Still grinning, she turned to Victoria and stuck her hand out to shake. "Hi. We haven't met. I'm Bridget. Bailey's younger sister. Obviously. From California. Are you with Ned?"

"Yes." Victoria introduced herself.

"Love it. Good for you. He's a super guy," Bridget said, winking at Ned, who nudged her shoulder like she was his own little sister.

A priest cleared his throat as he entered from a side door. "Are we ready to get started?" he asked with enough volume to get everyone's attention.

"Just waiting for the groom," David said, frowning. "Speaking of which…it's taking him a good long time, isn't it?"

Bailey glanced toward the doors. "He's still trying to find a parking spot."

The priest shook his head. "Our apologies for the parking situation. The city has to fix pipes that exploded underneath the road overnight. Unfortunate timing for everyone with special events this week."

Ned took out his phone, tapped the screen a few times, then held it against his ear for several seconds. "Scott's not answering."

"I know. I already called him," Jules said. "He must have turned his phone off. Was it really that hard to find a parking spot?"

"Don't ask me," Bridget answered. "I shared an Uber with Liam and David and Maria."

"I took an Uber, too," a man said as he stepped from behind Victoria to face her. His cheeks were still red from the cold

17

as he took off his gloves. He extended his hand and shook hers with a hard, tight grip. "Hi. I'm Dean. My wife is Katie. A bridesmaid. Bailey's best friend since childhood. There she is." Dean smiled toward the tall woman talking to someone in front of the altar. The woman who had been crying.

"I'm Victoria Heslin. I'm with the best man."

"Oh. Right. Right. Victoria." Dean looked her over and lowered his voice when he said, "I know who you are. Really sorry about what you endured. You know, the plane crash. That was when, December?"

"Yes."

"I gotta tell ya, the coverage of the missing flight had me glued to the television. Fascinating. And horrible, too. So horrible. I can't imagine what you went through. Did the two of you fly here? Or no plane rides for a while?"

Dean was a little intense, but it seemed he was just being friendly. "We flew," she answered. She and Ned were nervous, but they got through it. They'd managed to sit quietly in their seats like everyone else without panicking or having a flashback. That felt like an accomplishment. They still had to fly home. She hoped it would only get easier with time.

"Wow." Dean's brows inched upward. "That's gutsy. Not sure I'd get on a plane again ever. Anyway, how is the hotel? I heard it's nice. I haven't made it there yet. I work at Facebook. Long hours. Came right from the airport. Katie came a few days early, you know, to do all the required bridesmaid stuff with Bailey. How is it?"

"The hotel? It's beautiful." Victoria had an odd sensation someone was watching her. She looked up to see Jules avert her eyes and turn to Bailey.

"Why is it taking Scott so long?" Jules asked, sounding irritated. "Can you track his phone through Find Friends? See if he's still driving around?"

Bailey shook her head. "No. We don't have the same phone carrier."

"I'm going out to look for him. If he's still driving around, I'll park his car so he can come in," Ned said. "He still has a Jeep Wrangler, right? Or did he finally get something new?"

"Same old car with a new vanity plate. It says ER DOC."

"Be right back," Ned told Victoria. "You okay here?"

"Of course," she said with a smile.

They returned less than ten minutes later. Ned shook his head. "We didn't see him."

Mrs. Redmond frowned. "That's strange. It really is taking forever."

Kayla stepped forward, clutching her clipboard with one arm and pushing one braid off her shoulder with the other. "Perhaps we should get started without him?"

"Yes, we should," the priest answered. "Again, I apologize about the parking lot. Finding a legal parking spot on the roads can be difficult. But it's best we begin the rehearsal. I'm afraid we have another here in about an hour."

Mrs. Redmond placed her hand on Ned's arm. "You can stand in for Scott until he arrives."

"Best-man at your service," Ned joked. "I'll make sure I teach him everything we learn. He's a smart guy. I don't think he'll have a problem figuring it out."

Her lips pursed, Bailey glanced toward the doors before she and everyone else followed the wedding planner to the altar.

Victoria took a seat next to Dean in a pew. She set her coat, gloves, and purse beside her. Mrs. Redmond sat down in front of them.

Kayla corralled the bridesmaids and groomsmen, gave them instructions, then sent them to the back of the church to

19

practice the wedding procession. Meanwhile, Dean talked incessantly about his grueling schedule at Facebook. He was insecure, or he had an enormous ego. Victoria nodded politely and as soon as he paused, she interrupted him to say she had to check her messages.

"Right. Right. FBI stuff. You're a secret agent," he said in a conspiratorial whisper.

"Special agent," she corrected as she took out her phone. She wanted to check on her animals at home, and this was a good time to do it. The vet tech caring for them often sent photos and updates. When she glanced up minutes later, David and Jules were walking down the aisle together. Liam and Katie followed. They were both tall and attractive and, therefore, well matched. Ned and Bridget came next. Bridget strutted toward the altar, making exaggerated shoulder movements, then struck a runway pose, cracking herself up. Ned also laughed, seeming to enjoy her antics.

Bailey strolled down the aisle last, arm in arm with her father. When she reached the front, Ned left the other groomsmen and met Bailey in the center.

Victoria held up her phone to snap a photo of the bridal party on the altar, standing where Kayla had told them to stand with the men on one side and the women on the other. At the same instant the priest said something that made Bailey and Ned laugh, Victoria captured a fantastic photo of the moment.

At the back of the church, the doors opened. A high-pitched voice, oddly feminine and yet distinctively male, yelled, "Hey, who's that up there?" His own boisterous laughter punctuated his question. "I must be at the wrong rehearsal!"

Not at all what Victoria expected from Scott, but at least he was there. She swiveled around, expecting to see a handsome man in his late twenties with a fit runner's body. She'd imagined him with reddish hair like his sister, even though Ned had told her the nickname Big Red had everything to do with his last name and nothing to do with his hair color. Instead, a man in his sixties with a pinkish, mottled complexion and a potbelly lumbered down the center aisle with a striped scarf trailing from around his neck.

CHAPTER 5

"That's Duncan Simpson, the groom's uncle. Stephanie Redmond's brother," Dean whispered, as the older man plodded toward the front of the church. "He's an artist. The rare kind who actually makes good money. A few years ago, his paintings and sculptures started selling for big bucks. Katie told me he's retiring. Don't ask me why he'd want to quit now if he's doing so well. Must be nice, you know? Paint a few pictures, get rich, retire. If only my work schedule was a little more like that. There's no downtime at Facebook. I mean...Meta. Not for me, anyway. It's rare for me to even take a weekend off and go to a wedding like this. I can't even remember the last time..."

Victoria bobbed her head but mostly tuned Dean out. Listening to him rattle on was wearing on her.

Duncan wavered from side to side, stopping once to lean against a pew as he made his way down the aisle. She hoped he hadn't driven himself there. Duncan wasn't fit and trim like his sister. Lifestyle seemed to trump genetics. But his bespoke suit fit his barrel-shaped body perfectly.

With a tight-lipped grimace, Mrs. Redmond rushed from her seat to meet him. "Scott isn't here yet," she whispered, leading Duncan back to her pew.

"He's the main man. He needs to be here." Duncan's words and laughter echoed through the church, as if someone had hired him to entertain everyone. "He didn't get cold feet, did he?"

The entire bridal party frowned at him from the altar.

"No, of course not." Mrs. Redmond shook her head and did not sound amused.

The priest cleared his throat, regaining the attention of everyone on the altar, and resumed speaking. Victoria spent the rest of the rehearsal watching the bridal party on the altar, adding an occasional nod to Dean's incessant monologue, and scanning headlines on her phone's newsfeed which told her a new Covid pill hit the market, another airline employee strike was imminent, a couple went hiking in the mountains and only one of them returned, and—of particular interest to her—a group of hounds rescued from China's meat market now needed homes.

The rehearsal ended with the priest's blessing. Still carrying her clipboard, Kayla rushed to the center of the church and reminded everyone of the next day's schedule.

Still, there was no word from the groom.

Mrs. Redmond, Jules, and Duncan quietly left the church together through one of the side doors, leaving Scott's father alone in front of the church. He cleared his throat. The rest of the attendees quieted and faced him. "Listen, everyone," he said. "My guess is the hospital called Scott in for an emergency. Sometimes it happens. We'd appreciate if everyone would go on to the rehearsal dinner as planned."

"That would be just like Scott to save a few lives right before his wedding rehearsal," David said, revealing his good nature. "And you can bet we'll all have to forgive him for it."

"I'm worried something happened to him," Bailey said.

Katie wrapped her arm around Bailey and gave her a little squeeze. "He's fine. You know how it is when he gets called into an emergency. He can't call or text anyone."

23

"They wouldn't call him tonight. And I sent a message to someone who works at the hospital. She said he isn't there."

"She wouldn't really know that for sure. Not if there was a true, all-hands-on-deck sort of chaotic emergency," Katie said. "And doesn't he have privileges at a few different hospitals?"

Bailey dipped her head to the side, a noncommittal gesture, as if she was contemplating the idea.

"You know what I think?" Bridget said. "I think he got food poisoning. He ate at the Front Line with Liam and David today." She leaned over to nudge Liam in the back with her elbow. "I mean…ew. Just ew. I wouldn't put anything from that place into my mouth. And that's where you brought the groom before his big day. He's probably stuck on a toilet right now. You know, like in that movie where they try on the bridesmaid's dresses and get diarrhea. Would Scott be too embarrassed to tell you he's got explosive diarrhea?" she asked Bailey.

Victoria couldn't tell if Bridget was joking or not.

"He ate what we ate, and we're fine," Liam said.

The sanctuary doors opened. The people who entered ceased their conversations. One of them said, "Oh." They looked confused to see strangers inside the church.

"The next rehearsal is starting," Mr. Redmond said. "Let's go back to the hotel."

The Redmond/Ballard attendees gathered up their coats, gloves, and scarfs and left.

Victoria and Ned walked back to their car under a dark sky on a sidewalk lit by streetlamps and the soft glow emanating from house windows. Victoria clutched Ned's arm and leaned against him for warmth.

"It's really odd that no one has heard from him," Ned said.

"When you talked to him before we left the hotel, how did he seem?"

24

"Fine."

"What did he say?"

"He was bringing the wedding bands to the rehearsal for me to hold until the ceremony. He wanted to make sure I got them. He told me to remind him in case he forgot."

"Anything else?"

"He was just nervous about the wedding, you know. Uh…no, not nervous, that's not how I would describe him. Excited, is a better word. He was excited about everyone, his family and friends and coworkers celebrating with him."

"Bailey's mother wasn't there," Victoria said. "I was curious to see if her first name also starts with a B."

"She died a few years ago. Cancer."

"Oh, that's sad."

On the sidewalk not far from Ned's car, a hefty man wearing a down jacket and jeans, and a woman in a long dress coat with her hands on her hips spoke in heated voices. The woman's hat concealed much of her face, but her braided hair gave her away.

"That's Kayla. The wedding planner," Victoria said.

Ned walked right up to them. "Everything okay here?"

"Everything is fine," the man answered, folding his arms across his body.

"These people are part of the Redmond wedding." Kayla's tone contained a warning edge meant for her companion. "Everything is fine," she said to Ned. "My boyfriend is just…concerned for me. That's all. Thank you for asking."

Victoria studied Kayla for a few more seconds, searching for signs she might want help.

The boyfriend continued to glare at them. Eventually he huffed, swung around, and got into the nearest car.

25

"That was odd, the way he was looking at us," Ned said. "What was that about?"

"I have no idea," Victoria answered. "But this whole night…it's turning into the strangest of evenings."

***

Upon returning to the hotel, Victoria and Ned discovered someone had delivered a giant gift basket to their suite while they were at the rehearsal.

"Have a look at this stuff," Ned said, untying the silver bow from around the top of the clear plastic.

The basket contained two bottles of wine and a variety of local products: cheese and crackers, a scented candle, and a mouth-watering cinnamon streusel loaf. It also included a pair of men's and women's cashmere lined leather gloves, and a small, heavy item wrapped in white gossamer tissue.

Victoria unwrapped the gift and discovered a silver ornament engraved with the names of the bride and groom and their wedding date on the back. An attached handwritten tag proclaimed it a *Jacob Arroyo original created exclusively for the wondrous occasion.*

"What is it exactly?" Ned asked.

"It's a Christmas tree ornament."

"No, I mean, what is it supposed to be?"

"I'm not sure. A puffy cloud?"

"I don't think so. Doesn't look like a cloud to me."

"It doesn't matter. Every year, if the guests hang it on their tree, they'll remember the occasion. That's so nice. Don't you think?"

"I guess. Yeah. There's a wedding itinerary in here," Ned said, handing her a sheet of thick cream paper with periwinkle and silver ribbons woven through holes along the top edge.

Victoria opened the crackers and ate a few as she read over the schedule. Hand-printed in calligraphy, with a QR code on the bottom, it listed scheduled dinners, lunches, cocktails, a historic bus tour of the city, and a final "thank-you-for-coming brunch" on Monday morning—one last extravagance or a closing act of generosity, depending on how one looked at it. Apparently, Ned and Victoria weren't the only out-of-town guests who had booked a four-night stay at the hotel.

"There's a lot going on," she said, wondering if her brother's upcoming wedding would have so many organized activities. The long weekend would surely be an exhausting one for Bailey and Scott, being the center of attention throughout. And if Scott really was an introvert like Victoria, getting through the schedule would challenge him.

Ned grabbed a few crackers from the bag. "Let's head down to the rehearsal dinner."

They left the suite and took the elevator down to the first floor. Just outside the main doors of the opulent banquet room, an easel holding a large, professional photograph of Bailey and Scott greeted the guests. The photo presented Victoria with her first look at Ned's friend. She was happy to see he inherited his mother's nose rather than his father's. Scott possessed a rugged, solid physique, not at all like his sister. But they had the same dark eyes and thick lashes. In the photo, he and Bailey stood on the deck of a yacht with the sun setting in the background.

Victoria and Ned sat at a table with several others from the bridal party—Bailey and Bridget, Liam, Katie and Dean, and David and his wife. Victoria had met so many people since they'd arrived. Keeping their names straight now challenged her. It took a few seconds to remember David's wife's name. Maria.

The chair next to Bailey's sat empty, a reminder of Scott's absence.

One of the hotel's servers filled Victoria's glass with white wine and topped others around the table. Victoria took a deep breath and readied her smile. The time had come to get to know Ned's friends better. Ask questions. Make connections. Slot each one into an appropriate mental file. Victoria the profiler was good at it. Victoria the introvert sometimes dreaded it. But she was eager to learn more about Ned from his friends.

One seat over, Bridget swirled her wine and grinned at Liam. "No date for you this weekend? Too many women to choose from?"

Ned laughed and said to Victoria, "Liam was always a lady's man."

Liam shook his head, took a sip of his wine, and looked across the room. It seemed he had no interest in encouraging the teasing or continuing with the topic.

"And we've never held it against him," David said. "Well, maybe I used to during college. Just a little. But now that I have my dream woman, it doesn't bother me."

"Aww," Bridget said. "So sweet."

Maria smoothed her hand over her dark hair and gave her husband a warm smile.

"So…" Bridget turned her attention to Ned and Victoria. "I know Ned is your vet, as well as your significant other. Do you have a dog or are you a cat person?"

"Seven dogs and three donkeys," Victoria answered.

Bridget widened her eyes. "That's a lot."

Victoria laughed. "And those are just the ones I own. I also foster rescues. Thanks to Ned, I can take the ones in rough shape. Ned helps get them back to health so people can adopt them. Even though I'm happy to be here, I always miss them a little when I'm away."

"That's sweet, too," Bridget said. "Sounds to me like you absolutely should marry a vet." She grinned at Ned.

"Sounds right to me," Ned said without adding a laugh or a snort to show he was joking.

For a second, Victoria wasn't sure what to think. They certainly hadn't talked about marriage yet, though they'd been through so much together. Everyone seemed to look at her, waiting for a response. "How do all of you know each other?" she asked, turning the attention back to the rest of them. It had been clear since the rehearsal that most of the bridal party seemed comfortable with each other, even though some were Bailey's friends and family, and some were Scott's, and they came from different areas of the country.

"We met at Duncan's condo in Aspen," Bridget said. "In case you don't know yet, Duncan is Scott's uncle. Kind of hard to miss him if you were at the rehearsal." Bridget smiled before she continued. "Anyway, Bailey brought Katie and me. Scott invited Liam and Ned. And Jules was there too, because of something she was doing with the Redmond's art galleries."

"I couldn't get away from my job," Dean announced. "Facebook is demanding. Lots of weekend hours. I wish I could—"

"Everyone knows how much you work, Dean." Katie interrupted her husband with a smile that didn't reach her eyes, then raised her wineglass to her lips.

"Too bad, Dean. It was definitely memorable." Bridget's eyes gleamed as she leaned toward Victoria. "There was this blizzard, and we got snowed in for two days with Duncan's fancy wine cellar. The electricity didn't go out or anything like that, so it was amazing. He'd also stocked the fridge and ordered us boxes and boxes of gourmet foods. I'd do that trip again in a heartbeat. I felt like royalty. Aspen is fabulous."

"When was that?" Victoria asked.

"Hmm, I'd say almost two years ago," Bridget said.

"Before we met," Ned told Victoria.

"Yes, absolutely before he met you," Bridget added.

"Yes." Bailey's energetic nod emphasized her sister's comment and made Victoria think they were alluding to something beyond their words. Something they knew, and she didn't.

"Sounds like a memorable trip," Victoria said.

Across the room, sitting with Scott's parents and Jules, Duncan drained his cocktail and stared across the room with vacant eyes. The pensive moment contrasted with his boisterous, attention-grabbing behavior earlier. Perhaps he merely had indigestion, but it looked like something important weighed on his mind. He didn't have a partner with him at the table, and right then, Victoria got the impression he might be a lonely man.

"Are you and Scott taking a honeymoon?" Maria asked Bailey, drawing Victoria's attention back to her table.

"Leaving for St. Lucia on Monday. Ten whole days." Bailey hugged herself and beamed in a way that only then conveyed a similarity between her personality and Bridget's.

"Scott's such a workaholic," David said. "He amazed me by taking that much time off from the hospital. It's going to be a great, well-deserved trip for both of you."

In predictable form, Dean chimed in with, "I know what that's like. Boy, do I know. You wouldn't believe the hours I put in this past year."

Victoria thought a tropical island sounded perfect. She hadn't vacationed anywhere warm in a long time. Maybe she and Ned could go somewhere tropical with waterfalls. Or was she getting way ahead of herself? Best to see how this trip went before planning the next one.

During the rest of the dinner, Victoria learned Liam worked for Goldman Sachs in New York and David had recently left a job with Microsoft to work for a startup tech firm in Atlanta. Currently between jobs, Bridget claimed she was looking and willing to do anything, as long as it didn't involve over forty hours a week, working on the weekends, or getting to an office before nine a.m. As the waitstaff refilled drinks and the conversation flowed, Victoria occasionally forgot the groom wasn't there.

Across the table, Bailey acknowledged the conversations with polite and gracious comments, but her thoughts seemed elsewhere. Understandable. Every so often, she checked her phone. Her plate of food went untouched, as did the plate intended for Scott that the servers placed next to her.

When dessert arrived, Bailey's father stood and dinged his glass. "Thank you all for coming. None of us expected to have this dinner without Scott, but things happen. All that matters is that he's with us tomorrow."

Someone snorted loudly and everyone at Victoria's table whirled around to look at the critic, a man in his mid or late twenties with thick, tousled hair.

"Damn good thing the Redmonds are paying for most of the wedding, right?" he said. "At least it's their money down the drain if the wedding gets canceled."

"Ethan!" Bridget's hissed response cut through the shocked murmurs in the room.

Ethan unapologetically shrugged and kept his head up.

"That's Ethan," Bridget whispered as she leaned toward Ned and Victoria. "He's got, I don't know what to call it…issues. He's not like on a spectrum or anything like that, not that we know of, or I'd be a little more sensitive. But he can be tactless. He's never really had a filter. His mother and my mother were best friends. He's been Bailey's *biggest* fan since they were toddlers, if you know what I mean. Anyhow, so rude of him. My dad is a high school chemistry teacher, and as you can see, this wedding probably costs five times what he makes in a year." Bridget spoke of her father with pride. "Of course the Redmonds are helping to pay for the wedding. They're helping a lot. I mean, it's basically Stephanie Redmond's wedding. You know…for her friends."

31

Bailey didn't respond to Ethan's comment and acted as if she hadn't heard him, but her smile had completely disappeared. "I'm grateful for all the Redmonds have done," she said. "The wedding celebrations are...very special."

"Not exactly your style...all this flash," Bridget said. "But yes...it's certainly *special.*"

Later, the caterers cleared the dishes, and the guests left, thanking the Redmonds and Mr. Ballard and wishing Bailey well. Only the bridal party and immediate family members remained. Scott still hadn't shown.

"Listen, if no one has heard from Scott, we should get together and make a plan," Mr. Ballard said, beckoning everyone to a front table.

"Yes," Bridget said. "Absolutely. I'm the maid of honor. I'm supposed to help navigate family difficulties and other stresses. I researched my responsibilities. Don't anyone say the bachelorette party wasn't an enormous success, even though I got Bailey so drunk she lost her favorite shoes."

Victoria looked toward the door, ready to head back to her suite. "I'll meet you upstairs," she told Ned.

"Excuse me, Victoria," Mr. Ballard said. "Please stay."

"Oh, sure." She wondered why he'd asked her to join them. She followed Ned toward the convening group.

"So, is it just me, or does anyone else think we should call the police?" Mr. Ballard asked.

Bailey nodded whole-heartedly but Duncan answered, "I wouldn't do that now. Let's find out where he is first. No reason to let the world know."

Duncan's statement struck Victoria as odd. Did he know something the rest of them didn't?

Bridget flashed him an angry look and asked, "No reason to let the world know what, exactly?"

32

Duncan uncrossed his legs, lowering a hand-stitched leather shoe from one knee. "I'm not saying...Scott would never..." Duncan averted his gaze from the rest of them as his words trailed off.

"Then what did you mean?" Bridget asked. "Because it really sounded to me like you meant *something* with that comment."

"Forget I said anything," Duncan answered.

"Victoria, what would you do?" Ned asked, loud enough for everyone around them to hear.

Standing off to the side and not expecting to get drawn into what was becoming an emotional discussion, he caught Victoria off guard. "What would I do about what?"

"To find out where Scott is," Ned clarified. "The FBI handles missing people, doesn't it?"

"Sometimes. Usually at the request of local law enforcement. And if there's evidence of interstate travel." She knew what Ned was asking. "Scott is an adult. I'm not sure the authorities would consider him officially missing yet."

"I get it," Ned said. "But let's just say you got called at work because he was *officially* missing. What would you do first?"

Everyone stared at Victoria. She crossed her arms. "After going to his home to check on him, I'd check in with local authorities to make sure he wasn't in an accident. If nothing turned up, I'd call hospitals in the area to see if one admitted him. Did Scott have his wallet on him?"

"Yes," Bailey answered. "He always carries his wallet."

If something happened, there wouldn't be a problem identifying him, and one of you surely would have received a call by now. That was obvious and saying it aloud seemed cruel, so she didn't. "Has everyone checked their voicemails for calls?" Victoria looked from Bailey to Scott's parents to his sister.

33

"Of course we have," Jules answered, narrowing her eyes so that her dark top lashes touched the bottom ones.

"Yes. I've been checking," Bailey said. She stared at Victoria intently, as if hanging on her every word.

"You could try your insurance agent as well," Victoria suggested.

"Our insurance agent is a friend," Bailey said. "He's coming to the wedding tomorrow. Scott would have called him if he'd been in an accident. Although, if he could call the insurance agent, I'm sure he would have called me first to let me know what happened." She finished speaking so quietly that Victoria could barely hear her.

The room was silent for several seconds. The more explanations they came up with, the more one explanation rose to the forefront—Scott had ducked out of the wedding. It wasn't as terrible as Scott dying in an accident, but at the moment, from Bailey's perspective, it might feel worse.

"Let's make those calls Victoria suggested," Mr. Ballard said. "Much better than waiting and wondering. I'm going to see if the hotel has a whiteboard we can use. I'll be right back." He hurried from the room and returned a few minutes later with a whiteboard and a marker. "The hotel let me borrow this. No sense in duplicating efforts. Let's get on the internet and make a list of all the places we need to call. Then we'll split up the tasks."

Everyone except Mr. Ballard took a seat. They called out the names and numbers of urgent care centers and area hospitals as they looked them up on their phones. Mr. Ballard wrote them down, then assigned someone's name to each place. He was a natural at organizing the effort.

"Also, tell them he's a physician and someone there might have called him in to work an emergency there," Mrs. Redmond said. "Scott might be a patient *or* a care provider."

34

A flurry of cell phone activity followed. After exhausting their lists, they'd found no records of Scott Redmond at any emergency room or urgent care center.

Bailey got up from her seat and walked around the tables. "Our friend, the insurance agent, hasn't heard from him either. And he's still not answering his phone."

"And now more people know Scott isn't here," Bridget muttered.

Bailey stopped pacing and faced her sister. "I don't care who knows or what people think. I just need to know where he is."

"It's just that people are going to think he changed his mind," Bridget added, although she'd seemed irked with Duncan for coming close to making a similar comment earlier.

"He would never do that," Ned said to Bailey. "He would never do that to anyone, and especially not to you. He loves you more than anything."

"I know." Bailey wiped tears and smudged mascara from under her eyes. "That's why I'm so worried about him. Something happened."

"We should call the police," Mr. Ballard said, turning to Scott's parents.

Mrs. Redmond twisted a wedding band and a large diamond ring around her finger while Mr. Redmond slumped in his seat, his expression solemn.

"I don't think we should," Jules said. "Definitely not. Not yet."

"Do you know something you're not telling us?" Bridget asked, her tone sharp. She looked between Duncan and Jules. "Did your brother confide he was having second thoughts? Is that it?"

"No. Absolutely not." Jules softened her voice. "But think about what you're saying. The moment this gets out, Bailey and Scott's story will go viral. Let's not get ahead of ourselves and

35

embarrass anyone. He hasn't missed the actual wedding yet. I'm sure he has an explanation."

If this was Victoria's case, she'd grill everyone with questions to get to the truth. But she was a guest of Ned's, and it wasn't her place. Instead, she whispered to Ned. "It looks like Scott's family has reason to believe he didn't want to get married. That's how they're acting."

She thought Ned might want to take Jules and Duncan aside to confront them quietly, but Ned did just the opposite.

"Did Scott tell you he had reservations about getting married?" Ned asked, staring directly at Jules.

Bailey closed her eyes, and Katie wrapped her arm around Bailey's shoulder.

"No," Mr. Redmond answered for his daughter. "Absolutely not. Don't be ridiculous."

"Jules?" Ned asked, still waiting for her response.

Jules finally shook her head. "No. Just don't get the police involved yet. I promise you Scott would not want that."

Ned turned to Duncan. "What you said when you got to the rehearsal, about Scott getting cold feet, were you joking?"

"Yes, yes... of course I was joking," Duncan stammered. "But now...I agree with Jules. I don't think there's reason to involve the police yet. No reason to make things worse than they already are if it's not necessary."

Their responses weren't very convincing. Cradling her phone in her lap, Victoria googled *groom disappeared*. The search returned dozens of links. All were stories about grooms who reconsidered their marriage plans right before the wedding. Even more common were the brides who ditched their grooms last minute. It happened. But what would make Scott change his mind in the final hours? Had he discovered something he didn't know before?

"I'm sure there's an explanation," Mr. Ballard said. "We just need to know where he is. Then we can all relax. What would you, the FBI, do next to locate him, Victoria?"

Based on what they knew and especially how Scott's family was acting, Victoria doubted the Feds or the police would do anything. They would say it appeared Scott changed his mind and didn't have the guts to face anyone yet. But that's not what anyone else wanted to hear. Victoria cleared her throat. "If he was missing...every state handles missing persons a little differently. With adults, it's always on a case-by-case basis. You could file a report, but unless you have evidence something happened to him, they won't search for him yet. They'll want to give him a few days to turn up on his own."

"A few days?" Bailey moaned.

"But if they did search for him?" Ned prompted. "What would they do exactly?"

"They'd question people who were with him or who spoke with him recently." What she didn't say aloud is that they'd be specifically looking for indications of infidelity, an affair, or other signs he was having second thoughts about the marriage. "They'd track his phone or a GPS on his car. They'd also scan his credit and debit card transactions to see where he's been and what he purchased."

"There's no GPS in his car," Bailey said. "But I can access his credit cards. We already have joint accounts." She leaned forward in her seat, tapping away at her phone screen.

"I need a refill," Duncan said, having finished another cocktail. He got up from his seat and left. Mrs. Redmond and Jules followed, leaving Mr. Redmond behind.

"I'm in our account now. What am I looking for?" Bailey asked as she stared at her phone.

"Um, unexpected charges," Victoria answered. *Especially a last-minute flight.* She disliked feeling so cynical, but the most obvious explanation was usually the correct one.

"I see nothing like that," Bailey said. "Nothing unusual. Scott rarely buys anything besides meals and coffees."

"Is it possible he has cards you don't know about?" her father asked.

"I wouldn't know that, would I?" Bailey dropped her head into her hands. Bridget and Katie surrounded her.

Victoria might have been helpful earlier, but this now seemed a situation for close family and friends. "Excuse me," she said, pushing her chair away from the table and getting up. After leaving the banquet room, she picked a direction and headed down the main hallway in search of a restroom. At the end of the corridor, a wall placard indicated restrooms were located to the right. Heated whispers came from around the corner. Victoria stopped, not wanting to intrude on what sounded like a very personal conversation.

Jules's raspy voice rose above the others. "Well, he shouldn't have brought her. And I don't want anyone to talk to her."

Overhearing the ugly comment made Victoria embarrassed for Scott's sister. Who was Jules talking about? Clearly someone she didn't like. With no explanation for Scott's absence, this hardly seemed like the time for his sister to indulge herself in petty concerns.

"You can't avoid her, or you'll be the one who looks bad." The high-pitched response unmistakably came from Duncan, though there was something different about his voice. He sounded sober and rational, nothing like the buffoon he appeared to be when he entered the church. "She's Ned's girlfriend now," he said. "What would you have told him? The best man can't bring a guest? Get a hold of yourself, Jules, and think before you speak. People are watching."

A chill prickled Victoria's skin as heat rushed to her face. They were talking about her! How dare they? They didn't know the first thing about her. Actually, that probably wasn't true. The media storm following the plane crash in Greenland had seen to that. Anyone could google her name and learn she was an FBI agent, a former profiler. And even before the crash, it was easy to find out she was an heiress to her grandfather's fortune and that her mother had died a tragic death. All of it was out there. But still...they didn't *really* know her.

Deciding to take the high ground, she turned around before they could see her. She needed to calm down and wrap her head around what she'd heard. She was still feeling indignant and perplexed when she returned to the banquet room to let Ned know she was going up to their room.

Just as Victoria walked through the door, Bailey shouted, "Oh! Scott just texted me!" She read his message aloud. "I got pulled into an emergency out of town. I'll see you on the altar. I'll be there." She let out a long exhale through pursed lips, then her face relaxed into a tired smile.

Jules entered the room a few seconds later with her mother. "You're sure the text came from Scott?" Jules asked Bailey.

"Absolutely," Bailey answered. "It came from his phone. He ends every message and note with 'Love you, Bales.' It's him." Bailey narrowed her eyes at Jules. "Why would you even ask that?"

"I don't know, just forget I said it." Jules clutched one side of her silky dress and wrapped it across her tiny waist.

"Oh. I just got one also," Mrs. Redmond said, briefly holding up her phone. "He sends his sincere apologies."

"Thank you so much for your help, everyone," Bailey said. "I'm so sorry we went through all of this. I'm going back to my room to get some rest now. I'll see you tomorrow."

It's not you who should apologize, Victoria thought. Regardless of how busy Scott was, or how many lives he was saving, he should have called earlier.

CHAPTER 6

It was almost midnight when Ned and Victoria were alone again in their room.

Victoria grabbed her toiletry bag and went into the bathroom. As she washed her face, she debated telling Ned about the conversation she'd overheard.

She left the bathroom wearing a silk robe and smiled at Ned as he passed her and went in. She drew open the curtains and peered out through the balcony windows. They had a pleasant view of the lit courtyard below and city lights twinkling in the distance. Victoria gazed out, beginning to relax.

The bathroom door opened, and Ned came out wearing shorts and a T-shirt. He wrapped his arms around Victoria and leaned his smooth, freshly shaved face against her cheek. She inhaled the fresh scent of him. In silence, they stared out at the city together.

"This has to be one of the nicest suites in the hotel and with the best view," she said. "I hope you don't think I expect that."

"No. I know you don't expect to be spoiled. But after our last trip, I wanted us to be comfortable. I wanted to look out the window and see something other than an endless expanse of snow."

"It's very nice. Very comfortable. I love it."

"And it turns out I'm not paying for it. The Redmonds took care of it for us. I reserved the suite on my credit card and when I went to check in, I was told our stay had been taken care of. Compliments of the hosts."

"Really? Just for you because you're the best man, or are they covering rooms for everyone in the wedding party?"

"I don't know. And I won't ask anyone else, in case the Redmonds didn't pay for any other rooms. I was going to ask Scott tonight, but obviously I didn't get the chance."

"You know…I caught part of a conversation between Duncan and Jules earlier tonight."

"And?"

Victoria relayed the comments. "Do you have any idea why she would say that about me?"

"Are you sure that's what she said?"

"I'm positive."

Ned sighed. "Maybe because we dated. Just for a few months. It didn't work out."

"Oh. How long ago?"

"Before I met you."

"Did it start when you got snowed in together at Aspen?"

"Yes," he said, looking ashamed, though he had nothing to be sorry for. Victoria hadn't met him yet. And even if she had, it's not like they started dating immediately. Still, Victoria couldn't help comparing herself to Jules. Not a healthy thing to do, but there it was. Where Victoria was slender and athletic, Jules had a sophisticated, artsy vibe to her. Physically, Jules appeared almost fragile, but there was nothing delicate about her personality. She was a confident, assertive woman. The type of person who didn't get pushed around.

"Who ended things between you?" Victoria asked.

Ned raised his shoulders, but it wasn't a shrug because he kept them up as he sighed. "I guess I did. But I don't recall her caring much. I didn't break her heart or anything like that. Whatever was going on with us ended because neither of us were invested enough to make it work long distance. And I suppose I felt a little weird about dating my best friend's sister, even though Scott acted okay with it. Honestly, I don't know if that's why she said what she did. I can't imagine Jules getting hung up over something like that."

"You mean hung up over someone like you?" Victoria grinned. "You don't think you're worth the heartache?"

"I hope you think so." He chuckled. "I know Jules had a serious boyfriend for several years before we dated. She hinted about him being super rich enough times that I got the sense that was important to her. Good thing you don't care about that. I mean, I assume you don't care since…I better just shut up while I'm ahead."

Victoria laughed.

"I promise you that things were never serious between Jules and me. Not for either of us."

"I believe you, although you can't be sure what was going through her head. And if your past relationship isn't the reason she has a problem with me, then what else could it be?"

"I don't know. I'm sorry about what you heard. She doesn't have any reason not to like you. I promise." He turned her around to face him. "Who wouldn't like you?"

"Let's see…probably every person I've investigated and testified against. It's a long list. Few of them take responsibility for what they've done. In their minds, they're only behind bars because of me and the prosecutor."

His expression turned serious. "Right."

"What do the Redmonds do for a living?" Victoria asked, changing the topic.

"Scott's father is also a doctor. A primary care physician. The rest of the family is involved with the art world. Mrs. Redmond and Duncan own Redmond Galleries. Jules works with them. It's pretty upscale."

"Meaning what?"

"They really made a name for Redmond Galleries. Scott isn't involved in the business, he's busy working in the hospitals, but I know he's very proud of what his family has accomplished. They're like the King Midas of the modern art world. They make names out of unknown artists. And…any particular reason you're asking?"

"I guess because of the comment Ethan made at dinner, about the Redmonds paying for the entire wedding. It got me wondering."

"They're just generous. Now that they can be. For their wedding gift, they gave Scott and Bailey a painting worth over a quarter million dollars. Scott sent me a picture." Ned let go of Victoria and grabbed his phone off the dresser. He tapped and swiped at the screen until he had the image to show her.

Victoria was no art expert and didn't have the vocabulary to describe the painting. She saw a lot of different colors, the primary ones being shades of blue, each shaped like a roughly torn scrap of paper and fitting together in a collage-like presentation. Maybe it represented a master's work. Maybe it didn't.

"Hmm. At least it will go with almost any sofa color, right?" Amusement made the corners of her lips twitch. She looked up at Ned, could tell the feeling was mutual, and laughed aloud.

"I know, right?" Ned said. "I think that was Scott's reaction as well."

"They bought that painting for over a quarter million?"

"Well, no. I guess it's just worth that much, meaning that's what it would sell for at their gallery. Hard to believe anyone would pay so much money for something that can only hang on the wall, but that's how it is. It's the thought that counts, right? They can always sell it someday." He came closer to her. "I'm glad you got to meet the Redmonds and Bailey and some of my friends tonight. Of course, it's Scott who I most wanted you to meet. More like I want him to meet you. But that can wait until tomorrow. And enough about other people. Right now, I'm not interested in anyone but you. You were great tonight, by the way, helping everyone figure out what to do."

"Turns out they didn't need my help."

"They did. We all did. You helped us get through that awful unknown period until Bailey and Mrs. Redmond got Scott's messages."

"You're welcome, then." Victoria smiled up at him.

Ned leaned in and found her lips with his own. Victoria melted into his arms as he lowered her to the bed. His hands moved down her back and over her skin, working magic and making her shiver under his touch.

But a random thought snuck in and distracted her. "Ned?"

"What?" he whispered, without opening his eyes.

"This is important."

He pulled slightly away to look at her. "What is it?"

"Promise me that if you ever have a vet emergency when we have something significant planned, or anything, you'll text me first."

"I promise. And I want you to do the same."

"I promise, too," she said, and went back to kissing him.

45

CHAPTER 7

Detective Suarez sat at her desk, completing paperwork on the warehouse shooting. Notepads, files, binders, and a small stack of coupons covered the desk's surface. It looked messy, but she knew the exact location of everything she needed. A winter vanilla candle burned in a container to her left. As long as it burned, the scent filled her office and masked the odor of cigars that lingered in the hallway. The building didn't allow smoking and hadn't for decades, but that didn't seem to stop a few of her colleagues who worked at night. The same ones who made comments about Missy Blake's body when Blake wasn't around. Didn't they realize Suarez had ears that worked perfectly well? Suarez shook her head and focused on her laptop. She had to choose her battles carefully. Bitterness was getting to be a staple of her personality, and she didn't want it to take over.

Officer Blake tapped on the door. "Hi, Boss."

"Come in." Suarez flipped her file closed and stuck it in a desk drawer. In an effort to be more pleasant, she attempted a welcoming smile.

"I've got a name for the Tahoe driver. Facial recognition gives a ninety-three percent likelihood the subject is Richard Luna. He has a long-standing suspected association with organized crime. Eduardo Salazar's cartel, to be specific. We arrested him once for charges related to forgery. Never convicted. Somehow he stays clean."

"I've never met Luna in person, but I know of him," Suarez said. "Everyone who grew up in my neighborhood does. He's a local. Went by the name Ricky back then. Started out as an actor. Did some commercials, but nothing more. Now he hangs out with Eric Salazar, the cartel leader's son. He's smart and smooth, which makes him more dangerous. Done extremely well for himself without doing much of anything at all. Him and Tommy Sanchez. They stay clean because the cartel has excellent, extremely well-paid attorneys." The cartel probably had men on the inside as well, but Suarez didn't mention that. For all she knew, one of Blake's family members might be on the cartel's payroll.

"I remember hearing something about Tommy Sanchez," Blake said. "My brother charged him with forging contracts and receipts last year. That charge didn't stick either."

"Sounds about right." Suarez grumbled with disgust.

"Any info back from forensics on the DNA left behind?" Blake asked.

"No. Without proof of a murder, there isn't much of a case. That request is low on the lab's list. We'll be waiting weeks or months for that information, if they ever get to it." Which meant whoever was shooting people just blocks from her grandmother's neighborhood could keep on doing it. "Maybe we should pay Luna a visit and see what he has to say for himself. You have his address?" she asked Blake.

"I just sent it to you. It shouldn't take over thirty minutes to get there."

Suarez blew out the candle, stood up, and patted the gun at her side. "Let's check it out," she said, grabbing her coat. "I'd like to see where Luna lives now." Maybe he wasn't doing as well as she'd heard. She hoped he wasn't. She had nothing personal against Luna, besides him being a criminal. But it bugged her that if the rumors were true, he lived so much better than the men and

47

women like her who worked to keep people like him off the street. And now, here he was, coming back to wreak havoc on the neighborhood where he grew up. Not exactly giving back to the community in any positive way.

Luna lived on the north edge of the city in a trendy, posh area full of renovated condos and lofts. On the drive there, Blake did her best to make small talk about an unsolved homicide from a few weeks ago and a series she was binging on Netflix. When they reached Luna's street, she was babbling to Suarez about a sandwich she loved from a new cafe that opened off Boylston Street.

The rumors were true. Ricky Luna had certainly moved up in the world. His place was light years nicer than where Suarez lived, even though just about every dollar she earned that didn't go to helping with her grandma's bills went into Suarez's own mortgage.

Wearing civilian clothes, Suarez and Blake walked up a spotlessly clean path to a front door made of scrolled iron. Suarez rang the doorbell. Translucent glass blurred the figure approaching from within. When the door opened, a handsome man smiled at them. He wore jeans and a tight black T-shirt that clung to his trim torso, and held a mug in one hand. His buzz cut, mustache, and beard were all neatly trimmed. His face reminded Suarez of a young Benjamin Bratt from decades-old episodes of Law & Order. She had to admit Bratt was one of the main reasons she had enjoyed the show so much.

"Ricky Luna," Suarez said.

"Yes. But I haven't gone by Ricky in a long time. It's Richard. And you are?" He smiled at Blake in a way that was markedly different from the polite smile he offered Suarez.

The women showed their badges. "Detective Suarez and Officer Blake."

Luna epitomized coolness. His expression didn't change.

"Mind if we come in?" Suarez asked.

"Do you have a warrant, ladies?" he asked in an unfalteringly reasonable tone.

"Do we need one?" Suarez asked.

He shrugged as he stepped back and opened his door wider. "Come on in. And excuse the mess. I've been a little under the weather, hunkering down at home."

"You don't look sick," Blake said.

"Thank you, Officer Blake." Luna tipped his mug toward her. "Would either of you like some tea? This is peppermint green tea, but I've got an assortment you can choose from."

Both officers declined.

In no way did the word "mess" describe the inside of Luna's home. Everything had a place and resided there, as if a Feng Shui expert had arranged the sleek decor. Nothing mismatched or random existed inside, which was the unintentional theme in Suarez's own home. The wood floors gleamed. There was a neutral color scheme—white, beige, and accents of black—and every item adhered to it. Each wall held a large piece of striking modern art—strokes of black, gray, or blue across large white canvases. The kitchen had marble or quartz backsplash and stainless steel appliances, and a fridge with a screen built into it. The upscale sophistication of the place really pissed Suarez off. The rumors were true...and then some. Richard Luna was living large. Crime paid. If she had even a fraction of the money he apparently had, she could move her grandmother somewhere safer. And ironically, if it weren't for people like Luna and the cartel he worked for, she wouldn't have to.

People from her neighborhood spoke of Luna with a measure of envy and respect. Didn't they know there was almost no way to do as well as he had without crossing a line? She might enjoy nothing more than taking him down a few notches and

49

showing his admirers that crime doesn't pay, at least not in the long run.

She looked around, keeping her eyes peeled for anything that might get him in trouble. Traces of blood, perhaps. With the open floor plan, most of the space was visible from the living room, except for the bedrooms and bathrooms. "It looks like this place is for sale and you're staging it, Ricky." She intentionally used the name he no longer wanted to go by.

"It's Richard," he said calmly. "And what can I say? I like a nice place. And I'm handy. I installed new bathroom vanities myself. I'll show you…if you're interested."

She had to push waves of anger back and refocus. She resented that he possessed some actual skills. She hoped his bathroom vanities looked like crap. "Where were you Thursday night at 10:30 p.m.?"

"I was home." He answered without the slightest sign of stress.

"And yet we have footage of you driving a Chevy Tahoe at 10:30 p.m. ten miles east of here. You were speeding."

"Oh." Luna rubbed his beard. "I went out for some gelato. Ever had the stuff? Excellent, and it doesn't make my IBS act up." He chuckled. "Anyway, didn't realize I was speeding. Good thing no one got hurt."

"Where did you get your *gelato*?" Suarez asked.

"The Whole Foods on Danbury Street. The gelato is long gone, but I can dig the receipt out of my recycling bin for you." He raised an eyebrow as if he was offering her something special. "What's going on?"

"A shooting occurred a few blocks from where we saw your vehicle, right before you peeled out of the area. Know anything about that?"

Luna shook his head. "Nope. Can't say that I do." He smoothed his hand over his hair, squared his shoulders, and smiled at Blake.

"Several people got shot in that warehouse," Suarez said. "Lots of blood left behind."

"That's a shame," Luna said.

"May I take a look at your Tahoe?"

"I'd say yes if I could. But it's not here."

"Where is it?" Suarez asked.

"I lent it to a friend. He's taking a trip across country."

"How kind of you. Rather convenient, too." The SUV was probably in a hidden garage undergoing carpet and leather replacement to eliminate all traces of the men who bled out inside it. "What's your friend's name?"

"Marco."

"Mind giving Marco a call and asking him to come back?"

"He had a rough week. He wanted to get away from it all, if you know what I mean. He either turned his phone off or left it behind. One or the other. I've actually been trying to get hold of him and haven't been able to since he left. But I'm happy to leave him a message for you."

"Don't bother," Suarez said. "If your car has GPS, we can track it that way."

"If only." Luna sighed and gave her an apologetic look, appearing sincere. "It's broken."

Suarez huffed as she looked around the home. "Funny that everything in your house looks brand new, immaculate even, and you've got some computer screen I've never seen before built into your fridge there, but the GPS on your SUV is broken." She put a hand on her hip and studied him. She wanted him to know his

51

smooth charms had no effect on her. "Is the GPS really broken, or did someone deactivate it?"

Luna laughed as if they were having a nice time together. "It's just broken, detective, and I won't bother to get it fixed. Who needs GPS in their car anymore? If I need directions, I use my phone."

"I hope your phoneless friend doesn't get lost on his trip across the country then," Suarez said.

"Mind if I use your restroom?" Blake asked, speaking for the first time since they arrived. Suarez wondered if Luna had charmed Blake with his fancy home and polished demeanor act. Whether or not he was genuine, he was definitely charming. And charm like that went a long way. Perhaps if Suarez had a little more of it, she'd have a bit more sophistication and beauty in her life, too. But still...Blake should know better than to fall for Luna's act.

Blake smiled in a coy way. "I had a late night and drank too much coffee this morning to make up for it."

Was she flirting with him now?

"Go ahead. It's that way." Luna gestured down the hall. "Sorry if the seat is up. I wasn't expecting company."

"Oh, I don't think twice about the seat being up. I have brothers," Blake said, sauntering off.

Luna watched her go. "Wrong way," he said when she took a left. "That's my bedroom."

"It's nice." Blake didn't turn around right away. She moved her head slowly from side to side, taking in the room.

Suarez asked Luna a few more questions that failed to provide additional information. When Blake came out of the bathroom, they left.

"Were you checking the place out?" Suarez asked in the squad car.

THE GROOM WENT MISSING

Blake nodded.

"You see anything?"

"Nothing. No blood. Bedroom and bathrooms are clean. Forensics might find minor traces I couldn't see, but if he cleaned it up, he did a good job. And there's no one hiding in that house."

"I didn't think we'd find anything. Like I said, he's smart. And confident. I wouldn't put it past him to have stopped for gelato after a shootout. Though from the looks of his place—a little OCD if you ask me—he wouldn't be a fan of anyone bleeding out in his car." She picked up her handheld radio. "I'll post a lookout for the Tahoe. And then I could use a coffee. You ready for another?"

Blake grinned. "I never drink coffee. The stuff gives me the jitters."

Suarez tried to ignore it, but there it was, a flash of appreciation for Missy Blake. Perhaps there was more to Blake than Suarez imagined. Just like there appeared to be more to Luna than she'd given him credit for.

***

Luna sipped his tepid tea at a front window, watching the cops leave. The irritable one sure hadn't appreciated him. Probably jealous.

Luna's acting skills, particularly his winning attitude in a local car dealership commercial, landed him where he was today. Years ago, at a bar, one of Eduardo Salazar's sons, Eric Salazar, recognized Luna and remembered his energetic announcement about zero percent financing and no money down. Eric welcomed Luna into his entourage for the night, offering unlimited drinks, meth, and heroin. Luna was at his most charming, pleased to have fans.

At the end of the evening, Eric wanted to offer Luna a more permanent job. His father's organization needed more "classy" guys like Luna to handle some of their business. Luna didn't know what the business was, but after spying the thick wad of cash Salazar's son used to buy round after round and tip generously, Luna sure wanted to find out.

Once he was in, there was no getting out and everyone knew it, so no use even thinking about it. A colleague or two disappeared every so often. Luna didn't know if they got new identification documents and escaped, or if they had permanently vanished into the ocean's depths encased in a barrel of concrete. Thinking about it made him shudder. Salazar handled loyalty displacement issues with brutal violence and Luna would rather be alive and wealthy than honest and dead. Eventually, he'd become desensitized to the harsher aspects of the business, like Tommy and Marco spilling their blood all over his Tahoe and the broken, tortured bodies Salazar occasionally left out as reminders for those who worked for him. Luna liked to pretend his adventures with the cartel were part of a popular narco series now in its fourth or fifth season. He did what they told him when they told him. And though he lacked freedom, he otherwise enjoyed the life the cartel afforded him.

When those cops showed up unannounced on his doorstep, he relished the opportunity to use his acting skills and thoroughly enjoyed every minute. He'd imagined what he wanted them to see, what he needed his character to convey, and brought the performance to life. They didn't worry him. Not even the bad-tempered one who would probably love to see him fall. He'd been careful. The authorities had nothing on him. And even if they did...the cartel had inside people and the best attorneys to fix things. The charges against them never stuck.

CHAPTER 8

Ned left the hotel early Saturday morning to attend the scheduled bridal party breakfast. Afterward, the women would go to a salon for hair, nails, and makeup. The men would head elsewhere for a straight razor shave, a trim, and a massage.

Victoria didn't mind being alone in the hotel suite. Meeting so many people the previous day had drained her. Socializing in large groups always wore her out, even when she thoroughly enjoyed the company. Being an introvert didn't mean she was shy or uncomfortable in groups. She didn't mind public speaking or heading up meetings at work. It merely defined the way she got energy and preferred to interact with the world. With the wedding coming up, and a long day and night of social interactions, she needed to recharge her energy in solitude.

She plopped onto the couch and opened Facebook on her phone. Impossible to do now without thinking about Dean and his claims of working so many hours.

The FBI advised agents against sharing anything personal. She did, however, have a few fake accounts she'd set up during previous operations. She'd used them to dig into people's backgrounds, and that's what she was doing now. Her curiosity stemmed from caring about Ned. Doing a little research on his previous girlfriend was normal. That's what she told herself as she typed into the search bar and waited to see what came up on Jules Redmond.

Jules had a page, but it was mostly dormant. No pet pictures. No serious boyfriend. No vacation shots. Friends had tagged her in the most recent posts. Jules had posted nothing of her own in the past year.

Victoria searched for Redmond Galleries next. The business had an active presence on Facebook and Instagram. Weekly posts celebrated significant sales for various artists. A lot of those photos featured Jules and her many hairstyles. Long and straight, kinky curls, soft waves, and various updos. Rarely did she smile. Her go-to expression for the camera conveyed someone basking in their success. Someone arrogant. Or maybe Victoria judged her unfairly. If Ned had fallen for her—sweet Ned, who got along with everyone yet failed to tolerate unkindness and discrimination of any sort—Jules must possess some admirable qualities. She appeared to be a complicated woman. Her extreme thinness might result from deep-seated insecurities or repressed pain. Though more likely, especially in her case, a control issue. She struck Victoria as a woman determined to control every aspect of her life, including every ounce of her body.

After perusing Redmond Galleries' accounts, Victoria went to the hotel gym for a quick workout. Ned returned at ten thirty a.m., just after she'd showered and sat back down on the couch. He hung up his coat, greeted her with a tender kiss, and sat next to her.

"How was the massage?" she asked.

"Didn't get one."

"What happened?"

"Scott wasn't at the breakfast. We went to his condo to look for him."

"We who?"

"The other groomsmen."

56

"And…did you talk to him?"

"No. We haven't heard from him since the text he sent Bailey last night."

Victoria widened her eyes and slapped her hand on her chest. "Oh my God! No one has? Not even Bailey?"

"Yes."

"Yes, she has or yes, no one has?"

"No one has heard from him." Ned got up and took his tuxedo out of the closet.

"They're still moving forward with the wedding?" Victoria asked.

"Yes. He told Bailey he would be there."

"You mean in that text she got last night?"

"Yes. The limos arrive in half an hour. You're going to share a car with Dean and Maria."

"But…are you sure this is a good idea? What if he doesn't show?"

"It's not my call and he'll be there." Ned moved his tongue over his bottom lip, something he often did when he was thinking. He didn't seem to realize how sexy she found it.

Victoria still had to get ready, but it would only take a few minutes to slip into her outfit and put on a bit of makeup. She watched Ned dress, then crossed the room and pressed her body against his. She wrapped her arms around his neck and kissed him, trying to take away some of the stress he experienced worrying about Scott.

Ned caressed his fingers over her head and through her hair, kissing her neck and lips and awaking sensors throughout her body.

Breathless, she pulled away so they wouldn't be late. She held onto his shoulders and smiled up at him. "You look very handsome. Too good to let go of, but there's always later." She kissed him one more time. "I'll see you soon."

Before leaving the room, Ned called Scott again and left a voicemail message. "Hey, Big Red. We're all worried. Really worried. We're on our way to your wedding now." Ned stared at his phone for a few more seconds, as if willing Scott to call back with some explanation that would make sense of his absence.

***

Victoria entered the church just as Kayla hurried past, holding her clipboard against her chest as usual. Clearly preoccupied with her role organizing the ceremony, the wedding planner gave a harried nod and no indication their encounter with her boyfriend the previous evening had bothered her.

The church looked picture perfect inside. Thick rays of light seeped through the stained-glass windows. The florists had tied ribbons and white lilies to the end of every pew. Elegant white floral sprays adorned the altar.

A groomsman ushered Victoria to the front, where she joined Dean and Maria on the left side with the groom's guests. As she took her seat, Dean looked up from typing into his phone and whispered, "Katie said he's still not here."

A solo violinist played elegant, soothing music while the church pews filled. After several songs, a brief silence ensued, causing everyone to turn toward the back of the building.

Dean whispered, "Everyone is telling Bailey to stall, but she doesn't want to. She keeps saying he'll be here."

A stomach-churning sensation took hold inside Victoria. She hoped someone would postpone the ceremony anyway, before the situation got worse. Surely they wouldn't start the procession until Scott arrived.

A small orchestra began playing from the balcony as members of the bridal party lined up in the back of the church.

It was starting! Victoria shifted in her seat, her nerves on edge, her mouth dry. If she was that uncomfortable as a guest, she couldn't imagine what Bailey was feeling.

Escorted by David, Jules was the first to walk down the center aisle. Her periwinkle bridesmaid's dress hung loose around her hips and waist, as if she'd lost several pounds since the last fitting. As Jules's harsh words echoed in Victoria's mind—*I don't want anyone to talk to her.* Victoria had to force her smile into place.

As the maid of honor and best man, Bridget and Ned were the last of the bridesmaids and groomsmen to reach the altar. Wearing a black dress, Bridget's smile faltered, the corners of her mouth stretching, then falling back in a way that revealed her discomfort. Ned's expression was more serious, but as he passed Victoria, he acknowledged her with a lingering gaze that made her recall the electrifying sensations of his hands on her skin. For a quick second, she forgot the feeling of impending doom growing inside her. It returned full force when a cellist and pianist played Pachelbel's Canon in D. Everyone stood in anticipation of the bride's entrance. After several long, hold-your-breath seconds, Bailey appeared wearing a beautiful silk dress with spaghetti straps and a corseted waist that showcased her hourglass figure. Strolling down the aisle with her father, she-maintained a brave smile, reminding Victoria of something she'd read on social media— science says if you smile, you tell your brain everything is okay.

Everything about the ceremony was spectacularly elegant, beautiful…and wrong. She wanted to close her eyes and make it stop until the groom appeared at the altar.

This should have been one of the most wonderful days of Bailey's life, not the most uncertain and painful. How was she holding it together? The nausea in Victoria's stomach grew, and it was all she could do not to grimace. Bitter disgust for Scott blossomed inside her. Why hadn't they waited for him to show up before starting? The meaning of *jilted at the altar* unraveled before them, excruciatingly painful for everyone witnessing it.

59

Bailey and her father stopped at the front of the church and embraced in a long hug. When they separated, silent tears streamed down Bailey's face, but she made it up the steps with her head held high. Turning to face the guests, she looked over their heads toward the large double doors in the center.

All the bridesmaids were crying. Katie held her bouquet in one hand and wiped away tears with the other. Bridget's mischievous smile was nowhere to be seen. Her lips quivered. Yet they were all still standing up there, trying to act as if this was normal. All except Jules, who directed her impassive gaze forward.

The orchestra played their last soft notes, and the sanctuary fell silent.

Duncan cleared his throat and yelled, "You're the most beautiful bride ever, Bailey."

"Beautiful inside and out," someone else added.

Sounds came from the rear of the building. The church doors opened. The pews creaked as the guests pivoted in their seats.

A lanky teenager marched in and headed to the front of the church. Wearing jeans, a dark hoodie, and sneakers, he hardly looked like a wedding guest. He was tall, with a youthful spring in his stride and a smattering of pimples on his chin that made Victoria guess his age at fifteen or sixteen at most. Above a hard-set jaw and narrowed eyes, his eyebrows converged to form an almost uninterrupted line of hair. Victoria had worked with enough juvenile delinquents to recognize an attitude of defiance when she saw one.

Everyone seemed to watch him. No one questioned his presence aloud, so Victoria figured someone must know him. Though he hadn't dressed himself appropriately for the wedding, he might be someone's clueless nephew or friend or second cousin.

He stopped a few feet from the altar. "Who of you is Ms. Redmond?"

"I am." Jules and her mother responded at the same time.

Scott's mother raised her hand. "I'm *Mrs.* Redmond," she said, with more conviction. "And who are you?"

The teen glanced toward the back of the church, as if planning his escape. "This is for you," he said to Mrs. Redmond.

"Who are you?" she asked again.

Stone-faced, the teen pulled something small from his coat pocket and tossed it onto her lap. Victoria scooted forward in time to see Scott's mother close her hands over a small black box and an even smaller slip of yellow paper.

Duncan's voice rose above the commotion coming from the other guests. "This is a private wedding. Who sent you?"

"I'm just a messenger, dude." The teen hurried toward an exit door and disappeared.

"Hey, come back here!" Ethan jumped up from his seat and ran out after the teen, followed by others. In the commotion that followed, Victoria wasn't sure where to focus.

"What did he give you?" Bailey asked Mrs. Redmond. "Is it from Scott?"

Jules dropped her flowers on the altar and hurried toward her mother, almost leaping to get there. "Give it to me," she demanded.

Mrs. Redmond handed the box and paper over to Jules, who marched off to one side of the altar with them. With her back to the guests, Jules shook her head in a slight movement. Then she turned around. Her eyes blazed with anger as she tore up the paper, again and again, letting miniscule yellow scraps flutter down and land on the burgundy-colored carpet. Victoria might have missed the next thing Jules did had she not been closely watching. Jules made eye contact with Duncan, held his gaze, then looked away.

"Hey!" Carrying the train of her dress, Bailey marched toward Jules. "What was that? Why did you tear it up?"

Jules looked out at the church full of people, then back to Bailey and responded with, "Come with me and I'll tell you." She waved the bridal party off the altar and toward a side door. They all followed. Scott's family and Bailey's father got up and went after them. Only the priest remained on the altar. He removed a handkerchief from his pocket and wiped his brow.

Victoria didn't know what to think of the scene, and from the surrounding murmurs, nor did anyone else.

From the side door, Ned caught her attention and beckoned her over.

She pointed to her chest and mouthed, "Me?" She knew he was talking to her, and even though she was incredibly curious to know what the note was about, what was in the box, and if either had to do with Scott's whereabouts, this seemed another private moment for family and close friends. She did not want to join them. She didn't feel right bearing witness to Bailey's pain and Scott's family's embarrassment. She'd already seen more than enough of it. But Ned continued to gesture to her. With the buzz of murmurs building amongst the church guests, Victoria stepped sideways out of her pew, past Dean and Maria and several people she didn't know. She followed Ned into the smaller chapel.

Bailey stood in the center of the group, still holding the small box in her hands as if she couldn't bear to open it.

"Do you want me to see what it is?" Bridget asked.

The question seemed to get Bailey moving. She lifted the lid, revealing two gold bands nestled inside. She removed one and held it close to her face. "It's his. Scott's wedding band. We had our initials and today's date engraved inside."

"He had it with him on his way to the rehearsal last night," Ned said.

No one spoke until Bailey put the ring back in the box, snapped it shut, and turned to Jules. "What did that note say?"

"Um...I'm sorry," Jules said.

"You're sorry about what?" Bailey's face was tight, her eyes unblinking. "What did it say?"

"The note said, 'Bailey, I'm sorry.'"

Bailey shook her head. Her skin paled. The box fell from her hand as she swayed. Bridget and Katie rushed to her side and held her up.

"Here, sit down," Katie said, gathering Bailey's dress to one side and helping her into a chair.

Still holding her bouquet, which she mashed against her side as she put her hands on her hips, Bridget faced Jules and said, "Why did you tear up the note? I think Bailey would have liked to see it and...I don't know...confirm his handwriting or something...rather than take your word for it."

Jules stared down at the fallen box. "I think...I was just so angry."

"There's nothing she can do about it now," Mrs. Redmond said, wringing her hands as she jumped to her daughter's defense.

Bridget threw up her arms, sending white flower petals into the air like confetti. "I can't believe he did this. I'm going to kill him. What are we supposed to do now?"

Bridget didn't aim her question at anyone in particular, and it seemed rhetorical, but Bailey answered. "I don't know. I need to think." Wincing, she clutched her waist and lowered her head. "I need a minute."

"It's okay." Katie wrapped her arms around Bailey and held her tight, murmuring, "You don't have to figure anything out. Just...shhh. We're here for you. These things happen. They happen. It's okay. You'll get through this. Not every relationship is meant to be."

63

"What?" Bailey lifted her head and stared at Katie. When Katie didn't answer, Bailey said, "Please just tell everyone to go to the reception as planned."

"I'll do it," Jules said. As she marched back to the sanctuary, Victoria edged toward the chapel doorway, eager to hear what Jules would tell everyone.

She stood front and center, her shoulders squared. "We're so sorry. Something happened with my brother."

Murmurs and gasps followed.

"He's had an emergency, and he's…not able to come. We'd like you all to attend the reception later tonight, as planned. We'll see you there. Again, on behalf of Scott and our family, please accept our sincere apologies." Jules lingered there, as if she had more to say. She even got so far as to open her mouth before closing it again.

"Is Scott okay?" someone asked.

She didn't answer because Ethan reentered the church, waving his arms around and breathing hard, as if he'd been running. "He got away!" Ethan said. "And you know what, Scott is a douche bag! He better be dead. That's the only excuse that's gonna fly now." Ethan's outburst elicited gasps and shushes, but also comments that seemed to support him.

Victoria ran her gaze over the floor beside the altar. At some point, maybe during the commotion Ethan caused, someone had picked up the scraps of ripped paper. They were no longer on the floor.

CHAPTER 9

The bridal party huddled together inside the small chapel as the main church emptied of guests. Victoria could see them through the windows, congregating outside. Their wide-eyed expressions conveyed their shock. This was not the wedding they expected to witness, and like her, they would never forget it.

"Victoria." Ned's whisper drew her to one side of the chapel, away from the others. "Can you use your contacts to track Scott's phone and find his location?"

"I can't. Not without a warrant," she whispered back, noticing Jules staring at her from across the room. "Unless we have evidence to show he's missing, *not* of his own accord, it's an invasion of privacy. Per the Supreme Court."

"No one has heard from him since those messages last night. I just can't believe he would do this to Bailey. Something happened to him. Maybe when he was looking for a parking spot."

"Like what?" Victoria tried to keep her tone gentle. "What do you think happened?"

"I don't know." Ned exhaled loudly.

She angled her body so no one could see her face as she tried to plead some sense into him. "If Scott was looking for a parking spot, he couldn't have been more than a few blocks from the church. It was still light out. A mostly residential area. The chances of something happening to him right before his wedding, something that didn't involve a motor vehicle accident or a medical issue—which we've already ruled out—are so very small."

Things happened. Victoria knew that all too well. Carjackings. Kidnappings. Random disappearances. In this situation, none were likely. No evidence of foul play existed.

"Besides, he texted Bailey last night to say he got called out of town for an emergency," she reminded him. Again, she couldn't help wondering what sort of emergency it could be. She felt another surge of anger toward Scott. He had hurt and betrayed so many people. She had no desire to meet him now.

"He had those rings on him when he disappeared," Ned said. "It's a message that something happened."

Yes. The message is that he doesn't want to get married. She rested her hand on Ned's arm. "You said he was nervous before the rehearsal."

Ned curled his bottom lip in. "No. It wasn't like that. And if you're going to mention that apology note next…none of us got to see it. Only Jules."

He had a point.

Victoria didn't want Ned to feel any worse than he probably already did. "It's possible that Scott freaked out at the last minute and is more surprised than anyone about what he's done," she said, giving Scott more credit than he might deserve. "Sometimes we don't know we're going to do something until the very moment it happens. People act unpredictably in new, high-stress situations."

"High-stress? No. I don't think so. Operating on dying people when you might be their only hope, which is what Scott does for a living…that's stressful. Marrying the woman he loves is not. If you and I were to get—I mean, look, I know you don't know Scott, but you know me. Can you trust that I'm a decent judge of character? Especially since it's my best friend's character in question. I may not be a profiler like you, but I know Scott."

Perhaps Ned didn't know his friend as well as he thought he did. Maybe Scott had changed in the past few years. Victoria had investigated many people who seemed innocent or unremarkable to those around them but turned out to be criminals with ugly secrets. Ned was too close to Scott to believe the worst of him, whereas Victoria was one of the few people in attendance who could be objective, who could clearly see what the evidence showed. "The thing is—" she said, "—half the people we arrest...no one around them had any clue what they were capable of. Even people who commit murder. We don't know what people can do until they do it. I've seen it countless times."

"Doesn't matter, Victoria. I know Scott. When he decides something, he does it. He doesn't look back. He sees everything through. Especially something this important." Ned frowned. "You don't have a lot of faith in relationships, do you?"

His comment stung. It felt personal. And maybe there was truth to it.

"I'm going to see if one of those limos will take me back to the hotel." He turned away without taking her arm, without waiting to make sure she followed. "Everyone, check your messages and keep your phones nearby, in case Scott calls," Ned said as he left.

CHAPTER 10

A frosty silence marked the limo ride back to the hotel as Victoria sat across from Ned. She knew she didn't deserve it. He wasn't angry with her. Scott's betrayal had left Ned shocked and confused. He needed time to process the situation in his own way.

Once they got to their suite, Ned changed out of his tux and left. He didn't say where he was going, and Victoria didn't ask. She busied herself checking work emails, something she hadn't planned to do but might as well since she had the time. She was currently between cases—the only reason taking a long weekend had been a possibility. Actually, it had been a possibility for some time now. Murphy knew about a PTSD episode she experienced— her fault for telling the bureau psychiatrist about it. Her boss wanted to give her time before putting her back in the field. She hoped that watch-and-wait time was nearing its end.

After cleaning her inbox of recent mail, Ned still hadn't returned, and Victoria became increasingly aware of the utter silence in the suite. Because her life consisted of work or being home with her animals, she was never entirely alone. It wasn't that she minded it now, she didn't, only that it seemed strange.

Ned's absence presented an opportunity to catch up with a friend or check in with her brother or father. But it would be almost impossible to keep from sharing what happened at the trainwreck wedding, since it really was unbelievable. Spreading the word would mean further humiliating Bailey, and Victoria didn't want any part of that. Instead, she ate another chunk of cinnamon streusel bread and reclined on the couch with her feet up, several pillows behind her back, and read her mystery novel. Until yesterday, she'd imagined a romantic weekend with Ned in Boston. The reality—there was nothing romantic about being alone and reading about mysterious dead bodies in the deep woods, but reading relaxed her.

Over an hour passed before she heard someone outside the door. She closed her book and sat up. "Hi," she said as Ned entered and tossed his key card onto a table. "You doing okay?"

"Yeah. We drove out to Scott's condo again. Me and David and Liam. We talked to a few of his neighbors. None of them saw him." Ned sat down on one end of the couch, leaving a few feet of space between them. "Sorry I left you alone for so long."

"No worries. Are we still…is the reception still happening?"

"Yes." He sighed. "I don't have to give a speech anymore. I guess that's…something."

"Ned, I'm sorry."

"About Scott being gone? Or about not trusting me?"

"Both."

"It's okay. You could be right. You're probably right. I just don't want you to be."

"But wouldn't you rather he changed his mind than the alternative? That something happened to him."

"Of course. God, this is awful. There is no good outcome, is there?" Ned moved closer and picked up her hands in his own. "You know, we had our first argument."

"You think?"

"Yep. Because I'm not counting any arguing we might have done in Greenland, being at death's door for a week. But this was different, and it turns out I don't like being upset with you."

She smiled. "Turns out I don't like you being upset with me either."

They kissed, and it hardly took a few seconds for everything to feel all right between them. The making up, which ended with her lying in his arms on his bare chest and loving the feel of his arms around her, made their earlier disagreement seem worth the trouble.

***

Victoria didn't know what to expect at the wedding reception. She understood why the hosts wanted to go through with it. Their guests had traveled from all over the country and several from abroad. Everything was already paid for. But the question remained—was it okay to have a good time? People would probably take their cues from Bailey, assuming she would be there. If a jilted bride could make the most of the situation, then so should the rest of them, if for no other reason than to show Bailey their support.

As Victoria and Ned entered the elevator, Katie came out of a room. A different room than she'd come out of yesterday, almost at the opposite end of the corridor.

Ned thrust an arm out and held the elevator doors open.

Katie picked up her pace. "Thanks," she said, joining them inside.

They stood facing forward. The elevator beeped as it descended.

"Katie, why were you crying last night before the rehearsal?" Ned suddenly asked in an accusatory tone that surprised Victoria.

Katie turned and stared blankly at him. With her height and high-heeled boots, she was almost eye-level with Ned.

"Your husband said he hadn't checked into the hotel yet," Ned said. "Who were you with?"

Katie pushed her long blonde hair over her shoulder. "How is that any of your business?"

"Scott is missing," Ned said. "He changed his mind about the wedding, supposedly. And right before the rehearsal, you came out of a room crying."

"And?" Confusion muddled her features until his meaning hit her. "Oh, my God! You think I was with Scott? I would never." Anger radiated from her eyes. "Bailey is my best friend. I can't believe you would think that."

"I don't know what to think," Ned said.

"None of us know what to think or what to say," Katie snapped. "And it's because of *your* friend. You worry about what *he's* doing right now and stay out of my business." She jerked her head around so fast her hair whipped to the opposite shoulder.

They rode the rest of the way to the lobby in silence, facing front, the air thick with awkward tension. When the elevator doors opened, Katie turned to face Victoria. "Just a word from the wise for you, Victoria. If Ned is anything like his friends, then you really can't trust him." With that, she stomped away without looking back.

"What was that supposed to mean?" Victoria asked.

Ned's frown deepened. "I have no idea."

***

A private chartered bus waited outside the hotel to shuttle the wedding guests to the country club. Once on board, Victoria spotted Katie taking a seat toward the back, so Victoria chose two seats up front. Throughout the ride, the ambiguity of Scott's whereabouts hung in the air like the proverbial elephant in the

71

room. No one mentioned what everyone had to be thinking about. It was no different when they reached their destination. During cocktails and appetizers, everyone refrained from discussing it aloud, relegating his absence to whispered speculation in small groups of close friends and family members. Victoria caught snippets as she moved around the room.

A slender woman in a silver sequined dress leaned against one of the cocktail tables and twisted her champagne flute with long, manicured fingers. "It would have been the wedding of the year, with Stephanie Redmond at the helm and her daughter helping her. Everything they do is spectacular. Those gift baskets, weren't they just lovely?"

"Oh, yes," said another woman. "You know, Vince Redmond is so proud of his wife. He told my husband he could walk away from his practice if he wanted to and retire very, very comfortably thanks to Stephanie's galleries."

"The bride looked absolutely gorgeous, the poor dear," someone else said. "Unfortunately, that's not what we'll remember most about this event."

"How utterly and completely humiliating for all of them," said the woman in the silver dress before Ned led Victoria away.

Nibbling on a delicious vegetable tartlet she accepted from a passing server, Victoria and Ned stood near a cluster of guests in their thirties and forties. A man with a bowtie and glasses spoke in a hushed tone. "Maybe he arrived after my shift last night. But we all knew he was getting married. No one would have called him in. Does he even have privileges at Beth Israel?"

A woman in the group glanced over her shoulder before responding. "I asked a friend in the ER there who knows him. She was on last night and didn't see him." The woman raised her brows, letting the meaning sink in. "I have another friend who does the scheduling at Mass General. I asked her too." She shook her head. "No one would have asked him to come in…and if they did…he had every right to refuse."

It was sounding more and more like last night's out-of-town emergency wasn't work related and might have been a fabricated excuse.

Able to see above most heads, Ned scanned the large room. "I'm going to the bar for a refill. Would you like one?"

"Sure." Victoria set her empty flute on a nearby cocktail table. A man she had yet to meet made eye contact with her as Ned walked away. The man's outfit consisted of mostly black—his pants, shoes, and coat—with a bright orange shirt. An interesting outfit.

"Hi," he said to her. "Jacob Arroyo." His hair was longer than hers and he couldn't seem to stop touching it.

She was certain she hadn't met Jacob before, but his name sounded familiar. "I'm Victoria Heslin. A guest of the best man. Are you family?"

"I'm a close friend of Scott's family. Redmond Galleries represents me. You obviously know nothing about modern art."

"Oh." His name fell into context. Pleased she remembered, she spoke without thinking first. "You made the cloud ornaments in our gift baskets."

"The cloud ornaments?" Jacob's mouth gaped open leaving no doubt she had offended him. "The ornament is a dove."

"Oh." She concealed her surprise. "Of course. Forgive me. It's a lovely ornament."

"You know that it's a collector's item, don't you? Commissioned specifically for the occasion." He studied her as he took a gulp from his glass.

"That's what it said on the tag that was attached. Very nice. I love the idea of an ornament and I'll treasure it. Hang it prominently on my tree next year." She smiled, hoping she'd said enough to make up for her faux pas. "So...are there a lot of other artists here?"

73

"A few. But perhaps none who have the same relationship I have with Redmond Galleries. I'm extremely grateful to Duncan, Jules and Stephanie." He took another sip of his drink and stroked his hair again.

"I assume your work benefits them as well," Victoria said.

"Yes. It's unbearably frustrating when you know your work is special, yet no one knows you exist. Unfortunately, in the art world, it takes someone with credibility to establish you before people can appreciate what was right under their noses. If not for Redmond Galleries, I might have joined the ranks of the many universally celebrated artists whose work only sold well *after* their penniless deaths. Yes. I'm very grateful."

"Nice," Victoria said, thinking Jacob might have been a sensational artist, but he was still an arrogant man.

"Excuse me." A young woman in a catering uniform addressed them. "We're asking everyone to find their seats for dinner. Would you like help to find your assigned table?"

"Thank you. I think we'll be okay," Victoria answered, grateful for the interruption. "It was nice to meet you, Jacob."

Across the room, she found Ned leaving the bar with their drinks. They walked to their seats together. They were at the same table as David and Maria, Liam, and another couple with a college connection to Scott. Several of the tables were completely empty. Victoria could only imagine the vacant spots belonged to Scott's friends or coworkers; people who no longer felt comfortable being there.

As the guests took their seats, Bailey entered with her phone in her hand. She sat at the head table, next to her sister and the other bridesmaids. At most weddings Victoria had attended, guests inundated the bride with congratulations throughout the reception. That wasn't happening. Probably because they didn't know what to say.

Maria raised her wineglass toward the head table. Liquid sloshed over the sides, suggesting she'd had one too many drinks during the cocktail hour. "More power to Bailey for going through with this. I've got mad respect for that woman."

Ned reached for Victoria's hand, squeezed it, and let go when their entrees arrived. Conversations continued while people ate their dinners. Victoria glanced at the head table, where neither Bailey nor Jules touched their food.

Bridget dinged her fork against her glass and stood up. Chatter across the banquet room settled, then ceased as everyone gave her their attention. "I want to make a toast to my amazing sister," Bridget said, her eyes brimming with tears.

Beside her, Bailey straightened in her chair and looked up.

Bridget held her wineglass in one hand and rested the other on the back of her chair. "Over the past few weeks, I thought a lot about what I wanted to say during my maid-of-honor speech. I worked really hard to get it just right to honor my sister. And even though the situation has changed, what I planned to say still applies…so I'm going for it. The difference is that those of you who don't know Bailey as well as I do can now see the truth in my words." Bridget's gaze returned to her sister. "Since the day I was born, Bailey has been the person I've most looked up to. Bailey has always been strong and brave, sure of what she wanted. She's always held her head high and got through the toughest days, even when life threw its worst at us. She was the rock for me and our dad when our mother died. And when she had her accident—no one was more brave, accepting, and gracious. She inspired all of us. I've always been so proud to be her sister. So damn proud." Bridget closed her eyes and looked away, then finished through sobs. "And never more than I am today. I love you, Bailey, and you deserve the world."

At Victoria's table, Maria dabbed at her glistening eyes and the men looked uncomfortable. It had just become even more difficult for Victoria to think of Scott Redmond without an enormous ball of anger erupting inside her.

"I can't believe he paid a kid to return the ring," Ethan shouted. "What a coward. What a douche."

"Shut up, Ethan," Bridget yelled from the head table where she was still crying. "Just shut up! You aren't helping. You always thought you might marry Bailey someday, didn't you? Try not to be so thrilled about this."

People gasped. Victoria could hardly believe what was happening. Bailey might have been handling the situation with grace, but others weren't.

A stifled choking sound came from somewhere near the front of the room. Mrs. Redmond's chair scraped the floor as she moved it away from the table. She got up and rushed away with her arms crossed and her head down. Jules went after her mother.

"Aw, hell," Duncan exclaimed, taking his martini glass with him, and shuffling after the two women.

Mr. Redmond pushed his own chair back and craned his neck to watch them leave, but remained in his seat, as if he couldn't decide if he should stay or go.

Bailey stood up. "I think I better speak now, before *everyone* flees the room." Her slight smile disappeared quickly. She clasped her hands together. "It's been a really emotional day, but please, don't say things you might regret later. I know some of you think I'm in denial. But Scott wouldn't do this. I know him. He wouldn't do this." She looked around the room, silently challenging anyone to defy her. "I've spent the afternoon calling hospitals and waiting by the phone. I know many of you have asked me not to call the police, and so I haven't, even though I wanted to immediately. I don't know what's going on, but something happened to Scott. And I'd appreciate your help in finding him."

So…Ned wasn't the only one who refused to accept the evidence.

If Scott didn't change his mind about the wedding, then why did some of his family and friends look so ashamed? Why didn't they want to call the police? From Victoria's perspective, some of them knew more than they were saying.

CHAPTER 11

Ned stretched out on the bed, waiting for Victoria to join him.

"I just need a few more minutes," she said through the open bathroom door as she scrubbed her face.

Who would ever have imagined the weekend would turn out as it had? After the reception, many questions filled Victoria's mind. Ned might have the answer for one of them. She turned off the faucet and asked, "Do you know anything about the accident Bridget mentioned in her speech? Bailey's accident?"

"She was in a car accident about a year after she met Scott. The impact crushed her leg. They had to amputate at the knee."

"Oh, no. You said she was a runner, that had to be terrible for her."

"She still runs. Like Bridget said, Bailey is brave and she's tough."

Victoria dabbed moisturizer over her skin. "So…she must use a prosthetic."

"She does."

"I couldn't even tell."

"I know. I forget she has it."

As Victoria left the bathroom, she looked down at her own missing fingertips. She and Bailey had that in common. Losing fingertips wasn't as significant as losing a leg, but Victoria knew what it was like to lose a part of her body—the phantom pains and itches, the occasional regret that surfaced and needed to be quelled since it was nothing but a waste of time and energy. Victoria was not one to feel sorry for herself, and apparently neither was Bailey. Victoria would have enjoyed spending time with Bailey, getting to know her better. Maybe taking a trip with her, Ned, and Scott. Shame that couldn't happen now. Thanks to Scott, the whole notion of love and trust had taken a hit, trivialized by his behavior. But that didn't mean she and Ned should give up. She was alone at last with him. It wasn't too late to cultivate a little romance, maybe appreciate what they had while it was there.

His mesmerizing eyes did the trick as she slid under the smooth bed sheets beside him.

"This has not been the weekend I expected. Let's see if we can make up for it," he said, as if reading her thoughts. He stroked her bare shoulder under the silk strap of her nightgown, then kissed her with a hunger she'd never sensed in him before. His touch, always strong and confident, held a new roughness.

She slid his T-shirt over his head and tossed it away. He pulled off her nightgown and moved on top of her, one arm supporting most of his weight, his skin hot against hers. His body hard everywhere. She buried her hands in his hair as he gave her a crushing kiss.

And then, with no warning, she pictured Bailey's tear-stained face as she walked bravely into the church in her gorgeous wedding gown. Victoria tensed, no longer responding to his touch.

Ned stopped kissing her. He rolled onto his side. "What's wrong?"

"Sorry. I can't stop thinking about what happened today."

"I know. I wish I went after the kid who came to the church," Ned said. "I'd do anything now to find out who he was and how he got the rings. It's too bad Ethan didn't catch him."

A knock at the door made them sit up. The clock on the bedside table read eleven thirty at night. "Who is it?" Ned asked, his voice raised.

"Bailey," she said from the other side of the door.

Ned mouthed *sorry* to Victoria.

Victoria shook her head, letting him know it was okay.

"Just a minute," Ned called out to Bailey as he plucked his T-shirt from the bed and pulled it over his head.

Victoria grabbed her nightgown and headed toward the bathroom. "I'll be right back," she whispered. "I hope she's here because she finally heard from Scott."

From inside the bathroom, Victoria heard the door to the suite open.

"Hey," Ned said. "How are you doing?"

"I've certainly been better," Bailey said. "Sorry to bother you."

"Don't be. It's okay."

Victoria appreciated Ned's sweet, caring tone. He'd been incredibly supportive to Bailey, which made Victoria like him even more.

"Actually, I was hoping I could talk to you *and* Victoria," Bailey said.

"Oh, sure. Hold on. I'll be right back."

Ned tapped on the bathroom door. "Victoria, can you come out? Bailey wants to talk to both of us."

Victoria ran a brush through her hair and pulled it back into a ponytail. She left the bathroom, expecting Bailey to be inside their room.

"She's in the hall," Ned said.

"Ned," Victoria whispered, feeling terrible he'd left Bailey in the hall and now it must have been so obvious she interrupted something, which might make her feel worse. Or maybe she was too distraught about her fiancé to worry about such things. Although even now, in arguably the worst of times, Bailey had hardly seemed self-absorbed. Victoria opened the door wide and offered Bailey a close-lipped smile, doing her best to convey genuine welcome.

Bailey entered the suite. The stress and disappointment of the last two days had taken a toll on her glow, but determination radiated from her red-rimmed eyes. She'd changed into loose slacks and a burgundy sweater. Now that Victoria knew about the car accident, her gaze dropped inadvertently to Bailey's legs. Which leg was the prosthetic? Victoria still couldn't tell.

Bailey sank into one of the sitting area chairs. She put her feet on the edge of the cushion, wrapped her arms around her knees and rested her forehead against them for a few seconds. "First, I'm so sorry about all that's happened."

"*You* have absolutely nothing to apologize for," Victoria said. "I admire you for holding the reception. It was nice."

"You have Mrs. Redmond and Kayla to thank," Bailey said with a sigh. "Again, I'm sorry to intrude. I hope it's okay… I couldn't sleep. We all want to know where Scott is. Make sure he's safe. His mother is insisting we avoid the police. She's concerned about what it looks like. Everyone seems to want to keep things quiet. I guess I should appreciate their intent, but I don't agree. If the situation should embarrass anyone, it's me. And I'm not embarrassed. Just…confused. Anyway, Scott's parents are hiring a private investigator who will start tomorrow."

"That's good," Ned said. "At least we'll know he's safe. When they locate him."

"Yes, but I'm worried about waiting," Bailey said. "In case..." She made eye contact with Victoria. "Um...I know you're an FBI agent."

"Yes." Victoria knew what was coming, and she wanted to help Bailey, but wasn't sure it was the right thing to do. Scott didn't want to be found yet.

"It's killing me not knowing where he is. I just..." Bailey stood up, wringing her hands. "I can't help thinking...I can't believe he wouldn't call. I just have to know where he is." She stopped pacing and looked down at Victoria, her eyes pleading. "Can you help me?" Her bloodshot eyes held immense pain. Victoria understood it well, from personal experience. That's what happened when someone you loved went missing and you didn't have a clue where they were or how to get them back. Dealing with that pain was part of the reason Victoria became an agent. After her mother's abduction, Victoria never wanted to be helpless again, just waiting and praying, hoping for the best. Nor did she want that for others. Despite the circumstances, she took a long inhale. "What do you have in mind?"

"I don't know exactly," Bailey said. "I figured you had more clout than a private investigator. You have access to better information. What *can* you do?"

Victoria looked at Ned, who nodded, encouraging her. Bailey was right. There were several things Victoria could do. She had access to databases beyond the typical private investigator. Maybe if she located Scott, it would help Bailey come to terms with what happened and save her from the humiliation of dealing with the police. The authorities might be kind, depending on who she worked with, but they were just as likely to point out the obvious and refuse their help. After all, Scott hadn't been gone long, and the law allowed adults to run away and hide from their lives, their families, their weddings, no matter how cowardly that action may be.

Victoria headed toward her laptop. "I can put out a search for his car."

"That would be great," Bailey said. "I would really appreciate that. I'm checking out of the hotel tomorrow. I'm supposed to go to St. Lucia on Monday. Bridget said she'd go with me. But I'm still deciding. I guess it depends on what you learn."

"Let's exchange phone numbers," Victoria said. "I'll let you know if we get a hit on his car."

This was not Victoria's case. It wasn't a case at all. She was only helping Bailey find information. Helping her accept what happened. She hoped her involvement would lessen Bailey's pain, not make it worse.

CHAPTER 12

A text message electric chirp woke Victoria. She opened her eyes and rolled over to glance at the bedside table clock and get her bearings. Almost eight a.m. Sunday morning. They still had one more night in Boston.

Ned slept beside her, breathing deep in a slow, calm rhythm. He ought to be tired. They had slept little. Remembering their night brought a smile to her lips. Sharing a bed with him was more peaceful than with her dogs, who spread to their full length until she woke up hanging off the edge of the bed. At the slightest noise outside, they jumped up, barking. Incredibly annoying, but she loved them no less for it.

Victoria snuggled next to Ned for a few more minutes before sliding her phone off the table to read her message. It was a response to the all-points bulletin she'd posted on Scott's vehicle. She sat up, clicked the attached link, and read the information.

Boston's Airport Security staff had identified Scott's Jeep Wrangler in their short-term parking garage. Victoria wasn't surprised. The airport topped her list of places where she expected the vehicle to be found. According to the security staff, it entered the parking area on Friday night. The night before the wedding.

Victoria tried to anticipate what Ned's reaction would be when she told him. More disappointment. Perhaps anger. And yet, no matter how furious he and Scott's other buddies might be, they would eventually forgive Scott and move on, their friendships intact. His family would forgive him, too. But Bailey—well, that was another story. It would take an enormous heart for a woman to forgive him for taking off like he did. Victoria didn't know the real story. Maybe Scott had good reasons for not going through with the wedding. It may have been the right thing to do in the long run. The unforgivable part was not mustering the courage to let Bailey know. He could have spared her worry, humiliation, and public heartbreak.

Victoria was still thinking about Scott when Ned opened his eyes.

"Morning," she said.

Ned propped himself up on his elbow and rubbed his eyes. "Morning. You're awake. Did you hear anything about Scott's car?"

She wanted to laugh because he hadn't wasted a second before remembering and asking for an update, but there was nothing amusing about the news she had to deliver. "Yes."

"And?" he asked, pushing up to a sitting position.

"It's at the airport."

Ned shook his head and Victoria wasn't sure if it reflected his disappointment or if he'd returned to denying the facts.

"I know Bailey didn't find a flight purchase on their credit card, but he must have a card she doesn't know about," she said. "Or he used cash. He had the next ten days off for their honeymoon. He's probably trying to figure out how to face his family and friends and what to say to Bailey."

Ned groaned. "He wouldn't do that."

"His family seems to think he did."

"Can you call the airlines and find out what flight he took? Is that something you can do without a warrant?"

85

"I can. But Ned…Scott doesn't want anyone to know where he is, or he would have told someone by now. Let him come back when he's ready. He has to go back to work soon enough."

"What if he's in trouble?" Ned asked.

Victoria ran her fingers across the hard muscles of his shoulder and chest. Locating Scott was important to him. "If I do this, once we find his location, that should be it."

He pulled Victoria close and kissed her. "Thank you."

After using the bathroom and brushing her teeth, she drew the curtains open and booted up her laptop. While waiting, she grabbed a water bottle from the mini fridge and drank as she stared out the large windows at the city. Outside, a group of joggers crossed the bridge that arched over the river. Two women with fleece-lined boots walked terriers and cradled to-go coffee cups in their hands.

Standing near Victoria at the window, Ned stretched his arms overhead, then raked his hands through his hair. "I better call Bailey."

"Hold on, let's wait until we find out where Scott went." Victoria sat down on the couch and logged into the FBI's server, then the Secure Flight tracking system, which contained all airline passenger information for flights originating or landing in the United States. She typed in Scott Redmond and waited.

Ned joined her on the couch. He massaged her neck and shoulders while she stared intently at her computer screen.

"There's no record of Scott on any recent flights," she said.

"You checked all the airlines?"

"Yes. For Friday and Saturday. He didn't fly under his name."

Ned pressed his hands against his temples. "Believe me, Scott is not someone who has multiple passports or…a second family somewhere or anything wild like that. The guy works at a hospital and reserves any leftover time for Bailey and the gym. If he didn't get on a plane as Scott Redmond, then he didn't get on a plane."

Ned was too trusting and loyal, unwilling to believe his friend might have a devious side. And Victoria could hardly blame him. He hadn't witnessed firsthand the shocking things people could do. Scott's behavior was reprehensible, but nothing compared to some of the criminal activity on the FBI's radar.

"If only he would call from wherever he is and let Bailey know he's all right," Victoria said.

"Unless he can't call," Ned said, now pacing the suite.

If Ned was right, despite the evidence to the contrary, Victoria would regret not doing more to find his friend. "All right. I'm going to request the footage from the security cameras in the parking lot. This might take a good while." If they could see Scott getting out of his car with a suitcase or whatever, it might help everyone move past worrying and into unfettered anger.

On hold with airport security, she nibbled on a piece of cinnamon streusel bread from the gift basket and stared out the windows again. Sparkles from the sun's reflection danced across the river's surface. When someone from security returned to the line, Ned continued to pace with his arms crossed while Victoria put in the request. The airline sent her a digital form, which she filled out to include her FBI identification number and sent back. "They're going to email the footage to me," she told him. "It will take at least a few hours, if we're lucky. Want to go for a run? Looks like you've got energy to burn. We've got plenty of time before the historic bus tour."

"Sure. That would be great."

Victoria checked her weather app. "It's thirty-three degrees right now, but it's supposed to get colder and there's a forecast for snow around nine a.m."

They changed into cold weather running clothes and left the hotel. Once they got moving, it didn't take long for their bodies to warm up. They ran a few miles, mostly in comfortable silence, across the river, then into the city, choosing their route one turn at a time. The city seemed peaceful.

They passed a restaurant that made Victoria smile. "My mother took me here on a college visit years ago. Just the two of us. We had lunch in there."

Running through Boston brought back some vivid, happy memories, though she and her mother had argued about something during the trip. Considering Victoria couldn't remember what about, it couldn't have been important. If she'd known her mother would only be around a few more years, they wouldn't have argued over little things. Victoria would have appreciated her more in every moment. For instance, the way her mother arched her eyebrows and formed a lopsided grin whenever something amused her. And the I-don't-care-what-other-people-think attitude that made Abigail Heslin different from so many other parents Victoria knew.

Victoria stopped reminiscing when they came to a steep street in the Beacon Hill area. She focused on sprinting up, taking powerful strides, and pumping her arms. Beside her, Ned loped upward with an easy stride, his breath relaxed. Victoria trained regularly for her job, in case of a pursuit. She'd won a few 5ks in her age group over the years. But Ned trained harder for the sheer joy and challenge of it. She couldn't match his speed or endurance.

"Race you the rest of the way?" he asked, his eyes beaming.

She loved having a partner who could push her physically and mentally. But right then, his grin only made her laugh. "I'm already going almost as fast as I can!" she said between labored breaths.

"You've got more in you, I'm sure of it." He sounded like an encouraging coach and not at all as if he was matching her stride for stride.

Her laughter caused her to lose pace and made the uphill climb more difficult. "It's just so easy for you, isn't it?"

"Nah. It's never easy." He grinned. "Except when it is."

At the top of the hill, Victoria slowed to catch her breath. Something moving under a heap of blankets drew her gaze to an entryway. A homeless person huddled there next to a metal grocery cart filled with belongings. Between the man and the cart, a mixed breed dog lifted his head from a blanket and watched them approach.

Victoria felt compassion for the man, but as always—she couldn't help herself—it was the dog that really pulled at her heartstrings. "Hi." She waved to the man. "How are you doing?"

"Oh, I'm doing okay," the man answered.

"What's your dog's name?"

"His name is Fred."

"Hi, Fred." She kneeled near the dog but kept her hands to herself. "I bet you love hanging out with your owner all day, don't you?"

"He's my best friend and the best dog anyone could ever want," the man said. "Had him for six years."

Never taking his eyes off Victoria, Fred got up and moved to his owner's side.

"How does he look, Ned?" Victoria asked. "Can you look him over?"

"I'm a vet," Ned told the man, as he studied the dog. "I don't know what's going on inside him, but he's a good weight. Eyes look bright."

"He's a healthy boy," the man said.

"That's good. Bye, Fred and have a good day, sir," Victoria said, before turning away to resume their run.

"I brought a credit card but no cash," Ned told Victoria. "You have any?"

"No. I only brought my phone."

Disappointed, she thought about her own animals and the spoiled lives they enjoyed ever since she rescued them from shelters or adopted them from racetracks. They'd have a rough time adjusting to a more normal pet's life now.

She and Ned had run for over an hour when they returned to the bridge that would lead them back to the hotel. They jogged in place, their breath escaping in little white puffs, waiting to cross the street at a light. Ned unzipped his pocket and checked his running app. "That was eight miles."

During that time, the temperature had dropped, and clouds formed, coloring the sky a soft gray. Snow seemed imminent.

Near the hotel, they entered a café and bought breakfast sandwiches, a coffee for Ned, and a latte for Victoria. The heat from the drink seeped through her gloves. She took off the lid and let the sweet aroma float up to her face. "The perfect finish," she said, loving that they had time for the long run, a leisurely walk back to the hotel with coffee, and hours to go before the bus tour. She planned to take a long, hot shower. Maybe a bath. Maybe go back to bed. She glanced at Ned and grinned. She wasn't thinking about sleeping.

"Hey, can you check your email for the airport video when we get inside?" he asked, breaking her reverie, and definitely *not* reading her mind.

"Sure."

In their hotel suite, Victoria went to her email. "It's here. A video clip from the parking garage." She scooted over so Ned could see her screen.

THE GROOM WENT MISSING

She opened the file, checked the timestamp, and began fast forwarding from shortly after Scott dropped his family at the church. Logan airport was a busy place. Car after car entered the garage, stopped to take a ticket, then drove on. With the images sped up, it reminded her of watching a comedy reel. With Ned watching over her shoulder, she sipped her latte, ready to hit play at the first sign of Scott's car.

Two Jeep Wranglers entered the parking garage in thirty minutes. The first was red. The second royal blue. Twenty more minutes passed. At 9:48 p.m., a black Jeep arrived.

"Stop. Go back," Ned said, setting his coffee down.

Victoria rewound the video for a few seconds and pressed pause. She zoomed in on the license plate.

"That's his car," Ned said.

She rewound again and zoomed in on the driver. When he reached to take a ticket from the machine, he remained facing forward. Maybe even looking slightly away from the camera.

Ned slapped the desk with his hands. "That's not Scott. Why is he driving Scott's car?"

In profile, the driver was a handsome man with short black hair who would fit in well with Scott's circle of friends, although his mustache and beard might be uncommon. He appeared to be average height, though hard to say for sure, and in his mid to late thirties.

"Do you know who he is?" Victoria asked.

"No. Never seen that guy. Zoom in on the passenger seat. See if Scott is with him."

Victoria rewound the video and paused it again. The camera angle wasn't wide enough to tell if anyone else was in the car.

"Let's see if Bailey knows the driver," Victoria said.

91

Ned took one more look at the paused image of the stranger before hurrying from the room. "I'll go get her."

A few minutes later, he was back, tapping on the door. "Victoria, I didn't take my key. Open up."

Victoria opened the door. Bailey burst in barefoot, and for the first time, Victoria could see the lower part of Bailey's prosthetic. A normal shaped foot and ankle made of a smooth, skin-colored material.

"How long has his car been there?" Bailey asked.

"Since Friday night," Victoria answered. "It entered the garage approximately three hours after the rehearsal ended."

"Let me see the driver." Bailey hurried to the open laptop and leaned close to the zoomed-in image. With her eyes glued to the screen, she shook her head. "I've never seen that man before." The pitch of her voice rose. "I don't know who he is." She straightened and stared at Victoria. "I should go to the airport. Don't you think?"

"We'll go with you," Ned answered. "Do you have a key to his car?"

"Yes," Bailey answered. "I'm going to grab my things. I'll meet you downstairs in the lobby."

"I just need five minutes." Victoria grabbed some clothes and went into the bathroom. She yanked off her sweaty sports bra and panties and put dry ones on. That would have to do for now.

Who was driving Scott's car? And more important, where was Scott? She hoped the trip to the airport would finally get them answers.

CHAPTER 13

Ned remained quiet as he drove them to the airport, although he made a fist and tapped it against the steering wheel at each stop light. Traffic had picked up since their morning run. The cars no longer moved freely along the roads. A truck behind them honked, adding to the growing tension inside and outside their vehicle.

Victoria turned around to look at Bailey in the backseat. Bailey's hands rose to cover her mouth, then returned to her lap. She twisted her fingers together for a few seconds before she slid them under her thighs. She must have been emotionally depleted. The stress of the wedding, her groom disappearing, the not knowing…all of it had taken its toll and left her with tired, puffy eyes and worry lines crinkling her forehead. And yet she wasn't drowning in pity or having an emotional breakdown like most people would. That sure said a lot about her inner strength. A strong woman, despite her hardships. Or perhaps because of them. Victoria wanted to comfort her, but until they figured out what was going on, she wasn't sure what to say. Instead, she offered a sympathetic smile.

Snow began to fall, small wet flakes splatting the windshield. Ned turned on the wipers.

"I told you I checked our credit cards, didn't I?" Bailey asked. "He didn't buy a plane ticket."

"Does he have any friends with private airplanes?" Ned asked.

"No," Bailey answered. "Not that I know of. Do you think Scott got carjacked? Or he got kidnapped for a ransom? Do you think that's a possibility?"

Victoria had a visceral reaction to Bailey's question. "I would if his family received a ransom call. Have they?"

"No," Bailey answered. "Unless they're not telling me. And they wouldn't do that. No. The answer is no. I don't know what I was thinking suggesting it."

"That might be best thing that could happen right now," Ned said. "The Redmonds pay a ransom. Scott comes back. And everyone who said something terrible about him has to apologize big time."

Victoria wondered if he was throwing her into that category.

"Oh, no," Ned said, reaching over for Victoria's hand. "I'm so sorry."

"It's okay." Talking about a potential ransom hit close to home. She bit her lips and didn't respond.

"What?" Bailey asked.

Victoria didn't want to make Bailey more nervous.

"Please. tell me," Bailey said. "I've had enough of not knowing what's going on."

"Professional criminals kidnapped my mother for ransom," Victoria said. "She had a heart condition and needed daily medicine, which she didn't have with her."

"That's right. I read that somewhere but forgot. I'm sorry, Victoria. I know what it's like to grow up without a mother."

"I was already in college when it happened," Victoria said. "What happened to my mother shouldn't have happened, for so

THE GROOM WENT MISSING

many reasons. But I've handled other kidnapping cases. They all ended well. Anyhow, let's not get ahead of ourselves. We don't have any evidence someone kidnapped Scott."

"I know. But if Scott didn't want to get married, he would tell me," Bailey said. "He knows I would understand."

"I agree," Ned said. "And I assure you, he had no reservations about getting married. Zero."

Victoria wasn't sure if they were trying to convince her, or themselves. For Scott's sake, she hoped they were wrong. As she'd already told Ned, missing by choice was a far better situation than the alternative.

***

They arrived at the airport's short-term-parking garage, took a ticket to enter, and drove up to the fourth floor. When they arrived, Bailey said, "There it is!"

Before Ned came to a complete stop, she jumped out with the extra key fob in her hand.

"Wait!" Victoria shouted. Open-minded to all possibilities now, she had considered various scenarios and couldn't shake the terrible image of someone tied up in the back of the Wrangler. Maybe dead. Maybe alive. Airport security said they peered inside Scott's vehicle after identifying it. They reported seeing nothing suspicious. But how good a job did they do? Was it a quick glance as they walked past?

Bailey didn't listen. She pressed the key fob. The back of the Jeep slowly opened. She pushed aside a blanket and a small cooler. Victoria braced for the worst.

"Nothing unusual," Bailey said, leaving the back open and moving to the front of the car.

"Hold on," Victoria said, her voice louder and more commanding than before. "Don't touch anything."

This time, Bailey took a step back.

Wearing her winter gloves, Victoria opened the driver's side door. She shone her phone's flashlight around and searched for signs of a struggle or blood inside the car—things that would immediately tell her Scott was in trouble. She saw neither.

A center cup holder held the parking ticket stamped with a 9:48 p.m. arrival time. Next to the ticket rested a small, yellow paper. A post-it note folded in half. The same paper as the note delivered to the church. The one Jules destroyed.

In the tension of the moment, Victoria forgot she didn't have a full forefinger. When she picked up the paper, it slid from between her thick gloves. She scooped it up again, using her thumb and middle finger, unfolded it, and read the neatly printed note.

Bailey, something unexpected came up. Can't marry you now. Go to St. Lucia and have a blast. Don't love you, Bales.

Victoria held the paper up for Bailey to read.

"No. No," Bailey said, her hands balling into fists. "He would never write that. It's so...I don't know...cavalier. Like what he did is no big deal. As if he finds it amusing. He didn't write that."

Ned read the note next. "She's right. That doesn't sound like Scott at all."

"And that print is way too neat," Bailey said. "Scott's handwriting is barely legible."

If they were right, something strange had occurred. But why would someone pretend to be Scott and leave Bailey a note? What was the point? A carjacker wouldn't do it. And whoever wrote it knew about Scott's wedding and his honeymoon destination. That person also knew that Scott ended his communications to Bailey with, *Love you, Bales.*

The odd note made Victoria want to dig deeper. She didn't have any equipment with her to process fingerprints, hairs, and other evidence. But she knew someone in the FBI's Boston office, a woman who graduated with her from the academy. She might be able to help. Victoria called her friend.

Becca answered with enthusiasm. "Hey! It's been a long time. I've been thinking about you a lot since your plane crash. I hope you're doing okay. How are you?"

"I'm doing well. Thank you for the thoughtful card you sent. I really appreciated it."

"Yes, well, you were in my thoughts and prayers a lot. Still are. I miss you."

"Thanks. I'm actually in Boston and I could use a forensic expert to process a vehicle. Not someone from the FBI. I was thinking about a private forensic tech or consultant. Do you know anyone?"

"Sure. We've got a few good ones we use as consultants. Hold on. I've got their contact information on my phone. I'm going to forward you some names. But I'd try Lance first. He's a good guy. Dependable. I've never had to wait long for him to show up. He'll probably charge you by the hour plus travel."

"I don't even need him to process the evidence. Just collect it."

"He'll do a good job, regardless. Tell him I gave you his number and that I said, hey."

"Okay. I need to call him now, but thanks, and let's do a better job of keeping in touch."

"Yes. It was really great to hear from you, Victoria. Take care. And good luck with whatever you're working on."

Victoria said goodbye to Becca and called Lance. He picked up the phone immediately. After explaining what she needed, he agreed to bring the necessary equipment and meet her on the fourth floor of the parking garage.

"He said it will take him a little over an hour to get here." Victoria put her phone away and surveyed the garage. She spotted a camera mounted on a large column. "Lock up the car," she told Bailey. "Let's go inside and talk to security while we wait. I'll see if we can get more security footage showing who left the vehicle after it parked."

They rode an elevator to the level connecting the parking garage to the terminal. They walked a short distance outside, where the snow continued to fall in small, swirling flakes that left wet marks on their coats. Back inside, they located the security office and walked up to the counter.

"Hello," Victoria said.

"Can I help you?" The man behind the counter spoke without looking up.

"Victoria Heslin. With the FBI."

He gave her his attention then, scanning the badge she set on the counter in front of him.

"I need to see security footage from the short-term parking garage, fourth floor, row L, for Friday night," she said.

"Why?"

"A potential missing person situation." That's all Victoria intended to share.

"My fiancé went missing two days ago, the day before our wedding," Bailey added. "Someone drove his car here and left it."

The security employee snickered, a derisive sound that turned into a chuckle. "Sounds more like he changed his mind and went on the honeymoon without you."

"Hey!" Ned leaned across the desk toward the employee. "Is that how you help here?"

Victoria glared at the man. His comment represented the worst-case scenario everyone wanted to spare Bailey from experiencing. "Whom do I need to speak with to get access to the video?" Victoria asked, her tone reflecting her impatience. "Do I need to fill out another form?"

"Hold on. Wait here." With a groan, the man pushed his bulky body up from his chair and shuffled out through a side door. Almost twenty minutes later, he returned, and they followed him into a back-office room. A wall of monitors showed live views of the garage and airport. He led them to a corner monitor and showed them how to navigate the controls.

"I got other things to do," he said. "You got this?"

"Yes. Thank you," Victoria answered. "Go do whatever you have to do."

He studied her for a few more seconds, as if he wasn't sure if he could leave them. "We got eyes in here too, so watch yourselves. Don't mess anything up," he said.

"Hey, try to have a little respect," Ned told him.

The man grunted and ambled out of the office.

In short order, they found the best camera view and the time Scott's car entered the garage. They watched the man with the moustache exit Scott's car alone. He carried no bags. He kept his head down and shielded his face with his hands as if he was walking into blazing sunlight. After just a few paces, he was out of the camera's range. No one else got out of the Jeep.

"I still don't recognize the driver," Bailey said.

"Unfortunately, neither these images nor the ones from the other video are enough for the FBI's facial recognition software," Victoria said.

"That's okay. I wouldn't want you to get in trouble anyway, for doing all this," Bailey said.

"Don't worry about that." Victoria stood up and stretched her arms overhead. "I'm going outside to wait for the forensics tech. Why don't you two get some food?"

Bailey probably didn't feel like eating. It fell to others to make sure she did. She needed her strength to get through this. No need to be weak and dizzy on top of sad and desperate for the truth.

"Good idea," Ned said. "We'll meet you back out in the garage soon. What can I get you?"

"A vanilla latte if you see a Starbucks. Thanks."

Victoria returned to Scott's car and waited on a bench near the elevator bank. Her location kept her out of sight but allowed her to see if anyone approached the Jeep.

To her left, a family with four young children unloaded a slew of suitcases and backpacks from a minivan and rushed to the elevators. To her right, a couple parked and strolled along with carry-on luggage. They weren't wearing coats, and the woman carried a pink straw hat with a large brim, which made Victoria think about the honeymoon trip to St. Lucia. With so many unknowns, Bailey wouldn't go now. Unless she believed Scott was already there.

Ned and Bailey returned with Victoria's coffee right before the forensics consultant called to say he was in the garage. Victoria met him next to Scott's vehicle.

"Hi, I'm Lance," he said as he got out of a compact car. He was a young man, with thick-framed glasses and a wiry build. "Does the vehicle belong to one of you?"

"It belongs to my fiancé," Bailey said.

"Okay. The thing is…I just need to be sure this is okay…you know, me searching the car. Is it?" he asked, looking uncertain.

"Yes, it's okay, we have the keys to the vehicle," Victoria told him.

"So…you want me to comb for evidence and prints, that right?"

Victoria nodded. "Do what you normally do. And you can give me the findings when you're finished."

Lance went by the book and sprayed the car's interior with luminol to search for traces of blood. Finding none brought Victoria, Bailey, and Ned a measure of relief.

After gathering and labeling material from the tire treads, Lance vacuumed the vehicle's interior for hairs and other particles, checked for prints, and anything else that might be evidence *if* a crime had occurred. There were prints everywhere, including on the steering wheel, the gearshift, and the door handles. Most of them would belong to Scott. No one had wiped any surfaces clean, which seemed a good sign. Whoever was driving the car had nothing to hide...or he was very stupid.

"Did you check the back of the rearview mirror?" Victoria asked. "It's one of the first things I adjust when I drive a car that's not my own."

Lance shone his flashlight on the back of the mirror. "Got a good one here."

"Scan it for me before you leave," Victoria said. She wanted to check it as soon as she had the chance.

Victoria took a picture of the post-it note message in case they wanted to analyze the handwriting, then dropped the note and the parking ticket into evidence bags Lance provided. She also bagged a protein-bar wrapper, a water bottle, and two surgical masks. Finally, Lance got images of Bailey's fingers to rule out her prints from the others. His work completed, he left.

"It's possible none of this proves useful," Victoria said. "But we've got it just in case."

"Right," Bailey said, staring at the Jeep and rotating the key between her fingers. "I guess we leave his car here."

"Yes," Victoria answered. "Let's go back to the hotel. I'll run the print from the mirror. If we get lucky, we can identify the driver and talk to him. Then we'll have answers."

101

"Thank you so much," Bailey told Victoria. "How much did you have to pay Lance to come out here and do his search? I need to reimburse you."

"No. Consider it part of your wedding gift," Victoria said, realizing as she spoke that her response might not have been the best one, considering the marriage didn't occur. But Bailey didn't seem to notice.

"I can't let you do that. You've already done so much to help. We're so lucky you're here," Bailey said. "I couldn't just sit around and wait. Especially not now. I still can't come up with a good reason for a stranger to be driving Scott's car without him."

Neither could Victoria.

***

Victoria sat by the balcony windows in the hotel suite, waiting to connect to the FBI's database. Outside, the snow had stopped, leaving a thin white layer over everything. She'd taken a quick shower and her long, soft sweater and cashmere socks were perfect for her mood and the temperature inside the room. Under different circumstances, she and Ned would have just returned from the historic tour and Bailey would be preparing to leave for her honeymoon. Instead, Ned and Bailey were off telling Scott's family about finding his car.

Victoria logged into a fingerprint database and scanned the print from the rearview mirror. While the system did its thing, she unwrapped the cinnamon streusel bread and pulled off another chunk. The bread was delicious. So much so that she was reaching for a second slice when the database found a match. Richard Luna. Previously arrested on suspicion of falsifying documents. The charge hadn't stuck. Luna had one of the most attractive mug shots she'd ever seen. Nothing smug or defiant about his look. His mouth was closed, but his eyes smiled at the camera in a sultry way as if it was a modeling shoot rather than an arrest record. He had a beard and mustache like the man on the airport's security video, but longer hair hung over one side of his face in a soft, layered style. She wasn't positive he was the same person who drove Scott's car, but there was nothing in his photo to suggest he wasn't.

Victoria typed a quick text to Bailey. *I got a match on the prints from the car. Do you recognize the name Richard Luna?*

Bailey responded immediately. *No.*

Victoria typed Luna's name into an expanded database and discovered she wasn't the only one interested in him recently. Local police listed Luna as a person of interest in a shooting. The incident occurred on the outskirts of the city two days ago. The night before Scott disappeared. An investigating detective named Lisa Suarez questioned Luna, but she didn't press charges.

Victoria found a number for Detective Suarez and called her. The phone rang and eventually went to voicemail. After leaving a message, Victoria returned to her research on Richard Luna. She hoped to find a connection between him and Scott, but their upbringing told a story of two different worlds. The child of a single parent on welfare, Luna grew up in a Boston suburb with the highest crime statistics in the area. He dropped out of high school to pursue an acting career. Victoria found a reference to a former publicity agent, a few commercial credits, and multiple professional headshots. None were recent. Yet somehow, Richard Luna had found financial success. He owned a condo worth almost two-million dollars.

Footsteps and voices came from outside the door. The lock made a soft buzz a second before Ned and Bailey entered the suite. "Bailey said you found the guy's name," Ned said.

"Yes. Richard Luna. I've got some clear photos of him now." Victoria showed them several images.

Bailey leaned close to the computer screen. "That one is a mugshot. He's a criminal?"

"Police arrested him once but didn't or couldn't convict. I haven't found a connection to Scott yet, but Luna grew up around here. Maybe they're childhood friends."

Still studying the pictures, Bailey shrugged. "I've never seen him before. I'll ask Jules if she knows him." She snapped a photo of the images and forwarded them to Jules. Within seconds, she had Jules on the other end of her phone. "I just sent you a picture of a man named Richard Luna," Bailey said. "Do you know him? Or recognize him? Ever heard his name before?" Bailey pressed the speaker button and Victoria heard Jules reply "no" without hesitation.

"Thanks, Jules. I don't know him either. I'll keep you posted," Bailey said, ending the call.

"If we can't find a connection, I think I've got probable cause to put a trace on Scott's phone now," Victoria said. "I'll do that."

Did Scott and Richard Luna have a secret connection? Or was Scott a victim? Since they couldn't ask Scott, Victoria needed to speak with Luna.

CHAPTER 14

Richard Luna answered his door wearing navy slacks and a white button-down shirt, carrying a stemless glass of white wine. He smiled at Victoria. "Hello. Something tells me you aren't my sushi delivery, are you?" His voice had a hint of a Boston accent. "Are" came across as "ah." Not as strong as others, but it was there.

Victoria showed him her badge.

"Ah, the Feds. To what do I owe this honor?" Luna's smile hadn't faltered. "Is this about my Tahoe again?"

Not knowing what he was talking about, Victoria didn't answer and waited to see if he would explain. He didn't. "Mind if I come in and we can talk about it?" she asked.

"Be my guest." He opened the door further. "What about your friend? Is he going to stay in the car?" He gestured to Ned, who watched them from the rental car because Victoria thought it best that she spoke with Luna alone.

"Yes. I don't think this will take long." She turned and waved to Ned, hoping he wasn't worried about her going inside. She carried a weapon, after all. She stepped in and scanned her surroundings—a clean updated place in excellent condition. "How do you know Scott Redmond?" she asked.

"Oh. You're here about Scott? Is he okay?" Luna set his wineglass down on a sculpted concrete console table. Victoria's father owned a similar one.

"I asked how you knew him," she said.

"I met him at the hospital."

"Were you a patient?"

"Yes. I had a medical emergency. Appendicitis. He was my doctor."

"When was that?"

"Hmm, let me think. Last October? Yes. That's when it was."

"A doctor in a busy ER doesn't have much time to get to know patients." She studied Luna to see if he would counter her statement. He only smiled. For several seconds, neither spoke.

"When did you see him last?" she finally asked.

"A few days ago. I gave him a ride to the airport. In his car."

She hadn't expected him to tell the truth, but he'd gone straight to it without hesitating.

"Can I pour you a glass of wine?" he asked.

"No, thank you."

Luna took a few steps out of the foyer toward the white sectional in his living room. "Would you like to sit down?"

"I'm fine where I am. Why were you driving Scott's car?"

"He asked me to."

"Why?"

"He wanted to leave his car at the airport for his return trip but wasn't up to driving there. He was extremely emotional. I'm no doctor, but I think he might have been having a panic attack.

And with good reason. Not sure if you know this, but he backed out of his own wedding." Luna winced in a show of disapproval. "He didn't invite me to the event. We're casual acquaintances. Maybe that's why he asked me to drive him. I think he was ashamed to face everyone else. Can't say I blame him."

"Do you know his destination?"

"He said he needed to get out of town. And I think he mentioned somewhere tropical. St. Martin? I'm assuming you can't get in touch with him, or you'd be asking him rather than me."

"That's correct. His family and friends are worried."

"I hope he's okay and he didn't do anything rash. You know...You're the Feds—" Luna said, sounding concerned. There wasn't anything accusatory in his tone. "—can't you trace his phone? Track his credit cards?"

Victoria didn't answer his questions. Luna came across as likable, although so smooth it almost disarmed her, and cooperative—extremely cooperative. And now concerned. His connection to Scott and the reason he drove him to the airport were dubious, but without Scott to refute or explain, she had to take Luna's word. At least for now.

"How did you get back from the airport?" she asked.

"I took an Uber." He glanced at his phone on the counter. "You can check my account if that would help with the timing of things. I called the Uber as soon as I dropped him off."

"You drove Scott's car to the airport, and then you paid to get yourself back home?"

Luna smiled again. "Scott insisted on giving me cash to cover the ride, wouldn't let me refuse. Shame. Because it's not a big deal to do a friend a favor. And I really owed him one." Luna tapped the right side of his abdomen. "Not that I keep track, but I've found that what goes around, comes around. You believe in karma, Agent Heslin?"

107

At the moment, Victoria wasn't sure what she believed.

***

Only Ned had eaten at the airport earlier, so Victoria and Ned traveled from Luna's house to meet Bailey at a restaurant for a very late lunch.

Because of his training, Ned consumed thousands of calories more than the average person, yet Victoria had also seen him skip meals without once complaining. She liked that about him. No one would ever call Ned self-absorbed.

With their food, the three of them settled around a table in the corner, away from the hustle and bustle of busy Newbury Street, and tried to make sense of the situation.

Bailey stuck her fork into her salad, stared at it, then set it down and pushed the container away. "It just doesn't sound right to me that Scott couldn't drive himself and he asked someone he barely knows. But you think Luna was telling you the truth?"

"He at least told some version of the truth," Victoria said. "He didn't deny his involvement. I checked with the hospital. They verified Luna was a patient six months ago. That's all they could tell me without violating health care privacy rules." After taking a final bite of her own salad, she set her fork down. She checked her phone in case she'd missed a call from Detective Suarez. She had not. Next, she refreshed her emails and scrolled through them. "We might be about to find out. I got his phone records." She opened the email. "His cell phone pinged from a location fifteen minutes ago, according to the phone company." What she didn't say—his phone hadn't moved in almost forty-eight hours.

"Where is he?" Bailey asked. "Is he in St. Lucia?"

"No. He's still in Boston." Victoria showed Bailey the streets triangulating a territory approximately five miles from their current location.

Bailey frowned as she took in the information. "I know the area. It's not really anywhere…I mean…we better go."

108

"Yes, let's go." Ned finished the last of his hamburger and grabbed his coat as Victoria dropped a few bills on the table for a tip.

They rushed from the restaurant to the rental car where Victoria put the address into her phone's GPS and Ned started the engine. They followed the GPS directions and ended up on a highway overpass. "The signal came from somewhere over there," Victoria said.

With the last of the winter daylight waning, Ned parallel parked the car. Next to the busy road, walking trails meandered over small slopes and hills in a public, pedestrian area. People and dogs had trudged on and off the paths, disturbing the light snow cover.

"I don't think he's here." Ned turned in a slow circle, scanning the area. "Looks like we might just be searching for his phone."

"I'll call it," Bailey said, looking alarmed and already tapping her screen.

Standing close, Victoria heard a phone ringing through Bailey's device, but not from anywhere else around them. On a hunch, she walked to the nearest trash can but heard no sounds coming from inside it.

A sense of dread encroached as she studied a large cropping of trees dense enough to hide a body. A terrible image popped into her mind—Scott with a self-inflicted wound. "You two walk along the road," she said. "I'll check out that area over there." Over the course of the past few years, unsettling images had permanently seared into her memory. She wanted to spare Ned and Bailey from witnessing something that might haunt them forever.

"Wait. We should—" Ned never finished his sentence. She thought he was going to say something about not going alone. Perhaps he thought better of it, considering she was an armed FBI agent. He left with Bailey, heading down one trail as Victoria veered into the wooded area, praying Scott wasn't there. She ducked to walk beneath the trees, peering between the bushes and dead vegetation until an object partially covered by snow caught her attention. She froze in her tracks and stared at a blue shoe. Was it attached to a body? She couldn't tell. Careful not to disturb the area any more than she already had, she leaned forward. A few inches closer and she let out the breath she'd been holding. The old ratty sneaker with gaping holes and mildewed laces wasn't attached to anyone's foot, and she doubted it had ever belonged to Scott.

"Victoria!" Ned shouted from behind her.

Crouching, she walked back out of the trees.

Across the park, Ned waved his arms and yelled, "We hear something!"

Victoria jogged over to them.

"Shoot. It just went to voicemail again." Bailey tapped her phone screen. "Okay. It's ringing."

"I hear it," Ned said. "It's in here somewhere."

They plowed into the knee-high bushes, moving their phones' flashlights over the ground. Forty feet overhead, cars zoomed by on the overpass. Anything thrown from a vehicle in the left lane would land in the area with the drink cups, beer bottles, fast food wrappers, and other trash littering the underbrush. The soft ring persisted. The phone had to be nearby. Just as the ringing stopped, Victoria spotted it lying face down in the bushes. She picked it out of the snow with her gloves, surprised the moisture hadn't affected it.

The thinnest of red lines glowed inside the battery indicator. Had they arrived any later, the battery would have died, and they might not have found the device. Victoria used a stick from the ground to tap the phone's surface. Scott's phone wasn't password protected. The home screen appeared, showing dozens of unread texts and eighty-seven missed calls. The last outgoing call went to Jules just before the wedding rehearsal.

Victoria checked Scott's messages. The last sent message went out at 9:14 p.m. and matched the one Bailey received during the rehearsal dinner. The timestamp on the parking ticket in Scott's Jeep read 9:48 p.m. The timing fit for sending the text then tossing the phone on the way to the airport.

Victoria scanned Scott's other messages to Bailey. All ended in *Love you, Bales,* just as Bailey had said. It didn't elude Victoria that someone might have read those messages just as she had, then sent one pretending to be Scott.

Victoria remembered something else. "Didn't Mrs. Redmond say she received a text from Scott when you did?" she asked Bailey.

Bailey nodded.

"I don't see it here." Victoria wasn't sure what to make of that as they continued to search the area for any other signs of Scott, walking to the end of every trail and looping back. Considering the location of his phone, Victoria didn't expect to find him.

"What should we do next?" Ned asked.

"We wait," Victoria said. Detective Suarez still hadn't returned her call. Victoria was eager to hear why the detective had questioned Luna.

They got back in the car and joined the traffic.

Bailey leaned forward from the back seat. "I'm not going to St. Lucia. I can't go anywhere until I know what happened. I have to tell Bridget. I hope she has a friend who can go with her, even though it's last minute. If not...would you two want to go?"

"Thank you," Victoria said. "As much as I'd love to, I have to get back to my dogs and work."

"I'm scheduled to work this week, too," Ned said. "At the clinic. And for Victoria."

"Of course," Bailey said. "I understand. Do you mind dropping me at the hotel? My car is there."

"That's where I was headed," Ned said. "Unless you had other plans, Victoria."

"Hotel sounds good," she said.

They passed dozens of apartment buildings and a few shopping centers on their way back. When Ned pulled up to the front of the hotel, Bailey opened the door and said, "Will you text me if you learn anything else?"

"Of course," Ned answered. "And let us know the second you hear from Scott."

"Thank you for everything, both of you," Bailey said. "I can't tell you how much I appreciate it."

"We'll catch up again tonight," Ned said.

Bailey shut the door and walked toward the hotel's entrance.

"Before we go in, can we take a quick trip back to the last shopping center we passed?" Victoria asked. "There's something I have to do before we leave Boston."

"Sure," Ned said, but she could have sworn he gave her an odd look. "We haven't explored the city much, aside from our run. We missed the tour. I should have asked if you wanted to do any shopping."

"No worries. I don't really like shopping much, and we've had more important things to take care of, but this is different. After we go to the store, I need to stop downtown, too. It won't take long."

They drove back the way they'd come. Ned hit his blinker to turn into the shopping center. "Where do you want to go?"

112

"The pet store. And then the Trader Joe's over there. I'll be quick. Can you just wait for me here?"

"Um...okay."

Ned pulled over to the curb in front of the store. Victoria hurried inside and purchased a large bag of dog food and several cans of dog food with the purest ingredients listed on the labels. She also bought treats, a soft bed, a fresh blanket, and a five-hundred-dollar gift card. Her hands were full, and bags hung from her arms when she returned to the car. "Can you pop the trunk?" she asked Ned.

Ned got out to help her. "Why did you buy this stuff here?"

"It's not for me. I just need a few minutes in Trader Joe's."

"Sure. I'm coming with you."

Inside the grocery store, she bought two prepackaged sandwiches, two large bottles of water, and another five-hundred-dollar gift card. She got back in the car with the additional items. "Can we go back to that street where we talked to the homeless man and his dog?"

"Ah, I get it now." Ned smiled as he put the car in gear and headed back to the main road.

Victoria spotted the man's cart first. He'd moved and set up his camp farther down the street.

She got out and introduced herself. "Remember we met? I loved what you said about your dog. I hope you don't mind, but I bought a few things for you. Do you have room for them in your cart?" She opened the trunk and showed him her purchases.

"I can use all of those things," the man said, watching them unload the car.

Ned opened his wallet and gave the man all his cash. Only forty dollars, but the man accepted it with his mouth agape and tears in his eyes. Then he opened the gift cards. "Oh, my, God. This is amazing. Now I believe in angels."

113

"It's not enough," Victoria said when they were back in the rental car. She watched the man talking to his dog as he poured the food into a bowl.

"No," Ned said. "But it's something. You can't rescue every dog, or every person."

"I know. And not all of them need or want to be rescued." The concept brought her right back to Scott. Did he need saving or did he want to be left alone?

CHAPTER 15

On Monday morning, Victoria sat on the couch, after finishing a workout in the hotel gym. A news program blared from the television on the wall.

"David and Liam are stopping by," Ned said.

A few seconds later, they knocked. Ned muted the television and opened the door to let them in.

"Morning," David said to Victoria as he looked around. "Nice digs you got here. Maybe I should have gotten a suite."

"Morning," she said, taking her feet down from the coffee table. "Heading out soon?"

"Yeah," David answered. "Maria and I both have to work tomorrow."

"I have to get out of here, too," Liam said. A phone rang from somewhere on him as he plucked the last slice of Victoria's cinnamon streusel bread from the gift basket and unwrapped the plastic. He finished it off in three bites before taking out his phone. He punched a button to stop the ringing but didn't answer.

"I'm going out for a second," Victoria told Ned as she got up and put her boots on. "I'll be right back." Ned nodded and kissed her rather absent-mindedly on the cheek.

She turned to David and Liam. "If I don't see you again, it was nice meeting you."

"Likewise," David said, and Liam nodded.

Seeking privacy, she put on her coat and left the suite. She took the stairs down to the lobby and went out the front entrance. A mixture of salt and dirt ground under her boots as she crossed the parking lot to their rental car. Once inside, she started the motor and turned on the heat before calling Detective Suarez again.

"This is FBI Agent Victoria Heslin calling for Detective Lisa Suarez, please."

"One moment, please."

Victoria put her phone on speaker and scrolled through her phone's news feed while she waited. It didn't take long for the detective to pick up her line.

"Detective Suarez."

Victoria introduced herself. "Thank you for taking my call, detective. I left you a message yesterday."

"I was just about to return your call. Can I get your identification number so I can confirm you are who you say you are?" Like Richard Luna, Suarez had a Bostonian accent, only hers was more pronounced than his.

Victoria recited her ID number.

"Got it," Suarez said. "Agent Heslin from the D.C. bureau?"

"Yes, correct. That's me." If Suarez recognized Victoria's name from the recent media hype, she didn't show it.

"What can I do for you?"

"I've got a missing person. Potentially. Scott Redmond. Thirty years old. Disappeared the day before his wedding. I located his car at the airport."

"Did someone already report this to the local police?"

"Not yet. His family didn't want to. It's possible he got cold feet about the wedding. But there are also some oddities. From airport security video, we discovered someone drove Redmond's car into the short-term parking lot at Logan and left it there. I matched prints and images to Richard Luna."

Suarez grunted.

"I know you interviewed Luna at his place yesterday. That's why I called. I already spoke with him, but can you tell me why you questioned him?"

"A shooting occurred in an empty warehouse. No witnesses but we have video of Luna driving a black Chevy Tahoe, his registered vehicle, to and from the crime scene. It's not much. But it's absolutely the sort of thing Luna might be part of. You've heard of the Salazar cartel?"

"Yes, of course."

"Unfortunately, they have a large presence here. Luna works for them, though we never have enough evidence to convict him." The detective coughed and must have moved away from the phone or covered it with her hand because the sound muted before she spoke again. "I wouldn't believe a word Luna says. He's too smooth for his own good. What did he tell you when you spoke with him?"

"He told me Scott Redmond panicked and got a flight out of here. He wasn't certain of the destination. If that's true, Scott flew out of Logan under a false name."

"Have you considered that your missing man is complicit with Luna and his criminal associates, rather than just an acquaintance or an innocent victim?"

"Scott Redmond's background makes that unlikely."

"But you don't know for sure," Suarez said.

"I don't."

117

"Hmm. I can tell you this, if he's not working *with* Luna, he's probably in trouble. It's one or the other. You need to figure out which."

"If you give me the time of that shooting, I'll find out where Scott was then."

"It occurred at approximately 10:20 p.m. on Thursday. They couldn't even wait until the dead of night when people were sleeping. Pretty soon we'll have shootouts at noon if we can't stop these groups. The area's never been desirable, but crime never used to be this bad. I'm on a mission to stop it. I'm determined to find something on Luna that will stick."

Victoria wondered if a personal reason fueled the detective's passion.

"Where was Scott Redmond last seen?" Suarez asked.

"Outside Blessed Sacrament Church in Harfelt."

"Hold on. I'm looking for the address now."

Victoria appreciated that Suarez was the type of person who got right to something, rather than doing it later, which opened up the possibility of it not happening at all. While waiting for her, Victoria stared out the car window. Ethan's parents trudged out of the hotel. Ethan wasn't with them. Several yards separated the husband and wife as they crossed the sludgy parking lot. The father shook a pointed finger in the air and said something Victoria couldn't hear. Trying to keep up with him, Ethan's mother threw her hands up and scowled. Their gestures and their animated lip movements showed they were arguing or angry.

The SUV next to Victoria beeped as it unlocked. The couple headed straight toward her. She turned away as they got closer, pretending something on the passenger side required her attention. Once they reached their SUV, she easily heard their words.

"I still can't believe you would suggest such a thing," Ethan's father said. "For God's sake! Our own son!"

"After what happened last time…how can I not consider it?" Ethan's mother said from right outside Victoria's window.

"Nothing happened," he hissed. "How many times do we have to tell you? Nothing happened! He got a little carried away with his infatuation. That's all it was."

They got into their vehicle and slammed the doors just as Detective Suarez came back on the line.

"I see where the church is," Suarez said. "It's possible Luna went out to get a replacement car, if his *was* coated in blood, but that church is a long way off. Why would he go way out there to get a vehicle and then leave it at the airport?"

"What did you just say? Why was Luna's car covered in blood?"

"I didn't say it was. I said *if* it was. At least two seriously wounded people walked away from the shooting scene and got into a vehicle. Might have been Luna's Tahoe. He doesn't have it now. He said a friend borrowed it. Convenient."

"Any idea who got shot?"

"No. But my bet is there are no innocent victims. Probably a drug or money laundering transaction gone wrong."

"Hmm." Victoria massaged her fingers as she tried to connect some dots. "Scott Redmond is an ER physician. He's even got a vanity plate that says as much."

"Interesting coincidence." Suarez coughed away from the phone again. "If the shooting victims didn't die, they would need medical help. And no one with gunshot wounds went to a hospital Friday night or Saturday morning. If we find the injured men, assuming they aren't already dead, we might find Scott Redmond."

Victoria liked how Suarez used the pronoun we, as if they were already working together.

"Now that I know about the shootout, I could bring Luna in for questioning," Victoria said, thinking aloud.

"I wouldn't. Luna won't talk. He's a pro. You saw him. If your missing man is still alive and Luna or one of his colleagues has him—assuming he's not working with them, though maybe he is—anyway, pressing them further is the fastest way to get that doctor killed. We're better off watching Luna and seeing where he goes. That's what I planned to do. Luna told us he was sick. He didn't look sick. Eventually he'll have to leave his place."

Victoria agreed with the logic though the possibility still existed that Luna and Scott were nothing more than friends, Scott had left the country, and the surveillance would only waste time. "Does your department have the capacity to set up surveillance?"

"No." Suarez laughed. "You kidding? Definitely not. I'll do it myself. First shift anyway. I already got a warrant so I can track his phone."

"Scan it to me," Victoria said. "I'd like to have a look at Luna's phone record myself. I can probably access them faster."

"Yeah, you probably can," Suarez said, punctuating her thoughts with "mmf."

Victoria and Suarez exchanged emails.

"I'll check back with you tonight," Victoria said. "Or sooner if something happens."

"Agreed. Talk to you later," Suarez said.

Victoria stayed in the car for a few more moments to sort through her thoughts. Time enough for Suarez to email a scanned copy of the warrant. Victoria forwarded the warrant to an FBI contact at the phone company and requested access to Luna's phone records.

Satisfied they were on the right track to determine Scott's whereabouts, she trudged back across the parking lot toward the hotel.

Ned stood behind the glass lobby doors as if he'd been waiting for her.

THE GROOM WENT MISSING

"Hey, there." He seemed to search her face for information. "What were you doing outside?"

"I needed to make a call. I told you I'd be right back. Why?"

He studied her for a few seconds. She wasn't sure what he was thinking.

"Everyone is downstairs in the banquet room," he said. "They've got lots of questions. It would be best if they heard from you. Mind giving an update?"

Victoria frowned. "Ned...there's really no update to give."

"We have some information. We found Scott's phone and his car and you spoke to the person who drove it to the airport."

"And we still don't know what any of it means or where Scott is." She glanced across the foyer in the banquet room's direction. "They're waiting in there now?"

"Yes."

Victoria was unhappy about doing what might amount to a mini press conference concerning an emotionally charged and personal issue for everyone in the room. If the request came from anyone else, the answer would be no. But it was Ned asking.

"All right." She removed her coat and walked with him down the hall.

A small crowd had gathered. In fact, it appeared the entire bridal party waited. Bailey sat between Bridget and Katie at a table with David and Liam. Mr. Ballard stood behind his daughters with one hand on Bailey's shoulder.

Their conversations ceased as Victoria entered and made her way across the room. She grasped the back of a chair and leaned forward.

Scott's parents weren't there, but his sister and uncle were. Standing beside Duncan and drinking from a bottle of Fiji water in the center of the room, Jules wore a long baggy sweater with tight black leggings. Her red hair hung loose, flowing around her shoulders. Through dark, smoky eyes, she stared at Victoria's disfigured hands.

"You have news for us?" Duncan asked.

"Unfortunately, I don't think I have anything to tell you that you haven't heard already from Bailey," Victoria said. "Just let me emphasize, we don't know if anything criminal has occurred." She chose her words carefully, not wanting to disclose the possibility of Scott's involvement with a cartel associate, which would make him an accessory and therefore a criminal himself. "Has anyone heard from Scott since Friday?"

No one had.

"I just checked our credit cards again," Bailey said. "Still no charges."

"Besides his car and his phone, do you know anything new?" Bridget asked.

"No. We haven't located Scott. I want to make sure you all know that I'm helping as a friend, and not in any official capacity. This is not an official investigation. Otherwise, we might be crossing a line here, without knowing for sure that Scott is…that he isn't missing by choice." Victoria surveyed the room as she spoke, assessing body language. "I understand some of you were and maybe still are reluctant to involve the police. If there's a reason for that, if any of you have additional information as to Scott's frame of mind before the rehearsal dinner, please let me know." She looked directly at Jules.

Jules stared back at her while raising her water bottle to her lips.

Duncan cleared his throat and crossed his arms over his belly. "If you have something you're keeping quiet on—these leads Bailey said you're following—you need to tell us. The man who drove Scott's car, we heard you spoke with him. What did he have to say?"

"Richard Luna," Victoria said. "Do any of you know him? Have you ever heard Scott mention him before?"

No one spoke up.

Victoria shared the conversation she'd had with Luna. She expected Bailey had already told them everything and they weren't hearing anything new.

"So, this man no one knows, who claims he's a friend of Scott's, drove my nephew to the airport in his car." Duncan wasn't shouting, but almost. "Are you going to dig deeper on that, or take him at his word?"

"Hey, let's all be calm here. Don't be shooting the messenger," Ned said. He moved closer to Victoria and placed a hand on her elbow, but the comment hadn't fazed her. The situation had Scott's family and friends confused. They worried about his wellbeing. They needed someone to take those emotions out on. And truth be told, she was keeping the information on Suarez's investigation and Luna's criminal connections from them. If he was dangerous, as Detective Suarez believed, Scott's family needed to keep their distance and let the Boston authorities do their jobs. Neither could Victoria risk someone rushing to Luna's house and spooking him. Luna still might be their best chance of locating Scott.

The mystery surrounding the teen from the church still bothered Victoria. "Did anyone recognize the teen who delivered the ring and the note?" she asked.

Head shakes followed. Others murmured, "no."

"Are you worried Scott might have...you know...harmed himself?" Bridget asked.

Murmurs came from the group, most of them refuting the possibility, but in tones that told her they'd reached a point where anything might be possible.

"All of you know Scott well," Victoria said. "I'm sorry that I don't. I can only say that he could be under immense stress right now, regardless of what happened."

"So, did he get on a plane or didn't he?" Jules asked. "You must know that much."

Victoria met Jules' gaze. "If Scott boarded a plane, he did so under an alias and had the documents to back it up."

Bridget scowled. "Scott? That doesn't sound like him."

"You know…ah, no, never mind," David said.

"What is it?" Victoria asked David. "What were you going to say?"

"It's just that he had an impressive collection of fake IDs in college," David said. "We all did. Just until we were old enough to get served. Maybe we could remember some names he used?" David looked at Liam.

"No. We always used our real names and just changed the birthdates," Liam said.

Victoria cringed. "If Scott is traveling under a false name, it's a felony. I don't want to go down that road." She struggled to gather her thoughts. She didn't want to find anything that would make matters worse for Scott and his family. "My only goal is to help you locate him. To confirm he's all right."

"Good," Duncan said. "And we appreciate that. None of us are looking to get Scott in any more trouble if he's not in it already. We don't want to make things worse for anyone."

"Maybe you should stop investigating then," Jules said, her suggestion aimed at Victoria.

Bailey turned around to stare at her.

"Jules, did Scott tell you something?" Ned sounded exasperated. "Has he contacted you?"

"No. For the last time, no!" Jules tossed her hands in the air. "I'm just saying. If he's in trouble, going public with it is not the best strategy."

"Victoria isn't the 'public', if that's what you're implying," Ned said. "Scott is like family to me and so is Victoria."

"Okay," Victoria said, trying to diffuse the escalating frustration. "Scott's family and friends have the best chance of locating him and hearing from him. We can leave it at that. Ned and I are returning home this afternoon, but I'll continue to monitor the situation from D.C., unless you want to move forward officially with the police." She turned to Bailey, thinking it was her call to make. "He's been gone for over forty-eight hours now."

"I already made *my* thoughts on the matter clear," Jules said.

"You certainly have," Bailey said. She got out of her chair and went to Victoria. "We're very fortunate you're here and can help us." She gave Victoria a hug and whispered, "Thank you."

"You're welcome," Victoria said. "I'm sorry we still don't know where he is."

As Victoria headed upstairs to her suite, an idea came to her, based on her earlier conversation with Suarez. It was a long shot, building on the hypothesis they'd tossed around, that Scott might be providing medical treatment to those wounded in the warehouse shootout. If true, Scott would need drugs and medical supplies. Maybe he already had a stash somewhere, but maybe he'd need more. She wanted to alert the state's prescription database to flag anything Scott ordered.

She logged onto her laptop and researched how to put in the request, filled out some online forms, and successfully set up an automatic notification.

After completing that task, she checked her email. Her FBI contact at the phone company had come through with access to Luna's cell phone records. Victoria didn't expect to find anything incriminating. If Luna was as sophisticated a criminal as he appeared to be, he wouldn't use a registered personal phone for his shady business dealings. But she was eager to find out if the phone records would show a personal call from Scott Redmond.

She studied the log of Luna's outgoing and incoming calls. She didn't see Scott's phone number there. Instead, she noticed Luna had recently received three incoming calls from a local number. The last one came only five minutes ago. The calls went unanswered. Might just be marketing spam. Or not. If Luna suspected the cops or feds were watching him, maybe even listening, that might be the reason those three calls were ignored.

Victoria logged into a different database and traced the number. It belonged to an unregistered, prepaid mobile phone. Fortunately, they could trace burner phones through a virtual number operator to find the caller's approximate location. Victoria called the phone carrier, identified herself and asked for a manager, then waited until they provided an approximate location.

She typed the address they gave her into Google maps to see where it was relative to the hotel. She pressed enter.

Something wasn't right. She thought she'd made a mistake, somehow mixing her current location with the location of the burner phone. She entered the information again.

What the—?

No mistake.

A chill prickled slowly across her skin as if she was back in Greenland without a coat.

The three calls to Luna originated from somewhere in Victoria's hotel.

CHAPTER 16

Gritting her teeth, Victoria leaned back against the couch in her hotel room and stared up at the white ceiling as a flash of anger ignited inside her.

Someone wasn't telling the truth.

Who from the hotel made three phone calls to Luna from a burner phone?

She analyzed every interaction she'd had with the wedding guests and the bridal party. What had people said? How had they acted? Did anything seem unusual leading up to Scott's no-show? So many things and so many people came to mind.

Sitting up, she opened the photo app on her phone. She studied the one and only picture she had of the wedding party, taken during the rehearsal. In the center of the image, on the altar, Ned and Bailey smiled, surrounded by the rest of the bridal party. Groomsmen on the right, bridesmaids on the left. At that time, as far as they knew, Scott was merely late.

Or did *someone* know he wasn't coming?

Most of the people in the photograph had also been in the hotel's banquet room with Victoria less than twenty minutes ago. No one in the room claimed to know Luna. Had one of them been lying? Had one of them helped Scott disappear?

Another idea hit and it stuck, although it was as farfetched as the stuff of tabloid headlines. Maybe no one *helped* Scott disappear, but instead, someone *made him go away.*

What about Ethan? He wasn't in the banquet room. He hadn't left with his parents. Was he still somewhere in the vicinity? The conversation Victoria overheard in the hotel's parking lot between his parents still troubled her.

Ned and Bailey were the only people Victoria completely trusted. The only ones she was certain did not know what happened to Scott.

Perhaps the caller had nothing to do with Scott and Bailey's wedding. Other guests were staying at the hotel for different events. And then there were all the hotel's employees. But considering the connection Victoria had already established between Luna and Scott, it was more likely the caller knew the Redmonds.

She needed to question each member of the bridal party in person and analyze their body language and responses to determine who was lying. But that would take time, something she didn't have. She and Ned had to leave for the airport in less than an hour for their flight home.

Feeling pressure to get ahead of things before something or someone slipped away, she went with one of her surefire ways to move an investigation forward. She called Sam, one of the FBI's best intelligence analysts, and also her friend. For as long as they'd worked together, Sam had her back. He never seemed to judge her for personal dilemmas or give her a hard time about her family's wealth, as some of her colleagues had. Even though he was a super nice guy, he remained single. As far as she knew, he didn't even date. Or if he did, she didn't know about it. Work was pretty much his life and he seemed content. She bet he would be in the office or working from home even though it was Sunday.

Sam answered her call on the second ring.

"Hi, Sam. How is your weekend going?"

"I went out with a few friends and binged Netflix. Exactly as planned. I'm in the office now, catching up. You know. What's going on with you? I thought you were taking a long weekend for a wedding."

"The wedding didn't exactly happen. The groom didn't show."

"No kidding? Seriously?"

"I'm not sure what happened. I'm trying to help locate him for the bride and his family. There's something weird going on, but I don't know what. I want to check out some of the guests. I'm going to be traveling for most of the day. Could you help me with some background checks if I give you the names?"

"You think there's been a crime?"

"I didn't at first. But now I'm not sure. I want to investigate further. There's plenty of evidence he changed his mind, but no one has actually talked to him or seen him."

"I get it. I can help. Go ahead with the names. I'm ready."

She gave him the names she wanted to check out.

"I'll email the files. I should have them done by tonight."

"Perfect. I'll be home late this afternoon. Thank you so much, Sam."

"Anytime."

Their call finished a few seconds before the door to her suite opened.

"Thanks for giving everyone an update," Ned said. "I didn't mean to throw you into it. I should have known people would be emotional."

"It's not a problem."

"You still good to head out in an hour?"

"Yes. I'll be ready. I'm about to pack."

129

"Liam wants to talk to me about something before he leaves." Ned was still standing just inside the doorway. "Shouldn't take too long."

"I'll be fine."

"I know." He crossed the room to give her a kiss before leaving. It was slow and sweet with a sadness to it. Regret. An apology.

When he left, Victoria folded her clothes from the closet, gathered her belongings from the bathroom, and packed everything away in her suitcase. She left her laptop out and had just sat down in front of it again when her phone buzzed. A Boston area code. She didn't recognize the number, but she answered anyway.

"Hello," a woman said. "Is this FBI Agent Victoria Heslin?"

"Yes? With whom am I speaking?"

"This is Shondra. I'm a pharmacist at the CVS on Franklin. You flagged prescriptions for Dr. Scott Redmond?"

Excitement blossomed. "Yes. I did. Are you in the Boston area?"

"Yes. I am. Dr. Redmond left a message on our automated line a few minutes ago. Our pharmacy tech saw the flag. Usually, flags are for controlled substances. Narcotics. But this prescription is for two antibiotics."

Yes! "Thank you for calling right away. Who is the prescription for?"

"Dr. Redmond ordered the prescription for himself."

"Oh. I didn't know doctors could do that. Hmm." She tucked the info away to process later. "How do you notify the patient when a prescription is ready?"

"Our automated system calls them once we mark the prescription filled."

130

"Hold off on doing it. Don't mark it filled until I get there." Victoria jumped up, grabbed her boots, and stuffed her feet into them. She grabbed her coat and her purse next. "Could those antibiotics be used to treat someone with gunshot wounds? If that person were being treated in a home versus in a hospital?"

"I suppose. Yes. Flagyl and Cipro are appropriate for a wide variety of bacterial infections. What is the issue? Was Dr. Redmond shot?"

"I can't answer that," Victoria said. Which was true. She still didn't know if the prescriptions had anything to do with the warehouse shootings. But if they did, was Scott willingly aiding the cartel? Forced to help them? Or—something that hadn't occurred to her until now—was he one of the injured?

She scanned the room for the rental car key and didn't see it.

"Are you still there?" Shondra asked.

"Yes. I'm here." Victoria went to the closet, reached into a front pocket of Ned's coat, and wrapped her fingers around the key. *Got it.* "I need the address for your pharmacy."

The pharmacist recited the address and Victoria typed it into her phone.

"I'm leaving now. I'm on my way." She raced down the corridor and headed straight for the stairwell rather than wasting time waiting for the elevator. She ran down the stairs and out to the rental car, then hit the button on her phone to start the directions for the pharmacy. It was a thirty-four-minute drive. Once she was out of the parking lot and on the road, she called Detective Suarez and told her what happened. "I'm going to wait there for whoever picks up the prescription. From there...I'll see. If it's not Scott, I'll follow whoever it is."

"Are you armed?" Suarez asked.

"Always. Can I get backup?" Victoria switched lanes to avoid stalled traffic.

131

"Yes. I'm at my grandmother's place. I can leave here in five minutes."

"I'm sending you the address." Her phone rang again. "I think the pharmacy is calling me back. I've got to take this. It's a CVS on Franklin."

"I'll meet you there," Suarez said.

Victoria switched over to the new call.

"Agent Heslin?" The woman spoke so softly Victoria could barely hear her.

"Yes."

"It's Shondra. I didn't fill the prescription yet, like you asked, but someone came to pick it up. He's here right now."

Shoot! "Describe him."

"He's a teenager," the pharmacist whispered. "Tall and thin with long hair. Acne. Really thick eyebrows. He has a unibrow. He said the prescription is for his father."

It sounded like the teen who delivered the ring and the note to the church. He'd claimed Scott was his father? Scott didn't have children. Or did he? Victoria did the math. If the teen was fifteen or sixteen, Scott would have been around the same age when the boy was born. Definitely possible.

"I told him the prescriptions weren't ready yet," Shondra continued. "I said I had others to fill before I could get to it, but I'd take care of it as soon as I could. I asked him to have a seat. He's in the waiting area now. I can see him. He's just sitting there, sort of watching the counter and the doors. Are you almost here?"

"I'm about twenty minutes away. You've been an enormous help so far, Shondra. Please stall him until I get there."

"All right." Shondra sighed loud enough for it to come across the phone clearly. Not so much an exasperated sigh, more like the pharmacist had been holding her breath and needed a release. "I'll do my best."

"Get the prescription ready and give it to him when I arrive. I'm almost there. I have shoulder-length blonde hair and..." She almost said she was missing fingers but holding up her hands would not be a subtle gesture. She glanced down at her pants. "I'm wearing a black coat and jeans." *Ughh. Not exactly an unusual outfit.* "When I get there, I'll ask for a prescription for...I don't know...something different. What should I ask for?"

"Just ask for me," Shondra whispered.

"Okay. That will be your signal to give him the prescription. Until then, just act normal. Help your other customers and pretend he's not even there."

"Okay. I'll do that. We do have a big line now. We're always busy."

"I'll see you soon. Blonde hair. Black coat and jeans. I'll ask for you."

Up ahead, the three-lane road merged into one and detoured around a construction site. Victoria drove down one side street after another, each with stoplights and traffic signs. Once she returned to the direct route, she dictated a message to Ned.

"I took the car. I'll call you as soon as I can." She sent the communication. Seconds later, she realized the message wasn't enough and dictated another. "I've got a lead. Had to check it now or lose the chance. Please keep that to yourself until I know it's something."

Ned responded immediately with, *Okay. Where are you?*

She dictated, "Heading to a CVS on Franklin."

She did her best to navigate the busy traffic, switching lanes to buy a few more seconds while recalling everything she could about the teen who delivered the ring and note to the church. She mentally compared him to the photograph of Scott she'd seen

133

at the rehearsal dinner. Both were Caucasian with dark hair. Beyond that, she couldn't recall or rule out a resemblance.

Her GPS put her two miles from the store when Shondra called again. "Agent Heslin?"

Victoria could tell from the pharmacist's voice she didn't have good news. "What happened?"

"The teenager left without the prescription. After I talked to you, he got up twice and asked me what was taking so long. He was very rude. Then he left. I think he was suspicious."

"Did you see where he went? Did he get into a vehicle?"

"Uh, I'm not sure. I was behind the counter and couldn't see. But someone else might have noticed. We were all keeping an eye on him."

That hardly sounded discreet. Victoria might have laughed if she wasn't so disappointed.

Victoria arrived at the pharmacy and hurried inside. Two women wearing white coats waited at the front of the store, along with two young men wearing blue CVS uniform shirts and name tags. Victoria walked up to them. "Shondra?" she asked.

"Yes. That's me." Shondra was an attractive Indian woman with large brown eyes who looked just as excited as the people gathered around her.

Victoria showed them her badge. "Did anyone see where he went? If he drove or if someone picked him up?" The kid might not be old enough to drive.

"I think he got into a pickup truck that was waiting out here," an employee answered.

"The silver Dodge?" the other employee asked. "Nah. That old guy who buys all the vitamins drives that truck. He wasn't with the kid."

"How do you know?" the first employee snapped. "You didn't see him."

"Because I know what the old man drives. He's in here all the time. He was in here about fifteen minutes ago, and he wasn't with that kid."

"You talking about that kid you were all watching?" A man in his forties asked as he walked over carrying a red shopping basket. "I knew something was up. I saw him leave on a bike. He steal something?"

Victoria bit back her frustration. Even the customers picked up on the staff watching the teen. No wonder he'd bolted. "The store has video cameras?" she asked.

"Yes, it does," Shondra replied. "I don't know how to access them. I've only watched them live." She turned to her colleagues. "Does anyone else know how?"

No one did.

"We have to call Ernie," Shondra said. "He's the store manager."

"Call him now, please," Victoria said. "Tell him the FBI is here, and it's urgent."

A Latina woman entered the store and walked up to them. A tight bun held her hair away from her face. She wore no makeup and gave off a gruff, no-nonsense vibe. All-business. Under her sweater, a gun bulged against her left hip.

"Detective Suarez?" Victoria asked.

"Yes."

"I'm Victoria."

The detective extended her hand. Victoria took her aside and filled her in.

"Do you think the teen is Redmond's child?" Suarez asked.

"If he had a child, no one else seems to know about it."

135

"Maybe he didn't know about it either, until now," Suarez said. "Finding out might have screwed up his wedding plans pretty quick." She gazed toward the front doors. "What's taking so long? That manager coming in from New York City or something? I'm sure we could have figured out the camera system ourselves by now."

Victoria agreed as she checked her watch. Over an hour had passed since she left the hotel. Even if she returned now, it was unlikely she and Ned would make it to the airport on time. "I'm supposed to be on my way to Logan to go home," she told Suarez. "I've got to let my friend know I'm not going to make the flight. Excuse me, one second."

"Yeah, do what you need to do," Suarez said.

Before Victoria could make the call, a large man waddled into the store.

"What's going on, ladies?" he asked with an air of authority.

Shondra and two of the other employees rushed to tell him, all speaking at once. Victoria used the time to type a quick message to Ned.

Shouldn't be much longer. Can we reschedule the flights for later tonight?

But what if finding the teen led them to Scott? She couldn't leave yet. That's what happened when she got involved with a case. She had to see it through. Especially this one. Although it *wasn't* her case. She wasn't officially involved. Neither was the bureau. But that didn't stop her from wanting to make sense of the situation. Most of all, she wanted Scott to be the good guy Ned and Bailey believed him to be.

She deleted the last sentence of her message to Ned and typed a new one. *Will reschedule flight as soon as I know what's going on.* She pressed send and turned her focus to the store manager.

Ernie relished being in charge. That was obvious. He asked several questions before taking them into the back office. Once there, he made every step related to accessing the camera footage seem as complicated as possible. He logged in, typed codes, and switched screens with ample time in between staring at the tiny control board and grunting. Victoria wanted to yank him out of his seat and get him out of the way.

When they finally watched the video, the teen looked as she expected. Long hair. Lanky frame with bony shoulders under a flannel shirt. Might have been the same outfit he wore in the church. He sat slumped in a chair, watching everyone around him, especially the pharmacists. He never made a phone call or used a phone while he was there, which made him an anomaly among people waiting. Especially teens.

"That's the same kid who came to the church with a note during the wedding ceremony," Victoria told Suarez. "We need to find out who he is and where he came from. We can still trace the phone that called in the prescription, that might lead us to them. I'll get on it." She checked the time again. "But I've really got to get out of here. Before there are no more flights back to Virginia."

"Back to Virginia?"

"Yes. Things are getting weirder, but I have to get back home. Let's talk tonight, after I land, okay? Keep me posted on any developments, please. I'll do the same. There's some things I'm going to check on my end once I get home."

"Yeah, sure," Suarez said. "I've got an officer outside Luna's house still. I'll head back there and talk to you later. I want to know what's going on as much as you. The next time my grandmother asks me if I caught the people who were shooting at the warehouse, I want to answer in the affirmative. Safe travels, Agent Heslin."

Victoria programmed the hotel into her phone and started the directions before calling Ned from the car. He answered immediately, as if he'd been waiting. Which, of course, he was. A twinge of guilt pinged her. Undeserved. It wasn't like she'd lost track of time shopping. She was helping to locate Scott like Ned and Bailey had asked her to do, and since receiving the call from Shondra, there had been one thing after another. But after all that happened with Scott, and how she had criticized his lack of communication, mostly to herself, thank goodness, the irony was not lost on her.

"Where did you go?" Ned asked.

She told him most of what happened. "The person who came to pick up the prescription was the same teen from the church. We have to find out who he is."

Someone honked behind her. She glanced in the rearview mirror. A man in a Mercedes SUV flipped her the bird, though she did not know why.

"I'll tell you the rest later. I still have to get my stuff from our room. Is that where you are?"

"No. The cleaning service came. Wasn't sure if I should reserve the room for another night, but I didn't. I got us re-booked for a flight, but we've got to get to the airport in the next hour to make it. Or...do you want to stay?"

She hesitated before answering. "No. I want to go home. There's a detective helping here. Listen, I need to focus on my driving. I'll call you when I get closer, and I'll pull up to the front. Unless traffic gets worse, we should make the new flight."

CHAPTER 17

With Ned sitting beside her, Victoria leaned forward in her seat and gripped the wheel, willing traffic to move quicker.

Ned checked the flight status on his phone. "It's on time. No delays."

She parked the rental car in one of the return spots and dropped off the key while Ned grabbed their luggage. They joined a single file line waiting for the bus that would take them to the terminal. They were the last ones to board the bus. With no seats available, they stood in the center and held on to metal poles as the bus ambled along, stopping every few minutes to let passengers on and off.

"We're not checking suitcases, so that helps," Victoria said, trying to stay positive. They were so close and yet so far from getting on their plane, and she was suddenly anxious about getting back home to take care of her animals.

The bus finally reached their terminal. They jumped off and race-walked to security, pulling their suitcases behind them.

"I'll meet you at the gate." Victoria looked around for the separate security line for those carrying weapons. "If I get held up, go ahead without me."

He made a face. "I'm not doing that."

She was glad for his response. She didn't want to fly home without him.

After going through security, she ran to their gate, reluctantly passing a Starbucks and several ladies' rooms.

When she arrived, Ned stood at the gate's entrance, talking to an airline employee. He spotted Victoria and a smile spread over his face as he waved. "Come on, they're waiting on us."

The employee scanned Victoria's boarding pass. Once they were in the jetway, the door closed behind them.

"We made it," Victoria said, relieved they hadn't missed another flight. And with that sense of relief came a wave of fear. She'd been so rushed and concerned about getting to the gate that she hadn't worried too much about actually being *on* the plane. When she stepped inside the plane's cabin, a pressing, claustrophobic feeling enveloped her. She steadied herself with deep breaths and stuck her carryon in the first-class overhead bin. After sitting down, she secured her seatbelt and leaned back. Her heart pounded at an accelerated pace. She wanted to believe it was merely from her sprint through the airport, but she recognized the first signs of a panic attack.

She stared out her window at runway lights and focused on controlling the rhythm of her breath—deep breath in, *one, two, three, four,* slow exhale, *one, two, three, four*—willing herself to stay calm.

"I've got Xanax," Ned said. "Do you want one?"

"No, thank you." She stared at the bottle. She could use one, but also wanted to remain clear-headed.

Ned put the bottle away without opening it.

The flight attendant brought them waters. "Thank you," Victoria said, taking sips from hers.

Across the aisle, a toddler played an electronic puzzle game. His mother smiled as she pointed to something on his bright blue tablet. Having the child nearby comforted Victoria, as if they would all be safe because nothing terrible could happen to one so young and innocent, even though she knew otherwise.

During takeoff, Ned and Victoria gripped hands and stared straight ahead, the same thing they'd done on their way to Boston. Mercifully, if all went well, the flight would be a short one.

Once the plane leveled off, they exchanged tight smiles and let go their hands. Victoria took out her iPad and opened her mystery thriller novel. The book might as well have been in Chinese. She couldn't focus on the pages. Her thoughts revolved around everyone getting off the plane safely and without having a panic attack. She turned to Ned. His eyes were closed, but his hand still tightly gripped the arm of his seat. Victoria placed her hand over his. They were in this together.

"Attention passengers, we have a little turbulence ahead. Keep your seatbelts fastened and we'll let you know once we're clear of it."

Oh, crap.

Her body grew rigid with tension. To take her mind off the small but sudden lurches, she tried to sort through the events of the weekend, but the flight had her too distracted.

The plane lurched. Victoria gasped.

Ned squeezed her hand. "You okay?"

She offered a stiff nod, aware he was probably no less uncomfortable. She reconsidered the Xanax.

"We'll get through this," he said.

The ride smoothed out. Victoria's shoulders dropped from where they had clenched up near her ears. Another ten minutes passed smoothly.

"Sorry for being in a bad mood earlier," Ned said.

"No need to apologize. I didn't call you. I made us miss our flight."

"It wasn't that."

"It wasn't? Then what happened?"

"Remember when I said Liam wanted to talk to me?"

"Yes. What was it about?"

"He wanted advice. More like he just wanted to get something off his chest. He's having an affair."

"An affair?"

"Yep. With Katie."

"Bailey's friend Katie?" Comments and incidents from the weekend swirled through Victoria's mind. "But she's married."

"Yeah." Ned huffed. "I know. And so does Liam. That's what makes it an affair rather than a relationship we can all feel good about. They first got involved when we were at Duncan's condo in Aspen. None of us knew. They were definitely secretive about it."

"That was quite the week for hookups, huh?"

"Blame it on the blizzard. But it didn't end there. They've seen each other a few times since then. Katie told Liam she's in love with him. She wants to leave her husband."

Victoria had found Dean a little annoying and insecure. But now she felt terrible and embarrassed for him. He had a reason to be insecure.

"What does Liam think about her wanting to leave Dean?" she asked.

"He told Katie they couldn't see each other anymore. Having Dean around this weekend made him realize her husband is...I don't know...real?"

"What did you tell him?"

"Like I said, I don't think he was looking for advice so much as to get the matter off his chest. But I told him he needs to break things off until she figures out the deal with her marriage."

"Yes. Absolutely. That's the same advice I would have given."

"You know, I'm starting to think I really don't know my friends as well as I thought I did."

"Well…along those same lines…there's something I need to tell you." She watched his face fall as he prepared for whatever would come next. "The teen who came to pick up the prescription said he was Scott's son."

Ned made a face. "The one who came into the church? He was at least…what…fifteen?"

Victoria nodded.

"Wait…no. Absolutely not. There's no way."

"Maybe Scott didn't know he'd fathered a child until just recently."

Ned shook his head. "Impossible. Scott was a virgin until he was twenty. He told me that once and I don't know why he would randomly lie about it. I don't think he would. It was not a random hookup. He slept with a serious girlfriend. And even if he'd gotten her pregnant, that child couldn't be fifteen yet."

If Ned was right about Scott, then he hadn't backed out of the wedding because he'd fathered a child and they were no closer to an explanation.

***

Ned stopped his SUV at the end of Victoria's long driveway and pressed the remote on his visor to open the first gate. He drove forward and waited for it to close behind him before the inner gate opened. Victoria devised the double gate system so neither her greyhounds nor donkeys could escape the property when someone entered.

143

Inside the eight-foot iron gate, her estate home glowed with light at the end of the road. The home provided more space than any single woman needed. If not for the constant, enthusiastic presence of her dogs, she'd feel lost and lonely inside it. Most of the rooms were empty or nearly empty of furnishings. Fortunately, minimalism was in style. She'd purchased the property purely for the fenced acreage that surrounded the home—the ideal space for her animals—and also for the mountain trails behind it. She'd grown up hiking mountain trails with her family and their dogs. Now she did the same with her own pets. When she wasn't working, those trails were her happy place. Since becoming a minor celebrity after the plane crash, she appreciated the privacy more than ever.

They were halfway up the driveway when four sleek creatures came barreling from around the side of the house and raced toward them, faster than any animal on the planet except the cheetah.

"It's the welcome committee," Victoria said, her smile stretching.

Ned drove slowly up the side of the house and stopped the car. Victoria opened her door, and the overhead light came on.

"Wait." He met her eyes with a somber, sorrowful look. "I'm really sorry about the weekend. I hoped to sweep you away on a relaxing, romantic getaway, make you forget about work and everything else. Even though it didn't go as planned for anyone…it's good you were there. To help find Scott. To get everything in motion. I'm just grateful. I know Bailey's grateful. Whatever happens."

"I really like Bailey. I'm still going to help. I'll stay in touch with the detective working the case there. Suarez. She's focused on Luna. She's good. Which reminds me, did Bailey or Scott's parents say anything about the private investigator they were going to work with? He or she might have found something by now."

"I haven't heard. I'll ask Bailey about it in the morning." He brushed her hair away from her face and kissed her. "Go on in and get some sleep. I'll see you tomorrow."

"I had a great time when we were together. Good night."

She'd checked her email during the drive. The background files on the wedding guests waited in her inbox. She had reading to do once she got inside.

CHAPTER 18

Victoria left her suitcase and computer bag in the kitchen so she could return her dogs' affection. Whether she left the house for a week or an hour, they greeted her like a long-lost hero. Their constant adoration and enthusiasm had no bounds and never ceased to amaze her. Her animals provided a steady source of pure joy in her life.

"You missed me, sweeties?" She scratched Oliver's back, rubbed Izzy's head, and stroked Big Ed's ears. Myrtle, her smallest greyhound, and the alpha dog, rubbed against her like a cat.

Despite the dogs having free rein of the place, the house sparkled, thanks to the cleaning service. Victoria handed out treats before heading to her room, unpacking her suitcase, and changing her clothes. It was after midnight. The stress of rushing to the plane and then flying had tired her out, but the files beckoned. She made a hot cup of green tea with vanilla syrup, then entered her home office. She sat down at the gorgeous, handcrafted desk left behind by the previous homeowner, and logged into the FBI's server.

Sam's email awaited, but another caught her attention. A response from her contact at the phone company. She hoped it would tell her the location of the call to the automated prescription line and give her a solid lead on Scott's whereabouts. She opened that email first. If they could find Scott, she'd have no reason to go through the background files. Assuming they found him alive and well.

She read through the response. The call came from an unregistered pay-as-you-go device. The tech department triangulated the location to a stretch of highway in Boston. Another dead end. Although, if Scott made the call, it meant that as of that morning, he was still somewhere in the Boston area.

She finished her tea and opened the email from Sam. He'd attached the requested background files. Most would contain basic information from internet search engines: location of birth, known addresses, schools attended, employment records. But the FBI had programs to quickly pull the information together and access to sources outside of public records.

Sam had flagged Ethan White's file because he had a police record. Victoria clicked on the file and eagerly read through the details. Three years ago, a woman filed stalking charges and obtained a restraining order against him. It started after they went on two dates, and she told him she didn't want to be more than friends. Ethan began following her. She spotted him at a park where she'd gone to walk her dog. When confronted, Ethan insisted his presence in the park was a coincidence. She came home from a night out with her friends to find him waiting in his car across from her apartment. On two different occasions, she woke to find he'd left a gift on her porch or in her mailbox during the night.

Ethan made no explicit threats, but that hardly mattered. Stalking victims lived in a state of constant fear, nervous and anxious about what their stalker might do next. The behavior often escalated. A staggering number of homicides began with stalking.

After the woman's colleagues spotted Ethan sitting in his car outside their office building, the woman reported everything to the police and asked for a restraining order.

Good for her.

After that, no additional comments were noted in the file. Ethan's obsession with the woman appeared to have ceased when the law got involved.

Was that the incident Ethan's parents referenced in the parking lot when his father insisted nothing happened? Ethan's background was relevant, especially combined with the information Bridget provided—*Ethan has always been Bailey's biggest fan*. It was more than enough to raise suspicion.

Myrtle yipped from the hallway, imploring Victoria to stop working.

"Hold on, Myrtle. I'm not quite done yet. But I'm heading to bed soon," Victoria said, rubbing her eyes.

Myrtle yipped a few more times.

"Stop," Victoria told her dog. "I can't think when you do that, sweetie."

She tried to recapture her train of thought, but found she was fading fast. She needed to sleep. She hoped things would make more sense in the morning.

CHAPTER 19

After pushing through a quick but intense full-body workout and feeding her animals breakfast, Victoria took a cup of matcha tea onto the back patio. Dressed in an old Georgetown sweatshirt and sweatpants, she grabbed a throw blanket from a basket near the door and wrapped it around her shoulders. She turned on a heat lamp, sunk into a comfortable chair, and put her legs up on the edge of the firepit. Sipping her tea, she stared out at the gorgeous view beyond her backyard. The still rising sun glowed behind the mountain ridge.

Across the yard, Oliver, her white and brindle greyhound, trotted along the fence in the shadow of the trees. Victoria called to him. Oliver's ears perked up. He stopped moving and stared in her direction, then raced across the lawn, legs barely touching the ground, in a majestic display of his speed. He sailed over the patio stairs and slid to a stop in front of her.

"Good boy, Oliver. What a good boy you are."

He ducked away from her hand and tried to dive his nose into her tea, but she moved her mug out of the way in time.

There was no place like home and for a few more soothing minutes, everything seemed right with the world. She had paperwork to do, and some online training, but her boss had not assigned her a new case, which concerned her a bit. Since she didn't have to go into the office, she could bring her laptop outside and hang out on the patio all day if she chose. In fact, she could hang out all day every day if she quit the FBI. The trust from her grandfather made it possible, as long as she didn't go overboard spending on her animals and the rescue organization she funded. She could read, hike, and spend all day with her animals. Foster more dogs and help find homes for them. Hide out at her house and ignore the messed-up world growing more hostile and divisive with each passing day.

But that wouldn't happen soon. She'd worked hard to earn the respect of her colleagues and to train for her position. With training, experience, and the right attitude, she had become someone to watch out for rather than someone helplessly watching her back. And though she mattered immensely to her animals—who didn't know or care that she was an FBI agent—she wanted more than that. She wanted to make a difference. Protect people. Bring the missing home.

Sometimes when she was alone in the house at night, when everything was quiet and her animals settled, she remembered how it felt to be helpless. She shuddered, recalling her father's desperation and their dependence on others after thugs abducted her mother. She'd prayed the FBI knew what they were doing, were good at their jobs, and weren't distracted by another case or a personal crisis.

That desperate feeling still haunted her. Sometimes it drove her to go for a long run. Sometimes she wrapped herself in a blanket on the couch with several of her dogs for solace. Often it drove her to work through the night, even when no one asked or expected her to.

Would her mother still be alive if the FBI had found her a few hours earlier? It was a pointless question, and yet it seemed she would never learn to let it go.

She couldn't rewrite her history, but she could do her best to bring others a better outcome.

She typed a message to Bailey. *Any word from Scott?*

Bailey responded immediately. *Not yet.*

Victoria finished the last drops of her tea, swung her legs down, and went back into the house. Time to get down to business. The evidence suggested Scott was alive. But it was not clear if he didn't want to be found yet, or if someone else didn't want him found.

Walking through the kitchen, Victoria avoided the robot vacuums scooting around on schedule, scooping up dog hair and the dirt the dogs invariably tracked in from outside through the dog door. She set her empty mug on the counter and moved to her office, where she sat down at her desk and returned to the files. She quickly reviewed what she'd learned the previous evening and settled on Ethan White, the only guest with a police record. It was still early morning, but she called him anyway.

"Yeah, hey. Who is this?" Ethan mumbled, surprising her. Few people accepted calls from unknown numbers. From the sound of his voice, she had woken him.

"This is Victoria Heslin. I'm a federal agent. I was at the wedding."

"Yeah, I know who you are." There was a change to this voice. He sounded fully awake now. "You still trying to find Scott?"

"I am. I'm trying to give Bailey peace of mind."

"I don't know how that's going to happen after what he did to her. But she's better off without him."

"I have a few questions for you."

"Shoot."

"Where were you during the wedding rehearsal? Before the dinner."

Ethan exhaled loudly into the phone. "You think I did something to that douche bag?"

"I want to talk to anyone who saw Scott prior to the wedding rehearsal. And I want to find out where everyone who attended the wedding was during that time."

"I was at the hotel. I had a room there. Across from my parents."

"Can anyone confirm you were in your room?"

"I wasn't in my room." Muffled noises and static came across the line, then disappeared. "Before the dinner, I was at the hotel bar with two guys, other wedding guests, who went to high school with us. With Bailey and me. We met at five."

"Can you give me their names and numbers, please?"

"Sure. Got 'em right here on my phone." He read her the names and numbers. "Also, you can ask the bartender. She was cute. We flirted some. My parent's neighbors were in there too, getting sauced before the rehearsal dinner. Everyone saw me."

"Thank you, Ethan. That's helpful."

Victoria called Ethan's high school friends before he could give them a heads up. One didn't answer, so she left a message. The other backed up Ethan's alibi. He added they'd done shots, gotten a little too rowdy, and everyone in the bar would remember them.

Victoria changed her focus and opened the file on Duncan Simpson, co-owner of Redmond Galleries with his sister, Stephanie Redmond.

Duncan owned two multi-million-dollar properties. His primary address was in Aspen, Colorado—the place where Ned and Liam had hooked up with Jules and Katie. Victoria imagined a picturesque home with a peaked roof and unparalleled views of the snowy mountains. Before she could stop herself, that image evolved to a giant living room with a stone fireplace and a leather couch where Jules and Ned were getting cozy under a blanket. Victoria shook her head to get rid of it. What was it about Jules that kept getting under her skin?

152

Back to Duncan. He also owned a condo in Boston. Redmond Galleries had showrooms in each location.

Victoria looked away from her laptop and gazed up at the framed photograph mounted over the mantel. In it, a middle-school aged Victoria and her horse, Rodney, sailed over a fence during a hunter-jumper event. Victoria had painstakingly braided her horse's mane and tail into tiny, tight braids for every show and event. She wasn't that good at it. It took hours. She redid the braids again and again trying to get them perfect. It left her fingers cramped and aching. She usually wanted to give up halfway through, but she always persevered. Looking at the photo now, those braids made her think of Kayla, the wedding planner. That interaction with Kayla and her boyfriend hadn't sat right with Victoria since she witnessed it. She hadn't included Kayla in the list of names she'd given Sam and so she didn't have a background file on her yet. She decided to give her a call instead.

After finding Kayla's business number on the internet, Victoria flipped her notebook to a fresh page, and pressed the wedding planner's numbers.

"Hi. This is Kayla with Planning Your Big Event," she answered, sounding professional and eager.

"This is Agent Victoria Heslin, with the FBI."

"Oh. Is this…is this about Scott Redmond?"

"Yes." Victoria remained silent to see if Kayla would fill in the empty space, something people often did when they were nervous.

"So, um," Kayla said. "Is there something I can help you with? Why are you calling me?"

"You probably met with Scott and Bailey frequently, correct?"

"Yes. Mostly with Mrs. Redmond and Bailey. Not usually together, but separately."

"Did you note anything unusual leading up to the wedding? You know, relative to other couples and families whose weddings you plan?"

"No. Not really. If they were different, it was only in a good way. Bailey and Scott were probably nicer to work with, calmer than most couples. That's why it's incredible what happened. That Scott didn't show."

"It surprised you?"

"Absolutely. They were a really sweet couple. Totally devoted to each other. Scott treated Bailey well. He was attentive and actually interested in the details."

"The night of the rehearsal, you and your boyfriend were arguing. You asked him not to ruin this for you."

The line went quiet until Kayla asked, "How would you know that?"

"I was a guest at the wedding. I saw you outside with him."

"Oh. That was you with the best man?"

"Yes."

"But...you said you were an FBI agent."

"I am."

"You didn't look like an FBI agent. More like...I don't know. You're very pretty."

"FBI agents look like anyone and everyone," Victoria said, aware people often employed flattery as a means of distraction. "What were you arguing about?"

"Why are you asking? What my boyfriend and I were discussing has nothing to do with Scott Redmond's no show."

"But did the argument have anything to do with the wedding?"

There was silence and then Kayla said, "Yes."

"What didn't you want him to ruin?"

Kayla sighed, procrastinating again. "Casper is an accountant. He was just looking out for me."

Victoria grasped for patience as she asked Kayla to elaborate. "How was he looking out for you? Please explain."

"He has this thing about rich people. He doesn't trust them."

"Did he have any reason not to trust anyone in particular at the wedding?"

"No. But when I told him the groom didn't show for the rehearsal, he got concerned."

"Why? Did Casper have a reason to think Scott would not be at the wedding."

"No. Why would he? But it turns out he was right, wasn't he? We didn't know that then, not with Mr. Redmond telling everyone Scott had a work emergency. Anyhow, Casper worried that if Scott didn't show, the Redmonds would stiff me and the vendors. But it was never an issue. And that's what I told him. Stephanie Redmond and her brother, Mr. Simpson, paid for everything, including my fee, before the weekend. I submitted receipts, the Redmond family gave me the cash, and I paid the vendors."

"They paid in cash?"

"Yes. This was honestly the best wedding I've ever done. And not just because Scott and Bailey were so great. Stephanie Redmond is an established, respected businesswoman. She's always in the society pages. She paid up front and on time, even gave me extra for tips, which few people do. It's not expected. The Redmonds are very generous. I'm so sorry for what their son did to Bailey. Unless something weird happened to him, in which case I'm just sorry."

"Thank you for your time, Kayla. I'll let you know if I have other questions." Victoria set her phone down on her desk and leaned back in the large chair.

Myrtle used her wet nose to nudge Victoria's hand. Victoria closed her eyes and petted the dog while she thought. Her mind kept going to Jules. Something bothered her, but she wasn't sure what. Was Ned's dating history clouding her judgement? She didn't think so. There was something else there that went beyond Jules' involvement with Ned. Victoria didn't particularly like Jules. Probably because of her comments and her bossy personality. The way she had grabbed the box and the note, marched off alone with it, and gotten so angry that she ripped it into the tiniest pieces before Bailey or anyone else could read it.

Then the note vanished from the floor.

Maybe it didn't matter.

And maybe it did.

Again, unless they found Scott or the teen who delivered it, Jules' claim was irrefutable.

Still searching for answers but without having a specific question in mind, Victoria searched the internet for articles about the Redmond family and Redmond Galleries. She clicked on an article titled: *Redmond Galleries—Masters in the Art of Establishing Artists.* A large, vibrant photo, the interior of a contemporary gallery, graced the top of the article. Jules stood in the center of the photo with her hands resting on her hips, wearing a beautiful floral dress with an artsy vibe. Her long, red hair flowed down over her shoulders as she posed for the photographer. Most everyone else held champagne glasses as they gazed at art on the tall gallery walls, seemingly unaware someone was taking the photo.

Victoria zeroed in on the handsome man closest to Jules. Standing in front of a large modern painting, he wore a tailored black sports coat over gray slacks. He had a movie-screen-worthy hairstyle, a neat mustache, and a trim beard.

Victoria's pulse thumped in her ears. Ever since she discovered the calls made from the hotel, her suspicions about the wedding guests and bridal party increased. Now they spiked.

The man was Richard Luna. Inside Redmond Galleries. Standing only a few feet away from Jules.

PART II

CHAPTER 20

FIVE DAYS AGO

Scott Redmond shut the Jeep's door and hustled down the sidewalk with his phone in his hand, sending Bailey a message that he'd finally found a parking spot.

"Hey," a man shouted in a tone so startling Scott couldn't ignore him.

Partway through typing *Love you, Bales,* Scott looked up to see a man with a mustache and a beard in a black Tahoe.

"You a doctor?" the man asked through an open window.

How does he know that? "Yes?" Distracted, because he was excited and now late to meet the people he loved and cared about most in the world, Scott's reply sounded uncertain, as if he wasn't sure if he was a doctor or not.

"I need your help," the man pleaded.

Scott stopped walking but stayed on the sidewalk, looking between the man in the Tahoe and the path ahead.

"Please," the man said. "My wife got hurt. Can you look at her?"

The man sounded sincere and desperate, but Scott had an odd feeling about the request. Though that mattered little, as he couldn't and wouldn't refuse care to anyone. Instinctively, he treated others exactly as he would want them to treat *his* loved ones. Still holding his phone, he approached the SUV. "What's going on with your wife? Is she with you?"

The Tahoe's back door opened. A burly guy in a brown leather jacket got out. His nose looked like it had been broken and never reset.

Confused, yet already sensing trouble, Scott began backing away.

The burly guy grabbed Scott's arm.

That's all he remembered.

***

"Idiot, you killed him," a deep, accented voice muttered.

"No, I didn't," another man shouted. "Wake up, damn it! Wake up!"

Angry voices stirred Scott from a deep, all-consuming sleep. A large, callused hand cupped his chin and squeezed it like a vise. Scott jerked away.

"There you go, man. He's alive! Told you I didn't kill him."

Scott's body ached and a thick fog clouded his brain. The cold, damp concrete beneath him felt like a basement floor. Or a dungeon. He forced his eyes open. A single light bulb dangled from the tall ceiling. Under it, two ugly, frowning faces stared down at him. One was the man with the broken nose who had grabbed him. The other had pockmarked skin that made his cheeks look like a sponge. Both men were large and strong. At least one of them reeked of cigarette smoke. They carried guns.

159

A bolt of terror struck Scott. *Where the hell am I? Why am I here?*

"Get up," the man with the broken nose said.

"I don't know who you think I am, but you've got the wrong person." Scott swept his gaze over the huge, almost empty space. Definitely a basement. "There's been some sort of terrible mistake. I can't be here. I'm getting married tomorrow."

"What's your bride's name?" the man with the pockmarked skin had the deeper voice.

Scott kept his mouth closed. He couldn't bear to bring Bailey, even her name, into his current situation.

"Bailey?" Broken Nose asked. "Bailey Ballard?" He laughed. "Stupid name."

Hearing Broken Nose say her name with a derisive, frightening tone made Scott cringe. How did he know Bailey? That's when he realized the things he'd been carrying on his way to the church were no longer with him. His coat, his phone, his car keys…the wedding bands. His phone wasn't password protected. That's how they knew.

"There's no mistake," Broken Nose said. "Cooperate, doctor man, or Bailey's gonna suffer and die. You got it?"

Scott understood little about his situation, but he would do anything to keep Bailey safe.

His captors pulled him up the basement stairs. Pockmarked wheezed most of the way. He appeared to have more muscle than fat, but clearly his smoking habit wasn't doing him any favors. At the top of the stairs, they entered a large, clean, well-lit house. Not what Scott expected. Not at all. Rustic wooden beams crossed a soaring ceiling. Contemporary furniture pieces that reminded him of Restoration Hardware filled the large, masculine room. Paintings hung on every wall and pedestals displayed iron sculptures. A clock inside a realistic sculpture of a raven showed him the time. Seven p.m. His frustration escalated. He'd missed the wedding rehearsal and now he should be at the rehearsal dinner.

"Where have you taken me?" he asked. "I have a wedding to attend. *My* wedding!" He struggled, which only made them sink their fingers deeper into his arms and poke the barrel of a gun into his back.

They pushed him through another large room, past tall glass windows. Outside them, landscape lights illuminated manicured hedges forming a privacy wall around a huge yard. They kept going, past the windows and down a hallway. A modern painting caught his attention, specifically the signature scrawled in one corner. Totally unreadable, yet distinctive. Jacob Arroyo. Scott had met him a few years ago, just after Redmond Galleries signed him and sold several of his pieces for six-figure amounts.

A young woman wearing a classic, black and white maid's uniform that reminded him of a Halloween costume passed them in the hallway. She kept her head down but Scott caught the tension and fear in her eyes.

They veered into another room and let him go. The room contained two chairs, two dressers, and two beds. A man was lying face up on each bed.

"Fix them, doctor man," Broken Nose said, blocking the doorway.

Scott looked from one bed to the other. The men weren't moving. "What happened to them?"

"They got shot," Pockmarked answered.

"Then they should be in a hospital," Scott said. "Have they had any care?"

Pockmarked glared at Scott. "That's why you're here."

Scott moved to one bedside. It didn't take a medical professional to figure out that the man in the bed was in dire condition.

"You get to keep living as long as they do," Pockmarked grunted. "What are you waiting for?"

Scott tried to process the surreal situation. He'd treated hundreds of gunshot wounds, but these men might need more care than he could provide in a home setting. "What sort of medical equipment do you have?"

Broken Nose pointed to a pile of tools on top of a dresser. "Everything you need to operate. And lots of painkillers."

"What have you given them?"

"Heroin," Broken Nose answered.

At least they weren't in pain. Although, depending on what these men had done to end up in this condition...perhaps they deserved to be in some. Innocent men would have taken an ambulance to the hospital.

Scott inspected the sharp instruments atop a dresser. Scalpels, scissors, saws, forceps, clamps, and a stapler. Surgical instruments. It wasn't lost on him that all could double as implements of torture.

The occupant of one bed groaned and opened his eyes. "Get me another hit, man. This ain't fun."

"You got it, Tommy," Broken Nose said. He crossed the room and took a bag of powder off the dresser. His willingness to accommodate the patient told Scott his captors and the injured men were collaborators.

"I need to wash my hands," Scott said. "I'll need gloves, a mask, and a gown if I'm going to open them up to remove a bullet."

"Bathroom is that way." Broken Nose shoved Scott toward another door inside the room.

Scott closed the bathroom door behind him and locked it. The room had no windows. Only the one door. No other way out. He turned on the faucet, stuck his head under, and gulped the cold

162

water. He splashed more water over his face and stared into the mirror. Was this really happening?

Someone pounded on the door and then Pockmarked growled, "Hurry up in there."

Scott scrubbed his hands, then exited the bathroom, prepared to do what he could to help his patients.

Broken Nose handed him gloves and a mask, but no gown. Scott put them on. He moved closer to inspect the wounds, starting with Tommy, the man who had asked for another dose of heroin. Scott pressed his fingers against Tommy's neck and counted while watching the second hand move around his watch. "Weak pulse. And this wound is showing signs of infection."

"We got antibiotics." Pockmarked held up a medicine bottle.

Scott shook his head. "Not those. He needs intravenous antibiotics and a tetanus toxoid."

"We don't have a tetanus toxin or whatever it is! This is what we have!" Pockmarked growled and waved his gun at Scott. "And you're going to make it work. You got that?"

Pockmark's weapon made it harder to concentrate. Scott had endured supervising physicians who treated him and other interns terribly and barraged them with insults. But no one had ever pointed a gun at him while telling him what to do.

"Bring some lamps over here so I can see better," Scott said.

Broken Nose left and returned with a floor lamp and a flashlight. He plugged the lamp into the wall.

With the benefit of additional light, Scott checked the second patient. He was in far worse shape than Tommy.

"Marco lost a lot of blood," Pockmarked said. "Marco, you in there? You feeling any pain, bro?"

Marco didn't respond.

"I need you both to hold him still," Scott said.

Using the surgical tools, he removed bullet fragments, stabilized a fracture, and cleaned up the damaged areas as best he could without imaging to guide him.

The shot to Marco's shoulder wouldn't kill him. The one to his ankle might. That wound was more likely to develop an infection because of the soft tissue, the muscle coverage, and the limited blood supply. Marco was already behind in receiving the treatment he needed, treatment Scott couldn't provide there. The man's prognosis was poor.

CHAPTER 21

FOUR DAYS AGO

Sitting on the cot with his back against the cold concrete, Scott scanned the dank, windowless walls. A few yards from his cot, dried blood splattered the walls and coated the floor. He didn't want to think about what had happened to that person.

Scott's gaze returned to the half-eaten bowl of cold rice and beans on the floor. He'd almost vomited when he noticed one of the rice kernels wiggling around. And yet, his stomach cramped with hunger pains. Protein was protein, he told himself, picking the bowl up again. He couldn't escape this place if he had no strength.

He'd had so much time for the same thoughts to circle through his mind.

What does Bailey know? What happened with our wedding? Is my family looking for me? They must be worried sick.

The people holding him captive were criminals, obviously. Successful ones. Mafia or a drug cartel. All spoke English. Some with accents. So far, he'd only seen Pockmarked, Broken Nose, and the two men with the gunshot wounds—Marco and Tommy. He'd also seen two young maids around. The way they tip-toed through the rooms without looking at anyone, they might not be any less captive than he.

Scott sighed and turned over on the cot. Talk about being in the wrong place at the wrong time. The worst timing ever. How could this have happened right before his wedding? He'd pondered the question long and hard and now believed his ER vanity license plate was to blame.

His eyes had adjusted to the dim light. Gripping a small, sharp-edged stone from the ground, he pressed it hard against the concrete wall and scraped the curved lines of an Arabic S into the wall. Twelve years ago, as a first-year college student, he'd taken Arabic to fulfill his language requirement and embraced the mental challenge of learning a new alphabet and the associated sounds. He'd kept at it for three more semesters and hadn't thought about it since. Now, for something to do, and to avoid losing his mind, he struggled to recall the image of the Arabic letters before scratching them onto the wall.

When finished writing, he pried a small pebble from some broken concrete and rolled it across the ground, aiming for a rounded crack a few yards away. Off by a few inches, he retrieved the pebble and tried again. His own little golf game. When he couldn't bear to roll it again, he returned to his thoughts.

I missed my wedding. What is Bailey doing now? What is she thinking? What does she know? And all the people who made the trip to Massachusetts for us, what do they think happened to me? He tried to come up with the names and faces of the guests, the ones he and his family had invited. Liam, David and his wife, Maria. His best man, Ned, and Victoria, whom Scott had been eager to meet. Aunts and Uncles. Cousins. Colleagues. There were hundreds of people. Some he barely knew. His mother had insisted on a huge wedding.

His absence had to be major news. People didn't disappear before their weddings. Unless they got cold feet. *And no one who knows me would ever think that.*

THE GROOM WENT MISSING

The door at the top of the stairs rattled as someone turned the lock. They were coming for him. Scott scrambled to his feet, attempting to make himself a little less vulnerable.

The same two men came down the stairs. Broken Nose and Pockmarked. Scott still didn't know their real names.

Pockmarked held a gun in one hand. With his other, he pointed to the Arabic letters Scott had etched into the wall. "What's that? Are those words? What d'they say?"

"Nothing."

Pockmarked kicked Scott hard in the shin. "I asked you, what d'they say?"

"It's a prayer," Scott answered. "Listen, I'm going to be missed. I have a family. Coworkers. People are looking for me. Just let me go and I'll forget this ever happened."

Pockmarked scoffed. "Your job ain't done here. You know that."

"And no one thinks you're missing, estúpido," Broken Nose added.

"What?" Scott's heart sank. He didn't want to believe them. "Why don't they think I'm missing?"

Broken Nose laughed again. "Because they got sent messages from your phone. You said you couldn't get married because you have another honey on the side and she's having your baby."

Scott felt the blood drain from his face.

"Nah, I'm joking," Broken Nose said. "We told her you had to go out of town for an emergency."

"You spoke with her?"

"Just text messages. We said you'd see her at the altar. Just to mess with her. Then we made it real clear you weren't coming. That you couldn't marry her."

Scott shuddered at the thought of Bailey waiting for him at the altar. "She'll know that wasn't me."

"Nah. She won't. She'll think it was you." Broken Nose raised his voice a few octaves and taunted Scott by saying, "Love you, Bales."

Scott moaned and bowed his head as a wave of nausea crested through him. It was too much. He didn't know if they were telling the truth; he couldn't trust a word they said. But their words still cut him like a poisoned knife, making him sick with sorrow and anger. He had to get out of this place so Bailey could learn the truth.

Both men were still chuckling. They were monsters with no empathy. It shocked Scott that people existed without hearts.

"Come on," Pockmarked said. "We need you upstairs. Marco's not doing good."

Guns drawn, they dragged Scott upstairs. Pockmarked was still puffing from the effort as they crossed the house and pushed Scott into the room with his patients.

"I have to wash my hands first," Scott said. Inside the bathroom, he gulped all the water he could handle without it coming back up. Then he washed his face. A changed man stared back at him from the mirror.

Someone pounded on the door.

Scott scrubbed his hands, over each knuckle, in between his fingers, and under his nails, because the familiar routine gave him a tiny measure of comfort. He dried his hands and left the bathroom to treat his ailing patient.

Marco was feverish, coated in a sheen of sweat. The wound on his ankle was severely swollen and infected. "He needs a blood transfusion and IV antibiotics," Scott said.

"I'm doing better," Tommy said, sitting upright in the other bed. "Why aren't you helping Marco?"

"Different injuries," Scott answered, feeling incredulous that anyone would seriously ask that question. It seemed so obvious.

"You need to step up your game here," Pockmarked said.

"I know what he needs." Scott tried to keep his voice calm when he really felt like shouting. "You don't have it here. If you want him to live, he needs to be in a hospital. And if you won't take him to one, I need to stay up here and monitor him, make sure he doesn't seize."

"You can't stay up here," Pockmarked said. "Do what you need to do and then you're going back down."

"Hand me a scalpel," Scott said. "And I hope you've sterilized it."

"We did, man. You think we don't know about germs?" Broken Nose sneered.

"I don't know what you know. I don't know anything about any of you," Scott said, gripping the scalpel. It was sharp enough to slice a neck. But Pockmarked could get off several rounds before Scott could reach him.

As Scott opened Marco's wound again, he heard voices coming from another room. One rose above the others. It came from a confident and commanding man.

"Don't go near Luna," the man said to the others. "He's got the cops and the Feds watching. They've got nothing or they would have arrested him. They'll leave soon. I'll make sure of it. But for now…leave Luna alone."

Scott didn't know who Luna was, and he didn't know if law enforcement agencies were watching Luna because Scott was missing, or if it was something else, but he hoped the cops wouldn't give up.

Footsteps came toward the patients' room. A distinguished-looking man in his fifties stopped in the doorway and adjusted his sports coat. Two beautiful women with glazed-over eyes waited behind him.

Pockmarked and Broken Nose stood at attention. Tommy sat up straighter and with a slightly bowed head, faced the newcomer.

"So, this is the doctor," the man said. It wasn't a question. He looked Scott up and down. "Sorry about your wedding." He shifted his gaze to Tommy and nodded. Moving on to Marco, he gave his head a slight shake, then walked away, leaving Scott's skin prickling. The man's presence in the room made clear he was the one calling the shots. He was the one the others feared—the leader of the criminal operation. And he'd done nothing to conceal his face from Scott.

Scott couldn't provide effective medical care now. Marco was too far gone. Only the heroin could minimize his suffering. Yet Scott had to continue convincing his captors he was making a significant difference. Once his perceived usefulness ended—with Marco's death—Scott was a dead man.

THREE DAYS AGO

Scott found another stone to use as a writing implement and scrawled more Arabic across the wall. He threw the stone down just as footsteps and a rustle of noise came from the other side of the door.

Pockmarked ambled halfway down the stairs, his shoulders shrugging up and down with each heavy step. One hand rested on the gun at his side. "We need more of those pills," he said.

"The antibiotics?" Scott asked. They weren't strong enough to help Marco now, though there was a miniscule chance they would slow the pace at which he died, buying Scott more time.

"Yeah," Pockmarked said. "How do we get them?"

"You need a prescription. And I need one of my prescription pads to write him one."

"Get over here." Pockmarked pulled zip ties from his pocket and held them up.

"Why?"

"I'm tying you up, that's why. Get over here."

"No. Why do you have to tie me up?"

"This is the last time I tell you, idiot, and if I have to get help, you're going to be sorry."

"You need help down there?" Broken Nose shouted from the top of the stairs. "Doctor man not cooperating?"

"No. Why would I need help with this one?" Pockmarked shouted back.

Scott eyed the gun, noting his captor's finger near the trigger, and decided to cooperate. Once the zip ties were secured on Scott's wrists, Pockmarked went back up the stairs and locked the door.

With his hands tied behind his back, Scott paced the basement and tried to figure out what would happen next and what he could do to save his life; what he could do to get back to Bailey.

The lock on the door rattled. Pockmarked descended the stairs faster than he ever had before, his boots thudding and echoing on each step. His face contorted with rage as he stormed over to Scott and punched him in the head. Scott stumbled backward. Without his hands to help regain his balance, he slammed the floor hip first.

"You lied to me," Pockmarked hollered.

Scott rocked onto his side and quickly got on his knees so he could see the next blow coming. Ears ringing, he spit out blood and a tooth.

"We aren't stupid!" Spittle flew from Pockmarked's mouth as he yelled. "I looked it up on the internet. You can call those drugs in, and you can prescribe them for yourself." He pressed his phone screen. Scott heard it ringing and then an automatic prompt said, "This is CVS Pharmacy on Franklin Road. Press one if you are a physician."

Pockmarked cut off the call. "Tell me exactly what you'd say if you were talking to them."

Scott shook his head.

"You are really pissing me off. Think about Bailey." Pockmarked ended her name with a snort. "You want her to die? We know where she is right now. We're watching her. Remember what we told you. We mean what we say. You know that, right?"

That was all it took for Scott to cooperate. "I need two antibiotics. Flagyl and Cipro."

"That's what you say, exactly?"

Scott sighed. "I am calling in two prescriptions. One is for Flagyl 500 mg, one PO every six hours, number forty, no refills. The other prescription is for Cipro 500 mg, one PO every twelve hours, number twenty, no refills. They'll want my physician prescriber number, too."

"Hold on." Broken Nose held his phone in front of Scott. "I'm going to press record and then you say exactly what you would say, exactly how you would say it, again. No screwing with me. Or else you're gonna be sorry and so is Bailey."

CHAPTER 22

Whenever they brought Scott up from the basement, Broken Nose and Pockmarked always accompanied him with their guns. Scott believed he could easily outrun the men. But he couldn't outrun their bullets. Though soon, very soon, he'd have to take that risk.

Inside the patients' room, one bed was empty. Tommy now sat upright in a wingback corner chair. One of his hands held rosary beads, the other his gun. He wasn't in fighting shape yet, but would have no problem aiming and shooting his weapon.

While Tommy had quickly improved, Marco had only gotten worse. Each labored breath he took ended in a rattling gasp. Witnessing his rapid decline agonized Scott. He could have saved Marco's life under different conditions. The additional antibiotics that might have further delayed his death never arrived. Scott's captors seemed to know something about it—a screw up at the pharmacy—but they hadn't told him. He hoped whatever happened meant the authorities were close to finding him.

Scott went into the bathroom to take his fill of water before washing up. He gagged as the liquid hit his empty stomach but kept drinking, nonetheless. He could barely believe his reflection and how much he had changed in a few days. Leaning against the sink, his body weak from lack of food, he looked like a ghost of himself, and felt the same. Reluctantly, he emerged from the room when Pockmarked threatened to shoot him through the door.

"You're sure he's gonna die soon?" Pockmarked asked. His tone suggested he'd grown tired of watching Marco suffer and his death couldn't come soon enough.

A lie might save Scott's own skin, but not for much longer. The truth loomed closer with each passing minute. Marco's pulse had grown so weak it barely registered. "I'm sure. Unless you take him to a hospital. Which you could still do. Then he might have a chance." A razor slim chance.

"Then there's no need to make him suffer," Pockmarked said. He left the room, returned a minute later with a needle, and approached Marco. "Hey, man. You gonna feel better real soon. Salazar is going to take care of your family. So will we. We'll make sure they're good." He spoke with a calm respect as he depressed the contents of the needle into Marco's arm.

Marco's eyes flew open, and he gasped. Then his breathing ceased.

Pockmarked closed Marco's eyelids and pulled the sheet over his head. Scott shivered, knowing his own death was now imminent.

"You're done here," Broken Nose said. He grabbed Scott's shoulder, jabbed a gun into his back, then shoved him through the house. Scott dragged his feet on purpose. Though he had little strength only moments ago, his adrenaline now soared. He planned to bolt when they neared the front of the house.

"Go for it," Broken Nose said, apparently aware of Scott's thoughts. "I'd love it. I'll even give you a big head start to show off what an excellent shot I am."

"Let's just talk about what I can do to help you," Scott pleaded. If he could make himself seem useful and cooperative, it would give him more time to escape. But they weren't hearing any of it.

At the cellar stairs, they pushed him forward. Scott grabbed the railing to keep from plummeting down as the door slammed and locked behind him. Perched on the second step, he banged the door and shouted until he had no voice left. Exhausted and shaking, he clung to the railing until he had the strength to get back down the stairs. He paced slowly around the cellar in a cold sweat, his hunger and thirst forgotten. His fear and desperation made him feel more alive than he had in days. He'd spent so many hours alone with his thoughts there. But now that his time was running out, it hardly seemed like enough. Barring a miracle, he'd known Marco would soon die. But Scott wasn't ready.

He climbed the stairs again, rattled the handle, and banged on the door until his knuckles were raw and bloody.

No one came.

Finally, he trudged back down the stairs, sat down on the damp floor with his back against the wall, and dropped his head between his knees.

Oh, Bailey. I'm so sorry.

***

Sounds came from behind the door before it opened. Scott didn't get up from the cot. His dry mouth and throat burned from dehydration and shouting. He tried to swallow and find his voice as his captors descended the stairs. They'd left the door open behind them.

"Get up. On your feet." Pockmarked grabbed Scott's arms and pulled him up.

Scott wrenched away and put everything he had into a right hook. His fist connected with Pockmarked's face. He recoiled from the blow, giving Scott just enough time to make a break for the stairs. As he raced up, he heard Pockmarked swearing and Broken Nose laughing behind him.

He bounded to the top, bracing for the shot that would end his life. Halfway up and he was still alive. Only three steps remained. He leapt over them and landed inside the house...where Tommy waited and pointed a gun at Scott's head.

"Shame I'd have to kill you after you helped me, bro," Tommy said, grinning.

Then the other men were behind him—Pockmarked still swearing between his huffing and gasping, as if he'd just climbed a section of Mount Everest. They tied Scott's hands behind his back, jabbing and poking him as he thrashed to keep them free. When he could no longer move his hands, they shoved him toward the front of the house.

"Where are you taking me?" Scott shouted.

One of them dropped a thick canvas bag over his head.

"Keep moving," Tommy said as they pulled and pushed him forward.

A few steps more and Scott began to struggle. Flailing his body, he tried to shake them off. He had nothing left to lose. But they held tight and punched him in the face. His ears were still ringing when a second blow rammed his temple from the opposite direction.

"That's my payback," Pockmarked said.

Scott's head pounded as if it might explode. A wave of nausea made him almost pass out. They dragged him through the house, opened a door, and then cool air surrounded him.

"Watch your step," Tommy mumbled.

The warning came too late. Scott stumbled down a short staircase, landed hard, and twisted his ankle. The men's grips kept him from falling face first.

Scott heard the soft sound of a car door opening and hit his head on a metal edge as they pushed him down and into the vehicle. He sank into a cushioned seat.

"Move your feet in. Not going to do everything for you," Pockmarked said. He kicked Scott hard on the leg.

"Where are you taking me?" Scott pleaded, alarmed by the desperation in his voice. "I won't tell anyone about any of this. I'll say I got cold feet, just like your story, and I needed time to think. I won't tell anyone. Please."

"We know you won't tell anyone," Broken Nose said. "We're going to make sure of that."

Scott choked back a sob. "You need me. Something like this might happen again. I can be the person who fixes you. I can treat you in the ER, admit you under fake names. I'll have the right equipment. No one would ever know. You need me."

A garage door went up with a quiet hum followed by the car starting with a barely-there electric buzz. A lot quieter than his Jeep. The vehicle moved backwards, turned, and drove forward. Gravel or pebbles crunched under the car's tires. They stopped. Scott heard metal moving, perhaps a large gate opening, before the vehicle drove forward again. After several seconds, the sound of popping gravel ceased, and the tires glided over smooth road.

"Listen to me. Please. I helped you. I saved Tommy's life. And now I'm asking for one thing. Just one thing. I need Bailey to know I love her. I've loved her since our first date. I would never, ever desert her. She needs to know that. Please. Tell her I didn't suffer, and I'm so sorry, and I love her more than anything."

"Shut up!" Someone moved around on the front seat, the fabric of their clothes rustling, and then a fist rammed Scott's head hard enough to rattle his teeth.

Music blasted the car, playing so loudly Scott couldn't hear his own shouts.

I'm so sorry, Bailey. I'm so sorry.

All he could think about was her. He couldn't say how long they drove. Couldn't tell if it was ten minutes or thirty. It went so

177

slowly, and yet every moment he still breathed and could think about Bailey seemed precious.

Uneven terrain jostled the car. They'd pulled off the road into an unpaved area with dips or potholes.

The vehicle stopped and a fresh wave of fear spread through him. "Where are we? What's happening?"

A door opened in front of him. Cold air chilled his skin. Then his door unlatched.

"Get out," Broken Nose said.

The icy wind hit him. He had no jacket, no hat, no gloves. He would freeze out there. No, he wouldn't have time to freeze. They would shoot him first. *How far am I from a main road?* He hoped he was close and they would leave his body by the road so someone would find it and Bailey would know he hadn't left her by choice.

An owl hooted from somewhere not so far away. They were in a wooded area. His mounting fear made breathing difficult. He hyperventilated under the bag, sucking in air with big, gasping gulps. Hands came at his neck. He jerked away. They grabbed him again, more than one of them, and their strong fingers surrounded his neck. He struggled, smashing his head against one of his assailants.

"What the—damn you!" Broken Nose shouted.

Two sets of powerful hands now held him in place. He thrashed, breaking free for just a second, racing away without understanding where he was headed or what was in his path…until they yanked him back again.

"Hold still, Tonto," Pockmarked hissed.

Someone pulled at the rope around his neck.

"You saved Tommy," Pockmarked said. "Keep your mouth shut and Bailey Ballard lives. That's how it will work. One wrong move from you and our deal is off. We honor our word. Now it's up to you. Screw it up and she's dead. Got it?"

Scott had never been more confused. After abducting him, ruining his wedding, holding him hostage, starving and beating him, they were now going to trust him to keep his mouth shut? That made no sense. They were lying. He braced himself for a bullet or a blade that would slice across his jugular at any second.

Scott heard a twig snap and leaves rustle several yards away. Someone else was there.

The bag lifted off. At least Scott would see where he was going to die.

His captors moved away from him. Another figure approached.

"He's all yours now," Pockmarked said.

With his hands still tied, Scott blinked and squinted into the darkness, unable to make sense of what was happening and who was now standing in front of him. "Mom?" he asked, his jaw dropping. "What are you doing here?"

CHAPTER 23

"I'm so sorry about all of this," Scott's mother told him. Her voice conveyed her sorrow, but why wasn't she peppering him with questions?

"You're so thin," she said. "Didn't they feed you? Come on, hurry, get in my car."

As she walked toward her Audi, Scott remained frozen in place, his mouth still hanging open, relieved to be alive yet shocked and confused by his mother's presence.

She turned and beckoned him. "Come on, Scott."

He hurried after her. Inside her Audi, he grabbed the half empty Fiji bottle from the cup holder and gulped the water down. "What happened?" he asked. "Did you have to pay a ransom?"

"No, no." His mother turned on the car's interior lights and ran her gaze over his face and down to his bloody knuckles. "They hurt you. They really hurt you."

When Scott opened his mouth to speak, she whispered, "Oh, my God. Your teeth. You're missing a tooth. I'm so sorry." Biting down on her lip, she turned away. After a few seconds, she put the car in gear, drove out of the wooded area, and back to a main road. "We tried to protect you from all this. Never wanted you involved."

Scott was more confused than ever. "Tried to protect me from what? Who is 'we'?"

"Duncan and me. I'm not sure how much you've figured out or been told."

"No one has told me anything. I was captive in a dungeon for days when I should have been at my wedding!" Just when he'd thought his situation couldn't get more unbelievable, it had happened. "And you don't seem surprised by that. What the hell is going on? Why did you come and not the police?"

"Calm down. First things first." Despite the cold, she lowered the windows partway, confirming what Scott already knew. He smelled rancid.

"You're going to have to get your story straight," she said. "Listen carefully. This is very important. If anyone asks—and of course they're all going to ask, you can't avoid that—you're going to tell them you had a panic attack. You don't remember most of what happened next. You asked a friend, an acquaintance, to drive you to the airport. The man who took you there—he drove you in your car—his name is Richard Luna."

Scott had so many questions he didn't know where to start. "What are you talking about? Who is Richard Luna?" Scott asked, remembering his captors mentioning that name.

"Like I said, if anyone asks, Luna is an acquaintance of yours. You treated him for a ruptured appendix in July. Then right before the rehearsal, you asked him to drive you to the airport and leave your car there."

Scott could barely focus. Everything seemed surreal.

His mother used her blinker to turn right, though there were no other cars around them, only darkness. She wasn't using navigation. She seemed to be familiar with the area.

"You didn't get on a plane at the airport," she said. "You just wandered around the city in a daze. There must be a medical term for it, a specific diagnosis. Whatever it is, that's what you'll tell people. You wandered until you came to your senses."

His mother's matter-of-fact attitude made no sense to him. He shivered, whether from the frigid air rushing into the car, or his exhausted body's reaction to the situation, he wasn't sure. "I don't know what you're talking about. I have to see Bailey, and then I'm going straight to the police."

"No police, Scott. Not now. Not ever. You're sworn to secrecy about everything that happened. You can't tell anyone. That includes Bailey."

Scott's head spun with confusion. Bile rose into his throat from his empty stomach.

They finally reached a road with streetlights and other cars.

"Is it Wednesday?" he asked, trying to regain a small sense of normality.

"Yes, it is. By the way, not related to the day of the week, but to everything else…Ned and his girlfriend are causing trouble for us."

"Ned and his girlfriend? What do they have to do with anything? Enough of this cryptic crap. You need to tell me exactly what is going on here because I really don't know."

"I'm going to. Just as soon as we get home and get you some food. Duncan is waiting for us."

✲✲✲

Late Wednesday night, Bailey sat on her loveseat with a blanket wrapped around her shoulders and a large goblet of wine in her hand, alone for the first time in days. Ever since the wedding fiasco, someone had been by her side. Her sister. Her father. Katie. Jules. Mrs. Redmond. No one wanted to let her alone. What did they think would happen? The worst had already occurred. Scott was gone. Missing. She couldn't stop imagining him alone and suffering somewhere. The thought of it was unbearable. It was the reason empty wine bottles now filled her recycling bin.

Thanks to the Redmond's insistence about using a private investigator rather than going to the police, the situation remained relatively private. Bailey could return to work and her former life and pretend nothing had happened. She didn't want to do that. She wanted the truth. Regardless of the notes and messages Scott had supposedly sent, she refused to believe he would leave her. Maybe he'd hit his head and had amnesia. She'd accept that a hundred times before anyone could convince her he'd changed his mind. If he was still alive, he would find his way back. She just had to figure out how to help him do that.

Bailey was grateful for Victoria's help, although she wasn't sure what the agent believed. Did she think Scott was a victim or that he flew somewhere under a false name to hide away and avoid marriage? Either way, Bailey couldn't blame Victoria. She didn't blame anyone. She could see how things might look to everyone else. Mrs. Redmond has assured Bailey that the private investigator she hired was one of the absolute best. And according to him, there was no explanation to be found. At least not yet. But Bailey knew without a doubt that something had happened to Scott.

She finished her wine, got up from the loveseat, and went to the suitcase waiting on her bed. She unzipped it and removed the black and gold bikini from the top of her other island clothes. She'd loved the suit. Scott would have loved it, too. Every time she'd imagined them on the beach in St. Lucia, she'd pictured herself wearing that bikini. And now, she never wanted to see it again.

Her doorbell buzzed. She walked to the video cam in her entry, expecting to see one of her well-meaning friends who would then say, "Just making sure you're okay." How many times had she heard that phrase in the past few days? The texts and emails just kept coming. Of course she wasn't okay. She couldn't imagine ever being okay again until she located Scott.

On the video screen, under the security light, looking down, wearing the same clothes she'd seen him wearing the morning of the wedding rehearsal....it was Scott!

"Scott! Scott! You're here!" She almost didn't believe her own eyes. Was he really there? Was this nightmare finally over? As her heart fluttered and her knees almost gave out beneath her, she forgot to press the talk button. She had to push it and speak again. She was so giddy with happiness and relief she wasn't sure what to say or what she'd already said.

He looked up at her. He had several days-worth of growth on his face and there was something else there, a look she'd never seen before. Resignation? Exhaustion? Shame? She wasn't sure. And it hardly mattered. All that mattered was his presence. She pushed the button to unlock the door, then raced down the stairs to meet him. Two words repeated in her head. *He's here. He's here. He's here.*

They met halfway. Already crying tears of joy, she threw her arms around him and hugged him hard. His body trembled, he felt different in her arms, and he smelled as if he hadn't showered in days. She hugged him harder, not wanting to let go. They both cried.

Finally, he pulled away.

Bailey took stock of his battered knuckles, the dark bruises marring his face, and the gaping hole in his beautiful teeth.

"I love you and I'm so sorry," he said. "I panicked."

Bailey had engaged in wild speculation over the past few days in search of an explanation. She's prepared herself for so many things he might say, but not that.

He looked away, scrunching his face as if in pain. He couldn't meet her eyes.

"I'm not buying that, Scott. I don't know what's going on, but I deserve the truth."

He closed his eyes and hung his head.

"Come inside," she said. "We need to get you cleaned up and then you can tell me what really happened."

Before she could move, he pulled her toward him again. "I love you, Bailey, but I don't deserve you."

"Yes, you do. Cut it out. Because I deserve you *and* the truth about what happened."

Without putting his full weight on his left foot, Scott followed her up the stairs. Inside her apartment, Bailey carefully undressed him, trying to hide her shock when she saw more bruises on his torso and how much weight he'd lost. With almost zero body fat covering his taut muscles, they rippled under his skin.

"Wherever you were, they didn't have free drinks and chips and guacamole, did they?" she asked, uncertain if she could joke about whatever horror he'd endured. Something had changed inside Scott and Bailey needed to understand it. As long as it wasn't his feelings for her, they would get through this.

Scott turned the bedroom lamps off, leaving only scant light from the hallway. They finished undressing and got into the shower together. She gently soaped his body and washed his hair. She used her shaving cream and razor to shave his face. After getting out and toweling off, they made love. It was tender and gentle, and unleashed a desperate longing that left no doubt they were meant to be together. Scott needed her.

They held each other tightly without moving.

"You need to get a good night's sleep, and then we'll talk," Bailey said.

Scott murmured, his eyelids already drooping closed.

Bailey rolled onto her side, pulled the covers up to their shoulders and said, "Good night, Scott. I love you. And whatever happened, we're going to get through it together."

185

***

Bailey was the first one up the next morning. She got out of bed quietly, letting Scott sleep. She busied herself in the kitchen, making him the solid, balanced breakfast he needed. When she heard him stirring, she prepared a tray and carried it into the bedroom.

"Thank you," Scott said, sitting up.

He ate the food slowly. When he'd had enough, she moved the tray onto the nightstand and asked, "Are you ready to talk?"

"Yes." The look on his face told her it wouldn't be easy.

She sat next to him on the bed.

"It's about my family. And you're right, you deserve to know what you're getting into if you choose to stay with me."

As he held her hands, Scott told her the terrible, inconceivable truth.

Bailey believed every word, though she didn't know what to do about it. They held each other again for some time until Scott got up, clutching his abdomen. As he crossed the room, something made him stop in front of her dresser.

"Is that what I think it is?" he asked. "Are those our rings?"

"Yes," Bailey answered.

He stared at her, looking very confused before opening the small, velvet box. "I had them with me before the rehearsal. Where did you get them?"

She told him about the teen who delivered the rings. "It came with a note. You didn't send it?"

"No. What did it say?"

"According to Jules it came from you, and it said, 'I'm sorry.' She's the only one who read it. But if the note didn't come from you, I don't care what it said or didn't say. It doesn't matter."

Scott frowned. "It matters to me. I'll have to ask her. When I can bring myself to speak to her again. That might be awhile."

"There was also a note in your car. It said you didn't love me anymore."

He was at her side in no time. "I definitely didn't write that."

"I know," she said. "I never thought you did."

"Listen, what I told you…both our lives are in danger if you repeat any of it to anyone. Do you understand?"

"Yes, I understand. And I'm glad you can trust me. If we don't have that…"

"I know," he said before she could finish her sentence. His lips found hers again.

PART III

CHAPTER 24

Seated in one of the FBI's small conference rooms, Victoria took another sip of her latte, trying to get through the wave of afternoon sleepiness that came from having a quiet day in the office.

Payton Jennings, acting head of the FBI's forensic accounting department, entered looking as stylish and put together as always in a pencil skirt, silk blouse, and low heels. The sharp edges of her bob ended just above her shoulders. "Hey, there," she said.

"Hi, Payton. How have you been?" Victoria asked.

"Doing fine." Payton set her laptop down on the table and pulled out a chair. "Lots going on here, as usual." Then she smiled. "I just visited my niece, Ali, at University of Virginia. She's in the same sorority I was in when I was there. So that was fun."

"Oh, nice."

"And you…what are you working on?"

"I'm not assigned to any specific case right now. Starting to wonder what that's about, actually. I'm getting caught up with some paperwork and training. That's how I had time to delve into the situation I sent you. Did you have time to look at any of it?"

"I made the time. And I'm glad you sent the information my way."

Someone approached the doorway. Victoria and Payton looked to see who was there.

"Mind if I join you two?" Agent Dante Rivera asked.

Rivera looked good. His hair neat and trim against smooth, dark skin. His body lean and toned from hours on the basketball court and in the gym.

"Come on in," Victoria answered, though she wasn't sure why he was there.

He grinned. "It's always interesting to see what Victoria's got herself into next."

"That's not fair," Victoria said, a smile stretching across her face.

"Yeah, I know." Rivera smiled back at her as he took a seat. He opened a plastic container of gum, shook out two pieces into his hand, then offered the container to the women.

"No, thank you," Victoria said, before returning to her conversation with Payton. "Thanks for looking into it right away. When I started finding connections, I knew I needed an expert from forensic accounting to give their opinion."

"And you got the department director herself," Rivera said. There was something about his tone...an edge of pride. Rivera was always nice to his colleagues, but was it possible he and Payton had something beyond a colleague relationship? Of course it was possible. Why wouldn't it be? Months ago, Victoria had made it clear she just wanted to be friends. She'd chosen Ned.

"I'm very glad you sent it to me," Payton said, opening her laptop and turning it on. "I just got off the phone with the Financial

Crime Department. They want this. Homeland Security and the Organized Crime Taskforce will want in, too. So will Art Crimes."

"Oh." This surprised Victoria. "You talked to all of them about Redmond Galleries already?"

"Yes. This could be a big break for us."

Victoria felt a pang of discomfort. She wanted her suspicions confirmed, but she hadn't thought through what might happen next. The FBI had limited resources and so many active cases. Victoria certainly hadn't expected other departments to jump on board, never mind so quickly. When she'd asked for Payton's help, she wasn't sure if Payton would even get a chance to look at the information.

Payton settled back into her seat. "So, you know the family who runs the galleries? That's how you came across this information?"

"I met them last week," Victoria said. "At a wedding that never happened because their son, the groom, Ned's best friend, didn't show up. That's a whole other issue, but I think it's connected." She told Payton and Rivera that Scott was an ER doctor and about the suspected connection to the warehouse shootings, Luna, and the Salazar cartel. "Seeing Luna in the gallery next to Jules brings it all full circle. Though I still don't understand the exact nature of Scott's involvement."

"Wow." Payton's eyes went wide.

"You can't go somewhere without something like this happening, can you?" Rivera's tone was light, it was all good humor, but it cut a little because lately, it was true. Her last few vacation getaways had made headlines.

"Your instincts about Redmond Galleries were right on," Payton said. "How much do you know about fraud in the art world? Obviously, enough to recognize the red flags there."

"I know the basics. The secrecy and lack of regulation in the industry."

"Fill me in." Rivera leaned back against his seat and rested his hands on his lap.

Payton slid her glasses off and set them next to her computer. "Most high-end sales take place quietly and anonymously. Unlike a car or a real estate transaction, art sales don't have to be recorded. There are so many ways to launder money and profit illegitimately in the art world. I could give a full lecture on each."

"You don't have time for that." Rivera tapped his watch and Payton smiled, causing Victoria to wonder what he was referring to. Was Rivera working on a case with her? Or did they have a date?

"I'll stick to a basic summary of money laundering 101," Payton said, sliding her glasses back on. "We have a long list of red flags we use to identify possible money laundering. Based on my initial review, Redmond Galleries presents as a line of flashing, flapping flags."

Rivera laughed, but Victoria cringed inside, thinking about what this meant for the Redmond family. Though, if they were guilty, she shouldn't be feeling sorry for them.

"I looked at their tax returns," Payton said. "Their income skyrocketed over the past five years, and that's only what they reported. We found connections to layers of shell companies and trusts. I also looked through some purchases from Redmond Galleries. Of what I saw, more than half involve private, anonymous buyers that I wasn't able to track. Private dealers like Redmond Galleries can sell a toddler's paint-by-number piece for thousands if they wish. It's art, after all. Completely subjective. Who is to say a random scribble isn't worth half-a-million if someone will pay that for it? Dealers deem which pieces are good, and therefore expensive. Redmond Galleries has a trend of making previously unknown artists very famous with top-dollar sales. Jacob Arroyo, for example."

"I met him at the wedding," Victoria said. "He certainly thinks he's talented."

"A few years ago, Redmond Galleries started selling his work to undisclosed buyers for tens of thousands of dollars each. Why did an unknown artist's work suddenly become so valuable? It's possible his talent is so rare and special that it truly commanded those prices. So I looked at a few of his pieces where I could find photos online. It's very hard to believe anyone paid that much for them." Payton shrugged and offered an endearing, lopsided grin. "Another possibility, and what looks likely, is that a crime organization started buying his work at hugely inflated prices. The cash goes into the bank. Everyone takes a cut of it and the cartel gets clean money back. After that, it only gets more lucrative for everyone involved. The cartel lets the art sit around for a few years before putting it back in the market. Having already established its value, it now resells for even more."

"Allowing for more money laundering *and* a profit," Victoria said.

"Right," Payton said. "The new buyers might be legit art collectors, and even think they're getting a great deal, except that the original sales price was absurdly inflated. You can see how sketchy it can get."

Victoria pursed her lips and nodded. Everything lined up with what she had learned in bits and pieces about Redmond Galleries. They'd suddenly done very well financially. They had a *knack* for establishing artists. "And if a dealer like Redmond Galleries does this long enough, and always has someone disguised as a legit art collector lined up to buy from them, eventually it sure looks like they know exactly what they're doing."

"Impressive scheme," Rivera said. "And I can't say I'm surprised. Any industry with regulatory weaknesses becomes a magnet for crime."

Payton responded with a slight dip of her chin. "Just to give you an example—when the Mexican government passed a law requiring more information on art buyers, reported art sales plummeted by seventy percent, which strongly suggests the cartels had been major players in that market."

"Rather than inflating the price of unknown pieces, why not just buy the real thing?" Rivera asked.

"They do," Payton answered. "The FBI has found priceless works of art inside cartel homes. Some of it on display. Some carelessly stored in attics and basements."

"Interesting," Rivera said.

"Anyway, if we put together all the red flags we've found with the Salazar cartel connection you discovered…it doesn't look good for Redmond Galleries," Payton said.

Victoria suspected as much. Still, it was disappointing to have been right. She didn't want the loose ends to come together this way. Victoria had discovered some wild things during previous investigations, but the Redmond's criminal involvement…*possible criminal involvement*…was wholly unexpected.

"Is it possible that the gallery owners didn't know the identities of the buyers and therefore, they might not know who they're dealing with?" Victoria asked, hoping she was on to something.

"With the patterns I'm seeing here, that's doubtful," Payton said. "I'd go as far as to say it's completely impossible."

None of the Redmonds seemed like the type to be engaged in dangerous criminal activities. But wasn't that the same with most of the white-collar criminals she'd investigated? Still, she wanted to give them every benefit of the doubt. "What if they didn't have a choice getting involved?" Victoria asked.

"There's always a choice," Rivera said. "Don't you think?"

"I don't know," Victoria answered. "Once the cartel chooses you, can anyone really say thanks, but no thanks?"

Payton sighed. "Unfortunately, it's not an excuse to flout the law. They should have come to us immediately."

"Now what?" Rivera asked, looking from Victoria to Payton.

"We see activity similar to this often, especially when we go looking for it," Payton said. "But this is different. It's advanced. And you've already identified the cartel connection. We can act on this. I've got more than enough here to trigger an audit." She punched keys on her laptop and studied her screen. "I'm just checking my assignment schedule. I have three senior analysts I can spare for the week, and we'll go from there. I can have the warrant by end of day tomorrow and get the audit started."

Victoria kept her expression neutral, but inside, she grimaced. How long would it take the Redmond family to figure out her role in triggering the investigation? "Are they told it's just a random audit?" she asked.

"Yes," Payton answered. "But if they're engaging in illegal activities, they probably won't believe it's random. Neither will the cartel."

"Hold on," Rivera said. "The groom is still missing, right?"

Victoria nodded.

"Let's talk about what could happen when we trigger the audit," he said. "If the Redmonds are under pressure from the cartel, they can't launder with the FBI around. We'd make things worse for them. With one of their family members missing, is that wise? Perhaps the audit should wait until we have him back, or we know what happened to him."

"Excellent point," Victoria said.

Rivera faced her. "Unless…is the groom innocent? Or is he willingly working with the cartel?"

194

"I wish I knew," Victoria said. "If he had a choice, would he miss his own wedding? Push back his honeymoon maybe, but not show up for the main event? I doubt it. But does he know about his family's dealings? Is he part of them? Perhaps. But innocent until proven guilty, right? So let's go with the theory that the cartel forced him to treat their gunshot victims, *and* he's still alive. I want to keep him that way. I absolutely do not want to be responsible for anything that triggers his death. So...I absolutely agree with Rivera, we should hold off on the audit until we know what happened to Scott Redmond."

Payton sighed. "As I told you, I've already shared the information. Financial Crimes wants this case, but I suppose I can hold off any response for a few more days. If no one knows what happened to Scott Redmond by then, we may never know. The cartel is very good at eliminating their problems. I'm sorry to say it. I understand he's Ned's friend. But you must know that's true."

"I know." Victoria thought of Bailey and her heart ached.

Rivera pushed his seat away from the table and stood. "We have to get out of here or we'll be late."

Already closing her laptop, Payton checked her watch.

Rivera and Payton made a good team. And if there was more to it than that, they'd make a good couple. Payton was nice, respected at the bureau, and very attractive. She probably didn't have issues getting close to people and trusting them. She probably didn't have a house full of animals to aggravate Rivera's allergies. Which made Victoria wonder, if it hadn't been for Rivera's allergies, would things be different? No. She wouldn't let herself entertain those thoughts and was ashamed she'd been on her way to doing so. Ned deserved so much better. And yet here she was...responsible for sending multiple FBI taskforces after his best friend's family.

"Glad you trusted your hunches," Payton said. "If Scott shows up, if you find him, be sure to let me know right away."

"I will. And…we don't know with absolute certainty that the Redmonds are working with the cartel. There are other possibilities. Success can happen overnight if a business gets trending. Maybe a mega celebrity bought something from them and posted it to the world. That's all it takes."

"Yeah, maybe." Payton didn't sound at all convinced. "The audit will tell us for sure."

CHAPTER 25

Though Victoria had done the right thing by bringing her suspicions to her colleagues, upon seeing Ned's Toyota 4-Runner in her garage, she experienced a sudden pang of guilt. She felt as though she'd betrayed him.

Ned and Bailey had asked Victoria to get involved. They couldn't blame her for what she discovered. But that didn't mean they wouldn't hold her responsible for whatever consequences might befall the Redmond family. They'd asked her to find Scott, not to destroy his family.

What made it worse is that she couldn't tell Ned what she'd found.

If the audit moved forward and uncovered more incriminating evidence, that might mean everything Ned thought he knew about the Redmonds was a lie.

That's when it occurred to her—did Ned have even an inkling of how the Redmonds accumulated their wealth so quickly? No. He hadn't given her any reason to suspect that he did.

Victoria took her time getting out of her Suburban, gathering up a gas receipt, a plastic bag, and a few leaves from the floor mat. Her dogs snorted and yelped from behind the door. Their long tails thudded the walls in a frenzy of anticipation because they'd heard the garage door opening and closing. Once inside, she heard the kitchen faucet running and called out to Ned. "Hey! I'm back."

"Welcome home," he answered.

"Thanks. Any word from Scott?"

"No. Not yet." Ned shut off the faucet, wiped his hands on a dishtowel, then crossed the room and wrapped her into his arms. She closed her eyes, breathing in the scent of him, feeling his warmth and the hard strength of his body. She trusted him with her animals, her house, and her heart. He trusted her too, which made her discomfort rise.

Her dogs jumped and huffed, tails still smashing nearby objects and each other as they pushed their noses against her.

"Did you find out anything more?" he asked.

She pulled back and made her way through the mob of greyhounds while petting each of them. "Suarez is monitoring Richard Luna. That's all we can do with him right now. He's told us his story. Without Scott's word to refute it, there's not much to go on." She wasn't lying. Only omitting important information because she had to.

Victoria put her FBI weapon in the safe and set her purse on the counter. She wanted to relax with Ned and forget about the Redmonds for the night, but she couldn't stop thinking about them. She looked up to find Ned had caught her deep in thought and frowning.

"Come sit down," he said, dipping his head toward the couch. "We can figure out dinner and I can rub your feet...or something."

"That sounds amazing. I'd be crazy not to take you up on that opportunity. You are the absolute sweetest."

Her phone rang from inside her purse.

"Hold on one second." She crossed to the counter, pulled out her phone, and checked the screen. "It's Bailey," she told Ned before answering. "Hi, Bailey."

"Hi. How are you?"

"I'm doing well. Ned just offered to rub my feet, so I've got nothing to complain about. What's going on? Have you heard from Scott?"

"Yes. He's home. I called you right away because...in case you were still trying to find him. He's back."

"Really?" Victoria took a sharp intake of breath as Ned stared at her. She moved the phone away from her mouth and whispered, "He's back."

"I told him how helpful you were," Bailey said. "So, thank you again. Thank you so much for everything. I know Scott's family wants to do something for you, you know, for all your trouble. And so do I."

"That's not necessary. Please tell them not to. I can't accept anything."

Ned had moved to Victoria's side. "Where was he? Did she tell you what happened to him?"

The same questions raced through her own head and since Bailey didn't offer more information, Victoria asked, "So...did he tell you what happened?"

"Yes. It was just what others suggested. He suffered a severe panic attack. He calls it a dissociative incident. Almost an out-of-body experience."

Two days ago, Victoria would have bought that. Even said I told you so. But now...not so much. "Did he stay in the Boston area?" she asked, because asking yes or no questions was an effective way to test for the truth.

"Oh, well, he only remembers bits and pieces of the last few days. He was here and there. Just lost, really. Didn't know what to do with himself."

Bailey's convoluted answer set off alarm signals.

"But he's okay now," Bailey continued. "I understand, and I forgive him. We're hoping everyone else can too. We really want everyone to put the whole thing out of their minds."

As much as Bailey might want that, no one at the wedding would ever forget what happened. "Did he tell you why Richard Luna drove him to the airport?" Victoria asked.

"Well, Luna was available to give him a lift. That's all. The last few days are mostly a blur to him. But he's okay now. Everyone is okay. That's what matters."

Bailey's response to a direct yes or no question started with 'well,' which was often another sign of deception.

"Bailey, listen to me, if you want to talk to me about anything that happened…I can't right now… …but I'll get on the next flight to Boston if you need me." Victoria looked up to see Ned eyeing her strangely, as if he couldn't figure out why she'd said that. Good. She wanted him to be as confused as possible, which suggested he was ignorant of all crimes involving the Redmond family.

"What?" Bailey made a sound that was something between a laugh and a gasp. "I don't know…I'm not sure where that's coming from. We're not…we're fine. There's really nothing else to tell."

Bailey's answer failed to convince Victoria. "Is Scott there?" she asked. "Because I need to speak with him."

"He can't talk right now. He's still pretty traumatized about what he did, though it wasn't his fault. He has many people to apologize to."

"Is he with you at your apartment?" Victoria asked.

"Um, he's with his family."

Bailey still hadn't properly answered a single direct question.

"A local detective named Lisa Suarez will want to interview him," Victoria said. "Possibly even tonight."

"Oh." A few seconds of silence passed before Bailey asked, "Do they have to? I mean, I didn't think we involved the police. I thought it was just you helping us."

"It's because of Scott's connection to Richard Luna, who is currently under investigation."

"Oh, all right." Bailey sounded uncertain. "It was just a panic attack. A terrible panic attack. But I'll make sure he knows. Thank you, Victoria."

The call ended with Victoria wondering what really happened, how much Bailey really knew, and if she could convince Scott and Bailey to tell her the truth.

Across the room, Ned shook his head, his face clouding with anger. "He still hasn't gotten in touch with me. Still hasn't answered my calls and texts. And I still don't believe that he got cold feet."

Neither did Victoria. Considering the cartel connection, she believed the truth was worse. If Scott and Bailey thought they could handle things on their own and everything would be okay, they were gravely mistaken. Things might return to normal for the short term, but they would always be in danger.

"Hey, Ned, I have to make a couple of calls. Shouldn't be more than ten minutes, and then we can figure out dinner."

Inside her office, as she called Suarez, Victoria still didn't know if Scott was guilty of colluding with the cartel or if he'd been a victim.

"Scott Redmond is back," she told the detective. "Are you available to interview him?"

201

"I'll do it first thing in the morning," Suarez said. "I'm eager to hear his version of the truth. It should be interesting if nothing else."

One more thing remained before Victoria could return to the kitchen, discuss dinner plans with Ned, and continue trying to pretend that she didn't know more than she was saying. With Scott back home, she had to tell Payton the FBI could move forward with the audit of Redmond Galleries.

CHAPTER 26

Suarez sat in her car with Blake, outside Luna's house, feeling bitter.

The lingering odor of her fast-food takeout—a burger with a slimy tomato, a scrap of wilted lettuce, and French fries—now bothered her. Meanwhile, Luna had delivery from La Frond, a restaurant Suarez had never heard of, but according to Blake, it was 'fabulous.'

Was the man ever going to leave? Maybe she wouldn't leave either if she lived in his place. It was that nice. Which would make his adjustment to a prison cell that much harder.

Blake had clearly grown bored with their stakeout and Suarez would have preferred to continue it alone.

"He's still in there and we still haven't found his Tahoe anywhere, right?" Blake asked. She returned to slurping her milkshake through a straw.

"And now that he knows we're looking for the Tahoe, it might never see the light of day again," Suarez said.

"If there's not enough evidence for a case, and there never will be, then why are we still here?"

"It's called being patient. We're waiting to find that evidence. You have somewhere better to be, then go ahead and leave."

"Hey, come on," Blake laughed. "No need to cement your reputation with me."

"My reputation? What reputation?"

"Um...I figured you knew. They call you Lisa the grouch."

"Is that so?" Suarez was suddenly so angry; she felt her head might burst.

"Or Lisa the grump," Blake added. "No one knows what you're like when you're not working. Maybe you're happier then."

The truth was, Suarez's work made her happiest, even if she had an odd way of showing it. And it was her bitterness that often drove her dedication. Bitterness toward people like Luna. He represented everything that was wrong and unfair in the world.

Suarez was silently fuming when Agent Heslin called to say Scott Redmond was back and Suarez should interview him as soon as possible. A slight smile played on the corner of her lips as she put her phone away, her anger forgotten.

"Who was that?" Blake asked.

"The FBI agent who told me about the doctor who disappeared before his wedding. He's back. And he might be the connection to last week's warehouse shooting."

"You never told me the agent's name," Blake said. "Who is it? I'll look him up."

"Not him. Her. Victoria Heslin."

Blake scrunched up her nose. "Victoria Heslin? For real? That's who the FBI agent is?"

Suarez wasn't sure what had caused Blake's sudden enthusiasm.

"You met her? The FBI Agent from D.C.?" Missy Blake was literally bouncing in the passenger seat.

Suarez frowned, wondering what the big deal was. "Yes."

204

"The agent from the plane? Skyline Flight 745. You didn't remember who she was?"

"Uh...no." Then it came back to her. For an entire week back in December, the disappearance of a Skyline jet had captivated the world. Non-stop media coverage. And when only four of the 178 passengers and crew members survived, Agent Victoria Heslin was one of them. Interesting that Suarez had met a minor celebrity without even knowing it. And that explained the Agent's missing fingers.

Blake beamed like a child. "I would *love* to meet her."

"She went back to D.C."

Blake's eager smile remained. "What did she look like? Because she looks gorgeous in her photos."

"Yeah. She looks a little like you, but with blonde hair," Suarez said, thinking Blake would like that. "Not so curvy."

"Curvy? As in fat?" Blake said, looking genuinely offended.

Suarez shook her head. Trying to be nicer was exhausting. "Forget I said that. I'm going to interview the doctor. See what he has to say about all this and if his story syncs with Luna's."

***

"You sure I can't get you a coffee?" Suarez asked.

Sitting stiffly in a chair across from her, Scott Redmond shook his head.

"An ice-water?" she asked, because beads of sweat dotted his forehead, though Suarez was comfortable wearing a sweater in the interview room.

"No, thank you. I'm good."

Scott was a lean and muscular man, handsome by any account, but the haunted look in his eyes and the ugly purple and yellow bruises discoloring his skin reminded Suarez of her cousin

Andre. She'd recently taken her grandmother to visit him in prison. Andre fit no one's definition of attractive, and his life was a colossal mess of his own making. But he wasn't stupid. He knew better than to tell who beat him up in the shower or knifed him in the exercise yard. It came down to self-preservation—knowing what might wait for you if you snitched was far worse than what had already happened. Scott seemed to operate under that same understanding. So far, he had stuck with his humiliating story about having a sudden and severe panic attack. Suarez took mental health issues seriously. She knew they caused major problems. But there was something unlikely about this man having a mental lapse that explained away the bizarre set of circumstances and behaviors that followed.

"One more time for me," Suarez said. "How do you know Richard Luna?"

Scott cleared his throat. "He was my patient."

"And you asked a former patient to drive you to the airport?"

"I saw him near the church before my wedding rehearsal, right after my incident began. I couldn't think straight and didn't trust myself to drive."

"Hmm…you didn't call him? You saw him?"

"I don't remember really, like I said…I was suffering the effects of a panic attack so severe it caused a dissociation incident." The entire time Scott spoke, his eye twitched uncontrollably. He wasn't accustomed to lying, and it showed.

"Explain that for me again."

"It's a severe disconnection from physical and emotional experiences. A detachment from reality. Subconsciously, it's a means of avoiding or coping with a highly stressful situation. As a result, I was unaware of where I was and what I was doing."

"That's what I thought you said. And yet...I understand you sent your fiancée a text. And you left a note for her in your car."

"I wasn't in my right mind. I wasn't myself."

"We have video of Luna driving your car to the airport, but we can't see you with him."

"I don't know what to say."

"So even though you asked Luna to drive you to the airport, you didn't get on a plane?"

"No. I walked around. Tried to clear my head. Like I said, I wasn't thinking. I left my car there and took a cab back."

"A cab?"

"Yes. I paid cash. Listen, if we're done here, I need to go. And I'm sorry for wasting your time. I'm willing to reimburse the police department if that will help."

"I don't think that will be necessary, and don't be so sure you've wasted our time."

She'd already spent countless hours watching Luna's condo, and thanks to an angry call from her boss, neither she nor Blake could continue, but she didn't consider that wasted time either.

Scott's story was preposterous. Suarez could poke a dozen holes in it without even trying. Suarez would be furious with Scott if she didn't know better. Instead, she felt sorry for him. He was no hardened criminal. Far from it. He was in over his head. Scott Redmond was afraid. Very afraid.

What would it take for him to disclose the truth? Would he willingly put his own life and his family's lives in danger by defying the cartel? Would it be bravery or stupidity to do so?

CHAPTER 27

Four days after Scott's return, and two days after the FBI began their audit of Redmond Galleries, Victoria stopped at Costco to stock up on meat for her dogs. On her way home, her brother, Alex, a paramedic on an avalanche patrol team, called from Colorado. Last time she saw Alex was right after Christmas. They were at her family's vacation house on Lake Lucinda. He'd been a suspect in a young woman's drowning. Tragedies had a way of bringing a family closer together or tearing them apart. Though Victoria wished none of it had happened, the stress of the ordeal had brought Victoria and her brother closer than they'd been since their mother died years ago. With Alex's wedding coming up, Victoria didn't want to lose that bond.

"Hey, glad I caught you," Alex said. "I have something to ask you. Thanks to a cancellation, we got an earlier date at our wedding venue. May 10th."

"That's so soon. Will you be able to get everything ready by then?"

"Yeah. We can do it. The ceremony and reception are at the ski lodge. It's a night wedding. Should be beautiful up here by then. Might be a little chilly, but that's okay. Everyone just needs to wear coats. Minka is in charge of the details. Most of them."

"Sounds nice. And perfect for you. I went to a wedding in Boston about a week ago."

"Oh, yeah? Any ideas I should do for mine? Was there anything you thought made it really special?"

She considered telling him about the ornaments but changed her mind. "Just show up on time and it will be great. That's the most important thing."

He laughed. "You talking about me showing up? Why'd you say that? You think I have trouble being on time?"

"No, no, it's not that. Never mind. I'm really looking forward to it. Did you tell Dad yet?"

"Yeah. I called him right before I called you."

They talked about her brother's wedding plans all the way to Victoria's front gate. "Hey, I'm almost home," she said. "What is it you had to ask me?"

***

Victoria found Ned seated in a leather recliner in the sitting room with his phone to his ear and a serious expression wrinkling his face.

As far as she knew, Scott still hadn't spoken to Ned or the other groomsmen. Maybe they were finally talking now.

"I know nothing about this," Ned said into his phone. "I'll call you back after I speak with Victoria."

Victoria had planned to cross the room and give Ned a hug. She had news she wanted to share with him, but now wasn't the time or the place. His tone of voice had changed her mind. "Hey," she said, giving him a tentative smile.

He didn't return it.

An uneasy feeling took hold inside her.

"I just spoke with Jules," he said.

Her unease spiked. "That was Jules? What did she call about?"

209

"She wanted me to know the FBI is auditing Redmond Galleries." Ned left it at that and waited for Victoria to respond. When she didn't, he said, "Is that just a coincidence, or did you have something to do with it."

"Companies get audited randomly all the time."

"I know you called Sam when we were in Boston. Did that lead to the audit?"

"You and Bailey asked me to help find Scott. That's what you both wanted."

"Um...I guess your lack of an answer is my answer. You hoping to catch them on tax evasion or something?"

She shook her head. "I can't talk about it, Ned. You know I can't." She placed her hands on her hips as he studied her.

"Jules was acting pretty freaked out about the whole thing. She said the audit puts her family in real danger. I asked why. She didn't tell me, but she said you might know."

"Ned...I can't...I don't know what to say."

"Neither do I." He stared at her a few more seconds before he left the room.

Victoria watched him go. If there was ever a reason to separate her personal life from her work, this was it. Keeping information from Ned wasn't something she wanted to do, but she had no choice. Her job was to enforce the law and protect people. Whether that work was understood or appreciated wasn't her concern. But Ned's reaction still hurt.

CHAPTER 28

Scott parked his Jeep in front of the courthouse and turned to look at Bailey in the passenger seat. In a white sweater under a gray wool coat, she looked lovelier than any woman he'd ever seen before. He didn't deserve her. Not after what happened. And he should have never brought her into his family's misdeeds by telling her the truth. Maybe that was selfishness on his part. He didn't know. He loved her too much to lie to her; too much to think clearly about the matter. As the car grew colder, he took her hands. "I can't do this to you. No matter how much I might want this, I love you too much to do this to you."

"Scott, stop, please," Bailey said. "We're doing this, so lighten up and act like it's the best day of your life." She laughed. "I'm one hundred percent sure. I know exactly what I'm doing. I'm not leaving you to handle this alone. And besides, we have to act like everything is normal, right? What could be more normal than us going ahead with our marriage? Come on. My family is already in there." With that, she got out of the car and waited for him, and they walked to the courthouse under a blue, cloudless sky.

Inside, Mr. Ballard and Bridget waited.

"Hi, guys." Bridget's sparkling blue eyes matched the periwinkle color of her bridesmaid dress. "Glad you *both* made it.

At least I've got my dress this time around, right?" She handed Bailey a flower bouquet that had seen better days. Browning, wilted petals floated to the floor. "I kept them in Dad's extra fridge, which didn't seem to help much, but there you go." She picked up an equally decrepit bouquet from behind her. "Gotta have flowers. That's what they say."

Mr. Ballard stood off to the side, frowning. Scott didn't mind. What mattered was that Bailey's father was there. "You'd be in St. Lucia this morning if you hadn't panicked," he said.

Scott gave a contrite nod as he fidgeted with the buttons on his sport coat. He deserved whatever Mr. Ballard threw his way and so much more. Bailey's family couldn't know the truth about what happened. The less they knew, the safer they were. But it felt like he was being punched in the face all over again. It ate him up inside to have a man he loved and respected think the worst of him. Scott swallowed hard and nodded to Mr. Ballard, hoping the charade of lies would hurt less over time. "Thank you for being here, Bill."

"You can call me Dad, now, if you like, once you've sealed the deal here. Or stick with Bill if you prefer. Either is okay with me." Mr. Ballard smiled and placed his hand on Scott's shoulder.

His father-in-law's capacity for forgiveness amazed Scott and meant the world to him right then.

With only a circuit court clerk, and Mr. Ballard and Bridget as witnesses, Scott and Bailey exchanged their vows.

"I now pronounce you man and wife," the clerk said.

They kissed, and Scott felt like the luckiest and most conflicted man in the universe.

"Congratulations, you two." Bridget pulled them in for a hug, accidentally pressing dead flowers from her bouquet into Scott's mouth.

As they were leaving the courthouse arm in arm, Scott's mother called his phone. He ignored her. He wasn't ready to speak to her yet. He still had too much information to process. He planned to tell his father about the marriage soon. His father didn't seem to be aware of what and who the rest of the family was involved with. How was that even possible? Posing the question made Scott grimace, considering he'd been just as much in the dark until his mother told him. He'd been so proud of what she and Jules and Duncan had created. How many times had he bragged about their knack for turning unknown artists into celebrated phenomena? If only he could return to that level of ignorance. And that's what he was trying to do. Forget everything he'd been through and everything he'd recently learned. So far, it wasn't working.

When his mother called again, Scott turned off the ringer.

"Do they know we just got married?" Bailey asked.

"No. Not yet."

"Then she's not calling to congratulate us. Maybe you should answer it."

"No." He wanted a few moments of peace and happiness, though that was dwindling fast just thinking about the situation his family had created.

The phone calls from his mother stopped. Instead, she sent a text.

After reading it, Scott couldn't help but feel worried. Despite their stupid, selfish, criminal decisions, he loved his family.

"What is it?" Bailey asked. "Did something else happen?"

He showed her his phone.

Jules is in the hospital. It's very bad. She wants to see you.

***

The pitiful sight of Jules in the hospital bed shocked Bailey. Ugly purple bruises covered her sister-in-law's face, looking far worse than the beatings Scott received. One eye had swollen-shut. Her top lip had ballooned into something like one of those images for plastic surgery gone terribly wrong. Her left arm rested in a sling.

"Jules." Scott leaned close to his sister but didn't touch her. "You fell, huh?"

"Yes," Jules normally raspy voice came out a mere croak.

"I saw your chart and your x-rays," he said. "You didn't fall. They almost killed you. I know you can't press charges or anything like that, but do you at least know why they beat you?"

Jules glared at Scott with the one eye she could control, then looked away.

Ever since Scott told Bailey what happened, she'd been angry at Jules. Angry because of what Jules dragged Scott into, and because she must have known the cartel was responsible for Scott's disappearance. She knew Scott could be in grave danger. And yet Jules had said nothing. Instead, she had led others to believe Scott had misgivings about getting married. But seeing Jules like this, knowing how painful her injuries had to be, and imagining the violence that caused them, Bailey couldn't help feeling compassion for her sister-in-law. She gently touched Jules' thin arm. "What can we do to help you?"

Jules' gaze fell to the wedding band on Bailey's finger before she answered in a strange, garbled voice. "Get my dentist over here. I'm not leaving the hospital like this." Only then did Bailey notice the gaping black space in Jules' upper teeth. If she and Scott used the same dentist, he or she would start to wonder why members of the Redmond family kept losing their pearly whites.

"I have to talk to my brother alone," Jules said. She didn't know Scott had told Bailey everything.

"Sure. I'll wait in the hall. I hope you feel better soon." Before leaving the room, Bailey offered Jules a sad smile and wondered how much more violence would befall this family. It was Bailey's family now, too.

***

Scott hadn't seen Jules since the day of his rehearsal dinner when he dropped his family off at the church and went to find a parking spot. Now that he was alone with her, he had questions.

"When you were at the rehearsal, did you know what happened to me?" he asked.

"No. I didn't know."

Her words did little to reassure him. How could he trust anyone in his family anymore? "The note you got in the church the next day, what did it say?"

Jules shifted her weight, which moved the IV lines attached to her arm. "It was a message for mom and Duncan and me."

"What did it say?" he asked again.

"I don't remember exactly."

"Jules, really? What's the point in not telling me the whole truth now that you've dragged Bailey and me into this?"

She sighed. "It said something about them needing a doctor, and don't forget who we work for. Yes, I knew who it was from. I knew they were sending a message that they're in charge. I worried about you. Everyone did. But I didn't think they would actually hurt you. They'd done nothing to hurt us physically…until now."

"The violence is only new for us. Not them. It's what they do. But do you know why they did this to you?"

"Yes. It's because of an audit on our businesses. The thug who did this, with zero emotion I might add, said he had to give me a taste of what will happen if any of us talk. I promised them we wouldn't. And I told them the audit is just a routine one. That's what the FBI told us. But I need to know if that's true…or if the FBI suddenly descended because they know something."

"Is there a reason they might know something?"

"Did you tell anyone?"

"No," Scott lied, hoping to shield Bailey from his family's ugly business as much as possible, at least until he understood more of what it would mean for him and his wife.

"Then it has to be Ned's girlfriend. Victoria. She might have gone digging into our business dealings while trying to find you."

"The way you say it, it sounds like you're blaming me for going missing and screwing up your crime empire. I would have gotten married last week as planned, if it weren't for what you got yourself involved with."

"I see you've gotten married since then," she said, now looking at the gold band on his ring finger, below his scabbed knuckles. "Congratulations."

"We were just leaving the courthouse and Bailey's family when mom texted me you were in the hospital." Scott did nothing to disguise the bitterness he felt.

"We never wanted to involve you in any of this, Scott. Not you or Dad. We kept it hidden from you so you wouldn't have to worry. But now we need your help. Can you talk to Ned and Victoria and figure out if Victoria found something? I'd like to know if I'm going to jail. And if you're too angry with me to care, don't forget our mother would go to jail, too. She won't survive in prison, Scott."

"I haven't talked to Ned or any of my friends since you got me involved in this. I'm too ashamed. And jail might be preferable to more beatings whenever the cartel wants to send a message or ask a question." He wasn't sure if his mother or Duncan would make it in prison, although they were tougher than he'd realized.

But a beating like Jules received would probably kill them. She'd barely survived it herself.

"Please...for me. Find out what you can. I have to give the cartel an answer."

"Jules...I don't know how I'm supposed to find this out. I don't even know Victoria Heslin. I didn't get a chance to meet her." He refrained from adding thanks to you. "And what if it isn't a random audit? Then what?"

"I don't know. But I'm a lot more afraid of Salazar's men than I am the Feds."

Suddenly, Jules just seemed scared, which was uncharacteristic for her. She always acted tough and brave. But now that he thought about it, a tough exterior didn't mean she wasn't terrified. But surely there would have been a way out before she was in so deep. Anyone else would have gone to the authorities ages ago. Anger and frustration were getting the best of him. He couldn't talk to her anymore. "I've got to go. I know your attending doctor. She's a friend of mine. I'll check on your progress with her and make sure you're in excellent hands. See you later, Jules."

"Scott—" she called after him, "—please talk to Ned."

Scott found Bailey waiting in the hallway.

"Why did they do that to her?" Bailey asked, her voice soft enough that no one could overhear.

Scott looked around before quietly answering. "Redmond Galleries is being audited. The cartel wants to know what or who triggered it."

"And that's how they ask?" Bailey pressed her lips together and shook her head. "What if they think you're responsible?" She froze for a second. "Are you?"

"No. I know what's at stake. I haven't breathed a word about what really happened, except to you," he whispered.

"And I promise I haven't told anyone," Bailey said. "I wouldn't. Maybe it's just a coincidence."

"Jules thinks Victoria Heslin is involved," Scott whispered.

Bailey thought through the possibility. "I asked her to help. Maybe she found things when she was looking for you. I'm sorry. I was just so afraid. I had to know where you were. If it weren't for your family's insistence, I would have called the police immediately."

"Don't be sorry. I would have done the same for you, believe me. And as much as I'm afraid for her, for all of us, Jules can hardly blame what happens on anyone except herself."

"And Duncan and your mother," Bailey added, twisting her ring around her finger. "If Victoria has something to do with the audit…that means she might know what's going on. Maybe that's a good thing?"

"How is that a good thing?" Scott asked, looking around. "We shouldn't be talking in here. Come on." He headed down the hallway with Bailey.

Near the end of the corridor, Scott spotted his colleague and friend, Lilly, the attending physician caring for Jules. He'd worked with her since his residency, and he'd invited her to his wedding. She must have known Jules was his sister. "Hey," he said, addressing Lilly as he had several times a week for the past year or more.

The doctor gave him a curt nod as she moved out of his way. Her behavior confused him for a second, the time it took him to realize this was how it would be, with everyone who knew him believing he had walked out on his own wedding. And the irony is that if they knew the truth about his family's illegal endeavors, of which he was now complicit to some extent, they would have even greater reason to shun him.

When they got outside, Scott was still reeling from seeing Jules and being ostracized by his colleague. He inhaled the fresh, cold air and tried to clear his head.

About ten yards from the hospital entrance, a nicely dressed man in a wool coat sat on a bench, one leg crossed over the other, holding a to-go coffee cup in one hand. He gave off a relaxed, comfortable vibe, as if everything was all right in his world. Scott wondered if he would ever feel that way again.

The man waved.

Scott didn't think he knew the man, but he was glad not everyone was ignoring him. His hand rose instinctively to return the gesture. He froze as recognition hit him. The man on the bench was the driver of the Tahoe who had pretended his wife needed help. Turning away quickly, Scott guided Bailey in a different direction.

"Who was that? Do you know him?" Bailey asked, looking over her shoulder. "Wait. Oh, no. That's Richard Luna, isn't it?"

Scott knew it might be like this. He shouldn't have been so shocked, but he could barely utter his next whispered words. "Yes. And he's watching us."

***

As Bailey and Scott took a brisk walk to a nearby park, Bailey wrestled with her thoughts, something she'd been doing often since Scott's return. They found an empty bench and sat down. Nearby, children played on the playground while their parents watched from other benches. Two police officers stood talking and drinking coffee under a large, leafless tree.

"They really hurt Jules." Scott leaned forward and dropped his head into his hands.

"I know. I can't stop thinking about it and what it would take to cause those injuries." Imagining it sent a shudder rocking through Bailey's body. What if it was Bridget in the hospital? Was her own sister also in danger because of the Redmonds?

219

The newlyweds sat in silence for several minutes as cold seeped from the iron bench through their clothes.

"I'm afraid, Scott," Bailey said, finally voicing her thoughts aloud. "I don't think we can live like this, always looking over our shoulders. Wondering who they'll snatch next. Right now, it's just the two of us, but God willing, we'll have children soon. Can we protect them from this, or will the cartel go after them anytime they want to teach your family a lesson? And maybe they let Jules off easy this time, if you can call it that, because they need her. They don't need us. They wouldn't care if we lived or died, as long as hurting us sent a message."

Scott stared toward two kids chasing each other around a slide. "I know. Believe me, I know. I'm already so sorry you got dragged into this."

"You did not drag me into anything. Your problems are my problems. For better or for worse. I don't want a life without you. And we're married now." She held up her ring finger and smiled. "You can't get rid of me." Her smile faded as she continued. "But I think we have to do what's right, before we're in over our heads and we're just as complicit as Jules and your mother. Before we're criminals, too. I don't want that for us. We save lives, Scott. That's what we do. Helping the cartel…that just feels wrong. Very wrong."

What Bailey really wanted was to return to the day before her wedding and rewrite history. But that wasn't far back enough. Scott's family had been working with the cartel for years.

Things were already worse than she imagined they would be. She wasn't ready to admit it to herself or to Scott, but she'd decided what they must do. Something almost unimaginable. She wanted one more night to sleep on it, and then she'd try to convince Scott they needed to call the only person she knew and trusted who might be able to advise them.

CHAPTER 29

Victoria set her first coffee of the day on the desk and hung her coat on the back of the chair.

"Hey, do you have a minute?" Payton asked.

"Yes, come on into my office," Victoria joked, because her office in the FBI's building consisted of a desk surrounded by a chest-height partition to separate it from the others. She and other agents could reserve a conference room when they required privacy for a confidential phone call or a meeting. No special treatment for any of them except the big bosses.

"I thought you'd like an update on what financial crimes found on Redmond Galleries. Since you brought the case to us."

"Yes, thanks, I would. What's going on?"

"Everyone's excited and wants a part in bringing down the Salazar cartel. We've been looking for leverage like this for a while. We already found enough to arrest the people running Redmond Galleries."

Victoria knew this was coming, but it still made her uncomfortable. "What are their options if you arrest them?"

"Not if. *When*. If they cooperate with us, they'll plead guilty and testify against Salazar—if that's who they're working for—and receive protection. Or they can lawyer up and hope for the best."

Victoria twisted her hands together. "It's not in the cartel's interest to wait and see what the family decides. The Redmonds are in danger as soon as you arrest them. Or sooner than that."

"Victoria, I know you know this family, and maybe they're gracious people aside from their business dealings, but when you go into business with the cartel, rarely is there a happy ending. And yes, things are about to get worse for them. They're probably already feeling the pressure. The cartel might be watching the whole family carefully. If you already have a relationship with them, you can convince them their best option is working with us and getting into witness protection as soon as possible."

Victoria's phone rang. She checked the caller ID. The name on her screen surprised her. "It's Bailey. The woman Scott Redmond was going to marry."

Payton raised her brows. "Do you know why she's calling you?"

Victoria shook her head as she answered the call. "Bailey?"

"Hi, Victoria. Um, is this a good time?"

"Yes. What's going on?"

"Um, we…Scott and I got married. We had a small private ceremony at the courthouse."

"That's great. Congratulations." Victoria could tell that wasn't the main reason Bailey called.

"We'd like to get your, uh, advice on something." Bailey struggled to choose the right words. "Remember you said if we wanted to talk, you know about—"

Victoria cut her off. "About the adoption, right? I'd really like to talk about it, can't wait to hear everything, but I can't right now."

"What? It's not—"

"Are you home right now?"

222

"Yes. We're at my apartment. Why?"

"Text me your address. As soon as we get off the phone, I'm having your wedding gifts delivered. I should have given them to you when I was there, but better late than never, right? Hold tight until the package gets there, then call me back and tell me what you think. I should be able to talk then. Sorry. I have to go."

"Oh, uh. Okay."

Victoria ended the call before Bailey could say more.

Payton was still waiting. Again, she lifted her brows in question.

"It sounded like she and Scott might be ready to talk. I'm going to send a courier to her apartment with burner phones so we can communicate." Victoria thought about her schedule for the day. It was clear. "After I send the phones, I'm heading back to Boston to meet them in person."

"What do you think they're going to tell you?"

"I'll find out soon enough. Do you want to come with me?"

"I can't. Two court appearances tomorrow. Maybe Rivera can go."

Victoria was quick to shake her head. "No. I'll hear what they have to say and depending on what it is, I'll conference with you and Murphy on how to proceed."

"Sounds good. If they have evidence against the cartel and will talk, this might be the right time to arrest the gallery owners." Payton smiled as she tapped her pen on the top edge of Victoria's cubicle, then walked away, leaving Victoria with an odd, empty feeling inside.

***

Approximately seventy minutes later, Victoria received a call from an unregistered number.

"Um, it's Bailey. We got your wedding gifts and we're outside now. A few blocks from my apartment."

"Great," Victoria said.

"So…you know what we need to talk about, don't you?"

"I think so. Redmond Galleries. What really happened to Scott. And how we can keep you safe."

"Yes," Bailey said.

"It's best we talk in person. I can book the next flight and be in the Boston area tonight."

"Okay. Um…I guess give us your flight information and we can pick you up at the airport."

"You don't have to do that. I want to meet you somewhere you would normally go so that it looks like you're just meeting an old friend. Do you and Scott have a favorite dinner place?"

"Let me see. Not dinner, but on Thursday nights, when we're not working, we do a power yoga class together. The class is at 5:30."

"Perfect. Send me the name and address of the studio. I'll catch the first flight to Boston and meet you there."

"So…we really need to be careful about what we say and where we go now?" Bailey asked.

"I'd strongly advise it."

Victoria checked the flight schedules and booked the next departing flight from Dulles to Boston. She called Ned as she packed up her laptop. "Something came up at work and I need to go out of town. I might be back very late tonight, but I'm bringing an overnight bag just in case. Can you stay at my house?"

"Yes. I can."

He didn't ask where she was going, which spared her from not telling him.

CHAPTER 30

Victoria stepped inside the YogaFit studio and looked around the lobby.

"Are you here early for the power class?" the woman behind the desk asked her.

"Not tonight," Victoria said. "I'm just meeting friends." She took off her winter coat, her scarf, and the cute knit hat a friend made for her, and chose a seat next to a giant potted plant. From that vantage point, she could see both the front door and the entrance to the practice room, where more than a dozen bodies held a peaceful warrior pose.

Eucalyptus scented the air. New-age instrumental music played softly in the background and helped soothe her nerves. She'd flown back to Boston alone because there was no better way to get over a fear than to face it again and again. She felt pretty good when she got off the plane with her wits about her.

When the class ended, Bailey walked out of the studio first. Her appearance had changed since she entered the church for the rehearsal almost two weeks ago. Still beautiful, but a paler complexion had replaced her luminous glow, and a cold sore had sprouted on her upper lip. Victoria's college roommate used to get those whenever she got stressed. Bailey had also lost weight. Her yoga pants clung to her body and only now could Victoria see that Bailey wore a prosthetic device.

Bailey smiled in greeting, but her face tightened as her eyes moved to the glass front door.

"It's great to see you again." Victoria hugged her and whispered. "Just act natural."

Scott came out shortly after. He shifted a black yoga mat underneath his arm and extended his hand. "Hi. You must be Victoria. Thanks for coming."

"Nice to meet you finally," Victoria said.

"Same," he answered.

Victoria took in the faded bruises on his face. Whatever Scott had recently endured, whatever occurred to keep him from his own wedding, wasn't completely voluntary. Suarez had told Victoria as much after the detective interviewed him, but now Victoria saw it for herself. She was eager to get to the truth and hoped that's why they wanted to speak with her. "I heard the good news," she said. "Congratulations on being married."

"Thanks." Scott stared toward the exit as he pulled on a quilted jacket. "Should we go somewhere private to talk?"

"Yes," Victoria said, replacing her hat, rewrapping her scarf, and sliding her arms into her coat sleeves. "Actually, somewhere public where we'll have some privacy would be best."

They headed out to the street and walked the well-lit sidewalks to a public park. They made small talk along the way, and Victoria forced herself to be patient. Bailey and Scott needed to be comfortable to disclose the truth.

They came to a bench positioned far from any others, and sat down. The newlyweds leaned into each other, shoulders touching and holding hands. "Thank you again for coming all the way back here," Bailey said. "We weren't sure where to turn. We need advice."

"I'll do whatever I can to help you," Victoria said, zipping her coat up to her chin to protect herself from the chilly air.

Bailey looked at Scott and said, "You start."

"Okay." Scott ran his hand over his chin. "We're telling you this because we're in serious trouble. We aren't sure what to do."

Victoria waited while Scott seemed to gather his thoughts.

"I didn't panic about getting married," he said. "That wasn't true. When you hear what really happened, I hope you can understand why I had to lie." Scott made a fist with one hand and pressed it into his palm. "Eduardo Salazar's cartel kidnapped me right before the rehearsal. They held me captive in a house somewhere for five days while I treated two of their men for gunshot wounds." He looked at Bailey, who nodded. "It wasn't random. The cartel knew I was a doctor and knew exactly where I would be. They let me go because they trusted me to keep quiet. And they trusted me to keep quiet because my family does business with them. Actually, my father has nothing to do with this. He's not involved. And neither was I. But others in my family—my mother, my sister, and my uncle—are laundering money for the cartel through Redmond Galleries. My mother told me they've been doing it for years. Selling art to the cartel, depositing the cash, taking a cut, and giving the rest back to them."

Scott paused there. Maybe he expected Victoria to be shocked, that he would need to work harder to convince her it wasn't some wild, fabricated story. But none of what he said surprised her. In fact, his story made sense, and Scott showed no signs of deceit in telling it. "Did you actually see Eduardo Salazar or speak with him when he held you captive?" she asked.

"Yes. I think so. Though no one said his name."

"But you could pick him out of a line up?" Victoria asked.

"Yes. Definitely," Scott said.

"You don't seem at all surprised by what he just told you," Bailey said.

227

"I knew about Redmond Galleries and the money laundering," Victoria answered. "Not the details, but enough. I was looking into your disappearance and what I found triggered the audit. It wasn't intentional, but..." She wondered if Scott and Bailey now understood the entire lavish wedding had provided an opportunity to launder massive amounts of cash for the cartel. "I didn't know what happened to you, although I intercepted an antibiotic prescription you called in."

In some way, she was relieved the cartel kidnapped Scott. That explanation excused him from standing Bailey up at the altar. She was also grateful she'd kept most of her opinions of him to herself, otherwise she'd feel more terrible about them than she already did.

"And for the record, your wife and your best man never doubted for a second that something happened to you," Victoria said. "They had your back all along."

"I know," Scott said. He and Bailey exchanged a look that told Victoria just how much they loved each other. Then Scott lowered his head. "I honestly don't know what I'm supposed to tell Ned."

"Don't tell anyone anything," Victoria said. "It will only put you and them in danger."

"A couple of days ago, someone from the cartel beat Jules up to within inches of her life," Bailey said. "And then when we went to visit her, Richard Luna was outside the hospital, watching us. Or stalking us."

"When?" Victoria asked, alarmed by the news and grateful for all the precautions they'd taken prior to their meeting.

"Yesterday," Bailey answered.

"Does your family know I'm here? That you're talking to me?" Victoria surveyed the area, wary and alert. A couple with two standard poodles approached from one side. A twenty-something with a flannel shirt and baggy pants—either immune to

228

the cold or pretending it didn't bother him—rolled by on a skateboard.

"No one knows," Scott answered. "We wanted to talk to you first."

"What did you hope would happen by telling me this?" Victoria asked, trying to assess how much they knew about their limited options.

"We didn't know where else to turn," Bailey said. "We needed advice. If Scott tells everything he knows, what will happen?"

"Scott's testimony is enough to put some of the cartel behind bars. It's the right thing to do, but it comes with a significant risk."

"Could the FBI guarantee our safety? And that of his family?"

"You're talking about witness protection?" Victoria needed to make sure.

"Yes. I mean…if that's what it takes to get away from this." Bailey looked at Scott as if making sure he was still in agreement.

"To be brutally honest with you, I think it's your family's only good option, and the sooner you take it, the better," Victoria said. "You'd receive witness protection in exchange for testifying. Do you understand what it entails?"

"Yes," Bailey answered. "We have to give up almost everything…except each other."

Scott turned to face Bailey. "If we have children, your father will never see them."

Bailey pressed her lips together and took a few seconds before responding. "I know. I understand. I've done the research, as well as a lot of soul searching. As terrible as it is…"

"The research you did...was it on your phone?" Victoria asked as a wave of concern washed over her

"My phone and my laptop," Bailey answered.

Victoria tensed. Maybe it was fine, but Salazar's cartel had the best of the best of everything on their payroll. Including cyber hackers. Now that Scott had confirmed the cartel's involvement, she prayed the FBI's help wasn't too little or coming too late.

"I know you don't deserve what witness protection will do to your lives, but it's the only way," she said. "Otherwise, you'll live with this forever—the fear, the not-knowing, the danger."

"Unless the cartel gets taken down," Scott said. "That could happen."

"They only get taken down if people like you and your family have the courage to testify against them. That's the only way it happens. You can't wait in hope of someone else doing what you won't. I'll do what I can to convince your family this is the only way out, as self-sacrificing as it may be."

"Not sure how much of a self-sacrifice it is for them. My family is guilty," Scott said.

"Most people in witness protection are guilty of something. The government created the program decades ago to give mafia members a way to get out, to get a new life by agreeing to testify against more powerful, more dangerous members. Others in witness protection are like you, people who didn't know what their families were doing...right until the moment they found out."

"Once we do it...I mean...is it forever?" Bailey asked.

"No. The program is completely voluntary. You can leave any time. That's not advised. Few leave, but anyone can. Once you leave, you're at risk again."

Bailey touched a gloved finger to Scott's bruised cheek. "We have to convince your parents. Their lives depend on it. Now that they've seen what can happen—to you and Jules—surely they'll do whatever it takes to protect you and your sister."

"It won't be easy, or a life of luxury, but it beats the alternative." Victoria didn't feel the need to define the alternative aloud. She hoped they realized it was death. And at the hands of the cartel, it might not be quick or painless. "If your family agrees, I'll call the U.S. Marshals Service and get things started."

"And if my family doesn't agree?" Scott asked, turning to Bailey.

"I hope we won't have to answer that question," Bailey said. "We're going to convince them. Let's talk to them now. With Victoria."

Scott looked even more uncomfortable. "All right. Duncan is in Colorado. Jules just got out of the hospital and she's staying with my parents for a few days."

"Call your family," Victoria said. "Tell them you ran into a friend and you're bringing her for a late dinner. Or cocktails. Whatever your family would normally do with a guest. I'll do everything in my power to convince them this is what they need to do."

She hoped Mrs. Redmond could already see her family's lives were slowly but surely crashing down around them.

CHAPTER 31

The drive from the city to the Redmond's suburban address took over forty-five minutes. Bailey and Scott had more questions along the way. Victoria wanted to give them as much information as possible, so they knew exactly what they were getting into once they chose that route. They faced an enormous decision with life-altering consequences.

"You'll stay in a maximum-security site in D.C. while they set up your new life," Victoria said. "New birth certificates, social security cards, driver's licenses, credit reports. They'll try to place you in another city where you'll fit in. Somewhere you don't have any connections. They ask you a thousand questions and together you'll create a new background story. Education, employment history…all of it. They'll help you with the transition."

"I can't believe this might actually happen," Scott said.

"If we do this, I know we can't tell anyone where we're going, but I can't just leave Dad and Bridget to wonder," Bailey said. "They already know something, obviously. They know you love me, yet you missed our wedding…and then the bruises, and your family wasn't invited to the courthouse. My father is a smart man. He may not know what's going on exactly, but he knows something serious is underway and it's bigger than both of us. They'll understand what happened eventually, if there's a trial and Redmond Galleries and Scott's abduction are at the center of it."

Bailey sighed. "It's going to be a whole new world," her tone conveyed sarcasm, but then changed. "As long as we're together it's going to be a good one."

Impressive words coming from someone on the verge of giving up her family, friends, and career. Victoria admired Bailey's attitude. Most people would freak out about everything they had to leave behind. Jules' beating coming so soon after Scott's abduction seemed to have pushed Scott and Bailey in the right direction.

"The men you were treating for gunshot wounds—do you know who they are?" Victoria asked Scott.

"Only their first names. One of them didn't make it. Oh, and another thing, the cartel knows the police are watching Luna. I heard them say something about it."

That wasn't good either.

"Someone delivered a note to the church—I'm assuming that was also from the cartel," Victoria said. "Do you know what it said?"

"Yes. It was a message for my family. Something about the cartel needing an ER doctor more than my family needed a groom. Reminding them who was in charge."

Victoria was furious with Jules for lying when her brother's life was in danger…and yet, if she'd read the real message aloud, no one would have believed her. "It seems like the cartel was testing your family even before the audit," Victoria said. "Do you know if something triggered that?"

"My mother told me Duncan wants to close the gallery in Aspen. He has health issues. And now that my family's businesses have established reputations, they're selling lots of art to legit clients. The cartel wants a cut of every sale, no matter what. The wedding presented a great opportunity to remind my family of who is in charge. I'm not sure if Salazar planned to abduct me all along, or if their plans changed when two of their men got shot. The way it worked out, they got the medical care they needed and simultaneously ruined the wedding. I'd say my family got the cartel's message loud and clear." Scott huffed. "Damn it. Damn them all. I can hardly believe what they've done. What they've been doing."

Victoria wasn't sure if Scott referred to the cartel, his family, or both. "Once your family crossed that first line, they had little choice in their future decisions," she said. She wasn't convinced of this, but it would help Scott and Bailey with what needed to happen next. "Now is not the time for you to punish them for what they can't change. They'll have enough of that coming from external sources. You'll have to support each other. Going forward, you'll definitely need it."

"I agree," Bailey said. "We need to convince them with our love and concern, not with anger."

A mile from the Redmond's home, the road grew more private, darker, and winding. The homes had acreage between them and were set far back from the road. As they drove uphill, condensation formed on the car's windows, making it difficult to see out. Victoria scanned the console for a defrost button.

"They live at the end of this road," Scott said. "My mother is on her way back from the gallery. Jules and my father are there. They're all expecting us. They just don't know it's you we're bringing."

As the layer of fog thickened over the windshield, Victoria found the button she needed. With a whoosh of hot air from the vents, the condensation dissipated.

"We're doing the right thing for us and your family," Bailey said, reassuring Scott and it sounded like herself as well.

Two loud cracks rang out through the night, coming from somewhere ahead and not far away. Victoria tensed and leapt to a new level of alertness.

"What was that?" Bailey asked.

"Maybe only a car backfiring," Scott said with little conviction, as if he knew it wasn't that. The sounds were unmistakable gunshots.

Victoria sped up, then slowed for a tight bend. As the road straightened again, a Cadillac Escalade approached and shot past, traveling in the opposite direction.

Victoria watched the vehicle disappearing in her rearview mirror, its taillights becoming tiny sparks in the distance.

"That's your mom's car!" Bailey shouted.

A black Audi sat on the shoulder of the road. The tires on the left side were completely flat. Victoria had only heard two gunshots, so two flat tires boded well for anyone inside the car.

She flicked her high beams on and swept the area around the Audi and into the woods beyond as she pulled up to the driver's side of Mrs. Redmond's car.

Mrs. Redmond stared out the driver's side window. She'd raised her arm to shield her eyes from the light. Her wide-eyed expression conveyed her terror, but at least she was alive.

"Wait here. Do not get out of the car," Victoria ordered Scott and Bailey.

Holding her weapon, Victoria walked to the Audi. She signaled for Mrs. Redmond to roll down her window. "Are you hurt?"

"Victoria?" Mrs. Redmond's fear changed to indignation. "No, no. I'm not hurt. What are you doing here? Is Ned with you?"

Victoria kept her eyes peeled on the road and the woods lining it. She needed to be the one asking the questions. "What happened?"

"Um, I'm not sure."

"The Escalade that passed us—are they the ones that shot your tires?"

235

Mrs. Redmond looked away and reached for her glove compartment.

Victoria raised her weapon and her voice. "Drop your hands. Right now."

Mrs. Redmond looked shocked as she sat back in her seat. "I was only getting my wallet. This is where I keep it. I don't have a weapon of any kind, dear."

Victoria's voice shook as she said, "Get out of the car. I'll get your wallet."

Mrs. Redmond got out of the car and stepped away, saying, "I don't know what you think is happening here, but you really need to calm down. I think we've had some sort of misunderstanding."

"Stay right there and don't move." Victoria opened the passenger side door of the Audi, and then the glove compartment. Mrs. Redmond had been telling the truth. There was no weapon, only a small leather wallet that must have held her identification and credit cards. But Victoria wasn't falling for this innocent, its-all-a-misunderstanding-act. She grabbed the wallet and handed it to Mrs. Redmond. "Get in my car and I'll take you home." Victoria lowered her voice to a stern command so Mrs. Redmond wouldn't hesitate.

Scott got out of the rental. "Victoria is going to help us," he said. "The sooner the better."

Mrs. Redmond nearly hissed her response. "What are you talking about, Scott?"

"Please get in my car and we'll talk there," Victoria said. The gunshots and the Escalade had changed the situation. She wanted to get everyone off the dark road and somewhere safe as soon as possible.

"Mom, Victoria knows everything I know," Scott said. "So does Bailey."

Mrs. Redmond glowered at her son. "Now I understand why all of this is happening. Why couldn't you do what I told you to do? Oh, Scott. You have no idea what you've done."

"Whatever happened isn't because of anything I did," he said. "But that's going to change. I'm going to do whatever it takes to get us out of this nightmare now."

Mrs. Redmond finally got in the rental, slammed the door, and pressed her hands against her temples. "Take me home."

As Victoria started the car, the wails of a firetruck came from behind them, growing louder.

"I told you I was fine. I don't need a paramedic," Mrs. Redmond said.

Victoria glanced into her mirror at the fast-approaching emergency vehicle. "I didn't call them."

"Neither did we," Scott said.

Victoria pulled to the side of the road and the firetruck sped past.

"Oh, no," Mrs. Redmond said. "The men in the Escalade! Before they shot at my tires, they were coming from the direction of our house. Vince is there with Jules. Hurry!"

Victoria followed the racing firetruck to the last house on the private road, a mansion atop a hill. Golden flames shot up from one side of the roof and illuminated the black plumes of smoke rising into the night sky. As Victoria got closer, she expected to see Jules and Mr. Redmond outside, but there was no sign of them.

The fire crew scrambled from their truck, uncoiled hoses, and pulled them across the yard.

Scott jumped out of the car before Victoria came to a full stop. He ran toward the house, ignoring shouts for him to stop.

A firefighter in full gear jumped in front of Scott to keep him back. "Stay away from the house! Let us handle this!"

Scott dodged him and raced toward the side of the house, where he disappeared through a door.

Victoria, Bailey, and Mrs. Redmond left the car to stand on the lawn. Burning embers fizzled in the air and landed like fireworks. Heat warmed their skin. Smoke thickened the air.

"My husband and daughter are in there," Mrs. Redmond shouted to the firefighters. "My daughter is hurt. She was in the guest room. First floor on the right side of the house. But I don't know where my husband was. I have to go in there."

Taking Mrs. Redmond's arm and pulling her farther away, Victoria shouted over the blaring sirens coming from additional firetrucks. "Stay with me. The fire crew already have three lives to save. Don't make it any harder for them to rescue your family. Do you have any pets in there?"

"No," Mrs. Redmond said.

Bailey put an arm around her mother-in-law. "Someone inside the house must have called the fire department. That means Mr. Redmond and Jules are okay."

At least one of them was.

As another firetruck arrived, Victoria pulled off her coat, since she was already sweltering, and called Detective Suarez. "It's Victoria. I'm at the Redmond's house. Scott Redmond's parents." As she rattled off the address, an ambulance siren drowned her out.

"I can't hear you. Repeat that," Suarez said.

Shielding the mouthpiece with her hand, Victoria repeated the address. "Potential arson. All inhabitants not accounted for yet. Suspect or suspects are driving a newer model black Cadillac Escalade. Left the property ten minutes ago driving west. If one of your officers sees it, stop them. And make sure the officers know the Escalade's occupants are armed."

A firefighter burst through the side door. He carried a child in pajamas who had one arm in a cast. As he came closer, heading toward the ambulance, Victoria realized he was carrying Jules.

Two paramedics pushed a gurney toward the firefighter and helped him set Jules on top of it.

Victoria moved beside the gurney as the paramedics placed an oxygen mask over Jules' soot-covered face. "Did you see who was in the Escalade? Do you know who did this?" Victoria asked.

Above the mask, Jules' eyes radiated anger. Then, in a slow-motion show of drama, or maybe she really was that weak, Jules lifted her thin arm and pointed a trembling finger straight at Victoria. "You did."

The paramedics stopped their treatment and stared at Victoria. "Whoa," the female medic said, her gaze settling on Victoria's gun, clearly visible now that she'd removed her coat. "Step away from us. Step away!"

Time seemed to stand still, like the pivotal moment in a movie when the characters discover one of their own was actually the villain all along.

Victoria moved one hand to retrieve her badge.

"Don't move," the male medic shouted. "Keep your hands up!"

The firefighter lunged for Victoria. She noticed him coming and jumped out of his reach just in time. Stepping back further, she lifted her hands into the air and kept them there. "I'm a federal agent," she shouted. "I'm going to get my badge from my left pocket and show it to you." She couldn't blame them for being too careful. She'd just done the same with Mrs. Redmond.

"Why are you here already?" the female medic asked.

"I don't believe this fire was an accident. I'm helping the family," Victoria answered. She glared at Jules. "And that includes you."

239

The medics studied Victoria for a few more seconds, as if they didn't quite trust her, before focusing on their patient. As they lifted Jules into the back of the ambulance, she turned her head to the side, avoiding Victoria's gaze.

"Two more people are still inside the house," Victoria said. She moved away from the others to make phone calls requesting a police escort and protection at the hospital.

The mansion's side door burst open again. Scott and another firefighter emerged carrying a man between them. Scott held the man's legs, and the firefighter had his head and shoulders. They delivered him to another gurney waiting outside the ambulance.

"Dad? Dad, can you hear me?" Scott asked.

"Get out of the way," the male paramedic said, needing room to do his job.

Scott ignored him and continued to rouse his father, who wasn't responding. "He's unconscious," Scott said. "Maybe from the smoke, but there's also been blunt force trauma to the back of his head. He'll need a CT scan as soon as he gets to the hospital. Take him to General."

The paramedics put Mr. Redmond into the back of the ambulance with Jules.

Scott bent over with his hands on his knees and plunged into a coughing fit.

"A police escort will meet you at the end of the street," Victoria told the ambulance driver. "They'll go to the hospital with you and get you safely inside. We'll have guards outside the patients' rooms, also. They're in danger, and that means you are too. Understood?" Things had happened so quickly. She didn't want to overreact, but the potential consequences of not taking precautions terrified her.

The driver nodded.

The back doors shut, and the ambulance turned on its sirens and shot away from the house with Jules and Mr. Redmond inside. Bailey wrapped her arm around her mother-in-law. Scott kept coughing, his face blackened from the smoke, his eyes bloodshot.

Victoria watched the street, ready to fire if necessary. The sound of the gunshots from earlier reverberated through her mind. Whoever did this didn't want Mrs. Redmond to get home. Was it another "message" for the Redmond family? Or this time, were Jules and her father supposed to die?

CHAPTER 32

Driving away from the Redmond's smoldering house, an acrid, smoky odor overpowered the rental car, emanating from Scott. Victoria gripped the steering wheel hard, her hands at ten and two. A phantom tingling sensation coursed through her missing fingers and adrenaline still pumped through her veins. She checked the rearview mirror again to be certain no one followed them. Things had moved exponentially faster than she expected. She never would have come alone if she had any idea what lay ahead. How had she gone from discussing the possibility of witness protection with Scott and Bailey only hours earlier, to whisking them and Mrs. Redmond away to a safe house?

A disturbing thought flew into Victoria's mind. Might she be responsible for the current situation? She didn't have the luxury of thinking about it. Maybe later, she could give it some more serious consideration.

In the passenger seat, Mrs. Redmond sat with one hand pressed against the cold window, staring out as if she were alone in the car. Victoria didn't know where Mrs. Redmond stood on all this. Did she realize that as bad as things were, they could still get worse? Right now, her family members were still alive.

"You're not safe anymore," Victoria said, breaking the uncomfortable silence in the car. "You can't ever go back to business as usual. The FBI won't be the only people looking into your life. Things will get even more difficult for you because of the fire. Your insurance company will launch a criminal investigation into the cause. Even if you wanted to forgo the insurance money, there will still be an investigation. The firefighters found your husband unconscious after a strike to his head. The authorities will do their best to find out why someone wanted to burn your house down with your husband and daughter inside."

"They didn't know Jules was inside," Mrs. Redmond said, taking another step away from the pretense that everything had been a series of random, unfortunate events rather than the culmination of a criminal life catching up to her

"I called my boss before we left," Victoria said. "He's making arrangements for you as we speak. He's also assigned agents to meet the ambulance at the hospital. They'll guard Jules and Mr. Redmond."

Scott cleared his throat and coughed. "I should be there too, checking on them."

"No," Victoria answered. "Your presence will put others in danger."

"I can hire my own bodyguards," Mrs. Redmond said.

"They won't be a match for Salazar's men." Victoria checked her side mirror again and noticed a truck behind them. "I can't and won't make you do anything our way, but if you want the FBI's help, I need you to stay with me while we get things figured out." Another glance in the rearview mirror caught Bailey looking at her strangely, as if seeing Victoria for the first time. Understandable. Victoria wasn't acting like the reserved wedding guest she'd been. There was no time for pleasantries and politeness now.

"What's going to happen now?" Bailey asked.

"Once we get all of you somewhere safe, we wait for next steps," Victoria answered as the truck behind them took the next turn and disappeared into the night.

There was no right way to proceed. Only best practices and what had worked previously. There would be attorneys, agents, and marshals. Some were on their way to help, others were scrambling behind the scenes, their personal lives and sleep put on hold to handle the Redmond's situation as quickly as humanly possible. Local authorities, maybe even Suarez herself, were searching for the Escalade.

Victoria would not make the mistake of underestimating the cartel. She was afraid. And that was okay. It was smart to be afraid. The brutal and powerful Salazar cartel poured tons of money into their own self-preservation and protection. If they found out someone in their organization was preparing to spill secrets, they would do whatever it took to guarantee silence. Next time they might send an assassin rather than an arsonist. They had people everywhere, which probably included the FBI, though Victoria didn't need the Redmonds to know that. They had to trust the FBI completely for this to work.

In less than an hour, after taking several planned detours to ensure no one followed, they arrived at their destination. A safe house. Victoria parked in a concealed garage underneath the building. Exhausted and probably in a state of shock, the Redmonds climbed out of the vehicle and entered a basement.

Victoria had spent time in other safe houses. With the concrete, windowless walls, this one was as stark as she'd seen. Victoria wondered who would be the first to complain. But no one did. "We don't expect to be here more than one night," Victoria said.

"It's a lot better than I had it when I was with the cartel," Scott said.

Bailey hugged him. His mother said something Victoria couldn't hear, but it certainly looked like an apology.

Victoria had little time to think about what that apology might mean. After only a few seconds in the windowless room, something didn't feel right. The walls weren't closing in, but it seemed like they might. She couldn't believe what was happening. And with almost no warning. She'd make it through three plane rides only to have a PTSD episode occur in the basement of the safe house. She simply could not have an episode when others were counting on her. Not unless she wanted Murphy to stick her in a desk job forever.

"Are you okay?" Bailey asked, which meant Victoria wasn't doing a good enough job disguising her symptoms.

"I just need a second," Victoria stumbled before she managed to sit down on a cot next to a pile of blankets. She'd already broken out in a sweat as she closed her eyes and gripped the blanket underneath her. She forced away the irrational fear growing inside her, ignored her palpitating heart, and told herself to make it stop.

Pull it together. Deep breaths. Inhale. Exhale. Inhale. Exhale.

She heard footsteps descending the stairs and opened her eyes to see Bailey still watching her with concern. Behind Bailey, a man carried bags with toiletry supplies. A woman followed with two pizza boxes. They set everything down on a table that already held bottled waters and protein bars. "I'm Agent Rose, and this is Agent Louis," the woman said as she opened a pizza box. "Help yourselves if you're hungry. Sorry, no fruits or veggies tonight."

Victoria greeted the agents, doing her best to force a professional smile and not leave them with a terrible first impression. They probably knew who she was. Everyone at the FBI did. They also knew what she'd been through. All the more reason to prove they could count on her.

The aroma seeping out of the pizza boxes seemed to pull Victoria's mind out of spiraling, dark clouds. Her empty stomach tightened. Food might be just what she needed. Still trembling, she pushed herself up from the cot and crossed the room on wobbly legs. When she reached the table, she steadied herself on its edge and took deep breaths, struggling against the dizziness and nausea threatening to take over inside her. She focused on the simple task of getting her butt into a chair. Once she was sitting, a collection of magazines on a side table caught her attention. At first, she thought she might be hallucinating, but she wasn't. On the cover of an old People magazine, under the words *Forever Grateful* in a giant font, two familiar faces beamed up at her. Lizzie and Ashby. The teens were two of the four survivors from the plane crash. They stood close together, and between them, they held the cat who also made it out of Greenland alive. Seeing them gave Victoria renewed strength. They had survived against all odds, and now they needed to make the most of every moment.

Mind over matter.

She steeled her nerves, slid a slice of pizza onto a plate, and took her first taste of the warm, salty food. With each bite, she felt a little more like herself. Normal blood flow returned to her face and the shaky sensation faded inside her. The attack had passed. She prayed no others would follow.

While the Redmonds huddled together and talked, Victoria left the room and used a secure line to call her boss again for updates. She was finishing up the call when Scott came over and said, "My mother is on board. She sees there's no other way."

Relieved to hear that, Victoria set up a secure call between the Redmonds at the safe house and the Redmonds at the hospital. While they talked through their situation, she had a minute alone to entertain the guilt and questions that kept bugging her. What would life be like for the Redmond family that very moment if Ned hadn't brought Victoria to the wedding as his guest? Was Victoria partly responsible for what was now happening in their lives? Jules certainly seemed to think so and Victoria couldn't seem to ignore that. Then Payton's words came back to her. *When you go into business with the cartel, rarely is there a happy ending*. The Redmonds had already dug themselves into a deep and dangerous hole.

***

It was nearing eleven at night when Victoria and Mrs. Redmond entered an adjacent room to speak alone.

"Talk to me," Victoria said. "Tell me how this started."

Still elegant and stunning even after what she'd been through, Mrs. Redmond's red lips stood out against her pale skin. She held her shoulders back and her head high. Her dark eyes held the same intensity as her daughter's. Her sigh was the only outward sign something had changed.

"My brother and I opened the galleries years ago. I love the art world, and I thought of our endeavor as a hobby that might bring in some extra spending money. But Duncan had debts the regular gallery sales weren't close to covering. Gambling debts. He was growing desperate, and we'd already loaned him money several times. Then a charming man offered him a huge amount of cash for a painting…if Duncan agreed to some terms. He thought it would be a onetime deal. It wasn't. Still…it seemed a better alternative than declaring bankruptcy and selling his house. He wasn't dealing drugs or hurting people. He was simply facilitating the purchase of art at prices beyond their expected value. But the cartel wanted more opportunities to launder money. They forced Duncan to bring us—our Boston gallery—into their operation." Mrs. Redmond hung her head. "The cartel didn't ask us. They told us. We had no choice."

"You have a choice now," Victoria said. "It's not an easy one, but if you don't want anyone else in your family seriously hurt or killed, it's the right one."

This would be one of the last chances for Mrs. Redmond to protest or change her mind, but she didn't. "I know," she said. "We're ready."

"Good. The plan is to leave in the morning for a safer location in D.C. Your husband and daughter will meet us there. The FBI will bring Duncan soon after."

"What about...I need my things. I know I can't take everything. But a few suitcases, surely."

"Make a list. A short one. Agents will go tomorrow. It will look like they're with a fire clean-up service. Later, they'll get the rest—your valuables and anything else you really want to take with you. I know it feels like there are a million loose ends you're leaving behind, but you'll get to work them out over the next few days and weeks. In the meantime, do you have gallery employees who will open as usual for you, so it doesn't look like you're already gone?"

"Yes. Someone handles the day-to-day operations. So, this is it? We go right from here?"

"This is it. The sooner you're gone, the better it will be for your safety."

"I can't believe we'll simply disappear. It might be nice if at least one person knew what happened to us or where we're going," she said. "Will Ned know?"

Victoria shook her head. "No one can know. But speaking of Ned, I need to call him to let him know I won't be home tonight. Excuse me."

CHAPTER 33

They woke early, planning to leave the safe house at six a.m., anticipating an eight-hour drive to D.C. Victoria was eager to deliver the Redmonds safely to their destination and then sleep in her own bed at night.

Mrs. Redmond's cashmere pants had not held up well after sleeping in them. She'd removed her eye makeup overnight and her eyes weren't as dark and fierce. But what mattered was her attitude. With her shoulders squared and her head held high, she grabbed a bottle of water and a protein bar.

"I'll be riding with you to D.C.," Victoria said. "Mr. Redmond and Jules will travel separately and meet us there. And we've got Duncan flying with a U.S. Marshall. Put those on before we leave." She pointed to the bullet-proof vests everyone would wear over their clothes.

"Are those necessary?" Mrs. Redmond asked.

"We hope not. But we want you to wear them anyway." Victoria slipped her own vest over her head and tightened the side straps. "I know our driver. We're in excellent hands."

Victoria had met their driver, Pete Olsen, several times. His reputation as a dependable field agent preceded him. He'd turned down several promotions for managerial positions, preferring to stay involved with field work. He'd demonstrated calm in the worst of situations and prevailed in face-to-face confrontations with violent criminals, including the cartel. Most of Victoria's colleagues were dependable and well trained, but Pete had more experience than most to prove it. If the cartel were somehow able to track them down, Victoria felt good about having Pete with them.

A converted van waited for them in the garage beneath the safe house. The armored sides advertised Jose's Painting Service.

"What happens if someone calls that phone number?" Scott asked.

"Jose or his wife will answer and schedule a free estimate," Pete said. "I can vouch for them. They do quality work."

The Redmonds climbed into the back of the van, which contained two rows of bench seating, a small refrigerator, and a mini bathroom to facilitate the long ride to D.C. They would make no stops along the way. Victoria rode in the front seat next to Pete. Agent Louis and Agent Rose would drive behind them in an unmarked SUV all the way to D.C. The SUV did not have a bathroom, and for that reason, Victoria was grateful to be in the van.

"You're sure my husband and daughter have left the hospital already?" Mrs. Redmond asked as the van drove away from the safehouse.

"Yes. They're ahead of us," Pete answered. Traveling separately was a necessary strategy, which illustrated the risks involved. Should anything happen along the way, the prosecutors wouldn't lose all witnesses at once.

An hour into their drive, Mrs. Redmond asked Victoria to check on the rest of her family.

Victoria called the agents driving the other van. "It's Agent Heslin. Just checking your location."

"Hey, Agent Heslin. We just passed mile marker 163. Everything okay in your vehicle?"

"Yes. We're about eleven miles behind you. See you when we get there."

Two more hours passed. Victoria turned to see the Redmonds dozing in the back of the van. Bailey's head rested on her husband's shoulder. When Victoria faced forward again, she saw brake lights glowing on every car ahead of them. Pete slowed the van. The speed of traffic changed to a crawl. A steady stream of cars began drifting into the right lane for the upcoming exit.

"There's no construction scheduled on the route," Victoria told Pete, speaking so as not to wake the others. "Must be an accident. We're better off taking a detour than being stalled bumper to bumper."

Pete agreed, using the van's blinker to switch lanes like all the other cars avoiding the traffic jam. Victoria contacted Agents Rose and Louis behind them to say they were taking the exit. Once they were off the highway, GPS redirected their route.

"I thought we weren't stopping," Mrs. Redmond said from the back, rubbing her eyes. "Why are we getting off already?"

"We're not stopping," Pete said, his voice reassuring. "There was an accident. We'll get back on the highway on the other side of it."

The exit led them to a two-lane country road running parallel to the highway. They passed manufactured homes with sagging fences, junked cars, and rusting machinery on the front lawns. After less than a half mile along the detour which ran parallel to the highway, they could see the traffic jam they'd avoided off to their left. A jack-knifed semi-trailer truck blocked all southbound highway lanes.

Victoria studied their surroundings, including the stream of cars driving behind them. Agents Louis and Rose stayed on their tail, preventing any other car from slipping between them. Though they traveled at a good clip, any departure from their planned route gave reason to be concerned. Getting back on the highway would

251

bring Victoria some relief from the uneasiness inside her. According to her GPS, only three more miles to the next on ramp.

They had just passed a gas station with cracking asphalt and abandoned pumps that hadn't done business in years when a shiny, black Dodge Ram pulled out of the lot and edged in behind the other agents.

Agent Louis called Victoria's phone.

"Victoria, there's a truck behind us that might be looking for trouble," he said. "The passenger window just opened. Keep moving. We're going to hang back and put some distance between your vehicle and ours."

Still on the line with Louis, Victoria lowered her voice and repeated the information for Pete.

"I saw," Pete said. "Everyone got your seatbelts on?" he asked, his voice still calm but raised so they could hear him in the back.

"Yes," Bailey answered. "Is something wrong?"

"Just making sure," Pete answered.

The agents behind them reduced their speed, dropping farther back from the van.

Victoria grabbed a set of binoculars from the glove box and used them to look out the window as the road curved to the right. Two cars back, at the corner edge of the Dodge's passenger window, a glint of sunlight reflected off a gun barrel. A shoulder appeared. Before she could inform Agent Louis, the first shots rang out.

"Keep going! We'll block the road and take care of them!" Agent Louis shouted. "Rose is calling for backup."

Every precaution the agents had taken now proved justified.

"Is someone shooting at us?" Scott asked from the back, unable to see what was happening behind the van.

"We're okay," Victoria answered, running her finger over the edge of her own seatbelt. They'd reached a section of road with guardrails. They couldn't pass or drive off the road. They could only move forward.

Behind them, Agent Rose zigzagged the SUV from one side of the lane to the other so the truck couldn't pass. Agent Louis returned fire at the truck.

As soon as the guard rail ended, panicking drivers escaped the road, driving up onto front lawns and finally leaving open space on the road ahead. Pete accelerated toward an intersection with a green light. As they hit the center of the intersection, Victoria looked left. A truck barreled through the red light, coming straight toward them.

Pete floored the gas and jerked the wheel right. Victoria braced for impact, every muscle tense. Disbelief and this-can't-be-happening thoughts exploded inside her, blocking out all else. The truck smashed the van's back end and forced it into a spin. Pete yanked the wheel, fighting to resume control. The van careened toward a steep embankment. Facing backwards, the vehicle flipped toward the driver's side. Metal crunched as it did a complete rotation and crashed back down on its tires. The jarring motion slammed Pete hard against his window. It whipped Victoria to one side, then the other. Thoughts of Ned and her animals flashed through her mind.

The engine stalled.

Stunned by the crash, Victoria did a quick mental assessment of her body. It was all there. She looked over at Pete. No movement. His head rested against the glass. Blood trailed down his face.

Her ears were ringing, but she heard Scott asking if someone was okay and Agent Louis shouting. She still held her phone, her fingers wrapped tightly around the device in a death grip.

"Victoria! Can you hear me?" Agent Louis shouted again.

"I'm here. A truck hit us." She shuddered, reliving the instant it shot full speed through a red light coming straight toward them. Victoria shook Pete's shoulder. He didn't respond. She unbuckled her seatbelt and then reached to undo Pete's. He groaned. "Pete is unconscious," she said.

"Hold tight," Agent Louis said. "We're dealing with the men who were tailing us. But there's backup coming."

Blood streamed from Victoria's nose and into her mouth. She pressed the back of her forearm under her nostrils to stop the flow. The ringing in her ears persisted as she struggled to clear her jumbled thoughts. Someone had given their location away to those who wanted the Redmond family dead. She couldn't wait for whoever it was to finish the job. They had to get out of there. She turned and glimpsed Bailey's shocked expression and Scott hunched over his mother, his hands on her shoulders. "Is everyone okay?" Victoria asked.

"Yes," Scott answered. "I think so."

She moved toward the driver's side and tried to tug Pete out from behind the wheel.

"I'll help." Scott reached for the door handle.

"Don't get out of the van!" Victoria shouted. "Don't anyone get out!"

Scott let go of the door. Crouching behind the driver's seat, he helped pull Pete into the back.

"Can you help him?" Victoria asked as she scrambled into the driver's seat. She put the car into park, stretched her leg out straight to reach the brake, had to push the binoculars out of the way with her foot, and pressed the ignition button. The engine didn't start. She tried again. It wasn't turning over.

254

From her position, she couldn't tell if anyone was coming toward them. She moved to the front edge of the seat and swiveled around, craning her neck.

Two figures stood at the top of the embankment amidst a patch of tall trees. She couldn't see them clearly, and what she thought she saw made little sense. She grabbed the binoculars from the floor, raised them to her eyes, and looked again.

Both men were around six feet tall and carried semi-automatic weapons. They wore jeans, leather jackets, and frightening masks—pale monster's faces with giant bloodshot eyes and two twisted horns protruding from the tops of their heads. They stood holding their weapons and looking in the direction of the FBI vehicle. Their bullets couldn't penetrate the armored van. But...if someone on the inside had given the van's location away, they would have also informed those men the vehicle was bulletproof. And if the van didn't move, if the passengers remained inside, the cartel might have already planned another way to force the Redmonds out. A sharp shiver jolted through Victoria as she imagined the gas tank going up in flames.

She scanned her surroundings. A one-story brick structure sat about thirty yards away. If the masked men got much closer, the passengers wouldn't have enough time to make it safely there. Risks existed regardless of the choice she made, and she would not allow indecision to determine their fate. Bailey and Scott were runners, but what about Mrs. Redmond? "Can everyone run?" Victoria asked, looking directly at Scott's mother.

Mrs. Redmond nodded.

"Can you carry Pete?" Victoria asked Scott.

Pete moaned as Scott said, "Yes, I've got him."

"I'm going first," Victoria said. "Wait for my signal, then get out and race for that house while keeping the vehicle behind you. Do any of you know how to use a gun?"

"I do," Bailey said.

"Take Pete's gun. If something should happen to me and the other agents, you might have to use it." Victoria met Bailey's gaze. Bailey nodded.

Taking a deep breath, Victoria slid the van's door open and jumped out, gripping her weapon. Adrenaline made her heartrate soar.

The masked men still hadn't come any closer. They remained atop the embankment, mostly concealed by trees. What were they waiting for? Reinforcements? She wouldn't stay there to find out.

"Go!" she hissed into the open door. "As fast as you can." The Redmonds would have coverage from the vehicle for the first several yards. She would protect them the rest of the way.

Bailey ran by Mrs. Redmond's side. Pete was coming to. Scott got him to his feet and hurried away with the man's arm around his shoulder.

Victoria waited until the van no longer shielded them from the masked men on the embankment. She fired her weapon from behind the van's back corner.

One masked man returned fire in her direction. The other fired at the Redmonds, spraying bullets in a wide swath.

A woman let out a shocked scream behind her. What had happened? Was it Mrs. Redmond or Bailey? Victoria couldn't turn around to look. She had to keep her weapon and eyes trained on the approaching men.

One masked man stepped out from behind a tree. Victoria aimed and fired. His hand flew to his neck and within seconds, he had fallen to the ground.

The other assailant continued firing. If he stayed in his position, sheltered by a large tree, and Victoria remained behind the van, she couldn't get a good shot. She had to get a better angle. Exposing herself seemed akin to suicide, but if she didn't stop the shooter, he would move on to his intended targets. She took a deep breath and sprinted toward a junked tractor. Gunfire cracked and thumped like the grand finale of a firework display. Bullets ricocheted off the ground, zinged off a discarded riding mower, and buzzed right over her head. Racing low to the ground, Victoria tucked her chin and put everything she had into reaching the tractor before a bullet found her. From a few yards distance, she dove behind it, and flew into the air. She hit the frozen ground hard and slid. Something pierced her shirt and dug into her side. She jumped up to take a shot before she lost her chance. That's when she realized the shooting had stopped. The man's gun faced skyward. He dropped it, clutched his chest, and sank to his knees. Finally, he crumbled to the ground face first.

Victoria didn't think she'd hit him, but someone had. A few more seconds of watching to make sure he didn't move, and she turned to check on the Redmonds. Where she expected to see them, Pete stood alone. Holding a weapon, he watched the embankment behind Victoria.

"Thank God you recovered, Pete! Thank you!" she said.

"I wouldn't have had that shot if you hadn't forced him to move," he said.

"I heard a scream. Did someone get hit?" she asked.

He nodded.

"Who?"

"Bailey."

"Oh, no. No. No. Where are they?"

"On the other side of the building. Go," Pete said, looking at her strangely. "Get inside with them."

With a sharp sting on her side, Victoria jogged around the side and saw Bailey, Scott, and his mother standing against the brick wall. Bailey was on her feet. No signs of blood.

The building wasn't much, but they would be better off inside it. A broken window suggested previous tenants abandoned the property.

Victoria tried the door first. It didn't open. She pulled off her coat, wrapped it around her fist, and smashed through a glass pane. She reached through the broken glass and unlocked the door. "Get inside," she said.

Bailey limped inside with Scott holding her arm. Victoria directed them to an inner room so that multiple walls separated them from the outside. Once they were all in, she turned her attention to Bailey. "Did you get shot?"

Bailey did the one thing Victoria least expected. She laughed.

"My fake leg," she said, as she wiped debris off her clothes. "Of all places to hit—" Her expression changed as she studied Victoria. "Oh, my God. Are you shot? There's blood all over your face." Her gaze moved to Victoria's side. "And there."

Victoria wiped at her nose again and realized blood had already soaked her shirt sleeve. One side of her torso was also bleeding where a piece of junk from behind the tractor had pierced her skin. "I'm fine," she said, although she wasn't sure. Adrenaline had her too hyped to register if she'd gotten seriously hurt or not.

"Let me see your side," Scott said.

"Not now," Victoria snapped. She stood in the doorway with the Redmonds behind her, her weapon ready. They weren't out of danger yet. Somehow, the cartel knew the Redmonds' location on the route to D.C. Was it Agent Louis? Agent Rose? Or the agents driving the vehicle with Jules and Mr. Redmond? It couldn't have been Pete. He'd killed one of the masked men and probably saved her life.

Minutes later, the back door opened with a rusty creak. Someone approached.

"It's me, Pete." He carried a first-aid kit he must have retrieved from the van. "A helicopter is coming to take everyone out of here."

"What about my father and Jules?" Scott asked. "Are they okay?"

"They're fine," Agent Rose said. "Still on their way to D.C."

"And the men who were shooting at us?" Bailey asked.

"They're gone," Pete answered. "Dead."

"Are you sure?" Scott asked. "Should I check on them?"

"Positive. A witness said they were the men from the truck that hit us. I took pictures of their faces and I want you to see if you recognize them. But check Victoria first."

Scott turned to Victoria. "Here, sit down."

Victoria let him help her into an old wooden chair. Suddenly, her skin felt clammy. Her sodden shirt clung to her side.

"Helicopter is only a few minutes out," Pete said.

Scott used something from the first-aid kit and applied pressure to Victoria's wound. He mopped up the blood and poured something on it that stung like crazy, then applied pressure again. "We need to get you stitched up. You're going to need a tetanus shot if you haven't had one recently. Can you hold this here and press down?"

Victoria switched her weapon to her other hand and pressed her free one against her side as Scott moved his hand away. She felt light-headed as Pete showed everyone his phone with the pictures he'd taken of the shooters. "Do any of you recognize them?" he asked.

"I do," Scott said as he stared at the images of the criminals without their masks. "They were in the house where the cartel held me hostage. The first is one of my captors. I don't know his name.

259

I thought of him as Pockmarked. And the second is Tommy. He was one of my patients."

Pete leaned close and whispered to Victoria. "Jules made a call from her burner phone before the crash. We think she might be the one who gave our location away."

"What?" Victoria whispered back, completely shocked. "But how did she…." Then she remembered giving a location update to the agents who were driving Jules and her father. *We're eleven miles behind you.* They might have shared it with her. "Who would do that to their own family?"

Victoria heard the first faint rumblings of the helicopter. Still brandishing her weapon, she got up and went outside with the others. The helicopter lowered to the ground, its propeller stirring up debris and decaying leaves into a swirling frenzy around them.

Within seconds of landing, they loaded the Redmonds into the helicopter. The agents followed. Still wired and shaking, Victoria took a seat. Her nose throbbed, spreading pain between her eyes and across her forehead. Her side ached with a raw intensity, as if a wild animal had pierced her skin with sharp claws.

As the helicopter lifted into the air, she took a shuddering breath and closed her eyes.

CHAPTER 34

On her way down the corridor, Victoria ran into Rivera.

"Hey, I've been calling you to see how you're doing," he said as he studied her face.

"I know…things have just been crazy. Thanks. I'm good." She knew how awful she looked with her bandaged nose, but she didn't know how it broke. Her doctor said it would be fine once the swelling went down. The black circles around her eyes would soon disappear. And she hoped her head would stop pounding before the end of the day. Same thing she'd wished for yesterday. The stitches in her side would dissolve on their own over the next three weeks, leaving her with a nasty scar, but otherwise all in one piece. She'd never been comfortable wearing a bikini anyway. Once she healed, the wound wouldn't matter much.

"Jeez, I'll never be able to stop worrying about you, will I?" Rivera's voice was full of concern, maybe sadness, and he wasn't joking.

She wasn't sure what his comment was supposed to mean. "You don't have to worry about me. I'm fine. I have to go, Murphy called me into a meeting."

He stepped aside to let her pass. She could tell he was still watching her as she walked by him, down the hall, and into the crowded conference room.

Murphy and Payton stood and applauded her.

Still clapping, Murphy addressed the others around the table. "This is Agent Victoria Heslin. The agent who brought us this case." He turned to face her and smiled. "Congratulations on surviving a shootout. And here I was waiting to put you back out into the field."

Victoria preferred not to think about the shootout and the man she killed. She was grateful all the witnesses and FBI agents survived. Jules faced additional charges, now that they confirmed she'd called the cartel and given her family's location away. Victoria still couldn't imagine what possessed Jules to do such a thing.

Murphy crossed the room and slapped Victoria on the shoulder. The gesture wasn't surprising. Murphy had a habit of slapping backs and shoulders, despite a warning from HR. Victoria didn't mind, but this time it made her wince. The accident had happened in mere seconds, yet left her sore all over.

"I'm sure you've met Alexis Scope, the district attorney," Murphy said. "And this is the rest of her team."

"Yes, hello," Victoria said, aware of their collective gaze on her nose.

"Have a seat and you can listen in." Murphy gestured to an empty chair. He seemed in a good mood. The investigation must be going well.

Victoria settled in to listen to the progress the task force had made with the audit on Redmond Galleries and after having spent two days collecting testimonies from the Redmonds and Duncan Simpson. They were building a solid case against the Salazar cartel. Already they'd assembled enough indisputable evidence to make arrests for money laundering, wire fraud, and several other criminal charges.

"Excuse me," Victoria said, after the DA summarized the charges. "No one mentioned Scott Redmond's testimony. Are the prosecutors including an abduction and hostage taking charge?"

"No," the district attorney answered. "We won't be using Scott Redmond's testimony."

This surprised Victoria. "Why not?" she asked.

"Unfortunately, he told too many people he suffered a dissociative event. It's on record with the Boston police. The cartel's attorneys will make him into an unreliable witness. A liar. They'll say he's fabricating the abduction story now that it's convenient, to get out of ditching his bride the day before the wedding."

"You don't think his story is credible?"

"We believe him, but he has no proof."

"That's a shame," Victoria said. "What about evidence from Richard Luna or anything related to the gunshot victims from the Boston warehouse?"

"We brought Luna in for questioning. He had an excellent attorney representing him, and neither of them were talking. And without Scott's testimony, we don't have enough to link Luna to any of this right now. In the grand scheme of things, the kidnapping is one of many crimes they've committed that we have to overlook, at least for now. We have enough solid evidence of other crimes to focus on."

***

Victoria went from the conference room to an empty office to give Detective Suarez a courtesy call with an update.

After telling Suarez about the planned arrests, Victoria added, "They aren't going to arrest Luna." She knew the news would disappoint the detective. Suarez was eager to see him put behind bars.

"Why doesn't that surprise me?" Suarez said with a snort. "He wouldn't be of any use to their trial, anyway. He'd never flip on his bosses. He'd just spend time in prison with their protection. I almost have to admire his loyalty, even if it's misplaced."

"Is it really loyalty if it's driven by fear and self-preservation?" Victoria asked. She'd been thinking a lot about things like that lately. She wanted to have more compassion for the Redmonds and what they'd gotten themselves into. She wanted to believe self-preservation and fear were their motivating factors, rather than greed or stupidity.

"I don't know," Suarez answered. "Is that what the Redmonds are saying in their defense?"

"Yes, they are."

Officer Suarez scoffed.

"Oh, one more thing," Victoria said. "Our agents are raiding Eduardo Salazar's last known location as we speak."

***

The first of two FBI vehicles stopped at the gate to the mansion, Salazar's last known location. "This is the FBI with an arrest warrant for Eduardo Salazar and a warrant to search the estate," Agent Rose said into a speaker. Her heart pounded a steady, fast beat she could suddenly feel in her neck. She wiped her sweaty palms on her pants legs as they waited for a response. She didn't want to die today. Salazar usually dealt with authorities in a civilized manner, relying on his attorneys to clear his name. But after the shootout on the way to D.C., she was prepared for a violent encounter.

The gate opened.

The Feds drove through and stopped in the circular, gravel drive directly in front of the mansion.

Men with guns stood on the mansion's front terrace.

The agents got out of the cars. "Put your weapons aside, gentlemen. This is not the time for heroics," Agent Louis told the guards.

With looks that could kill, the guards set their weapons down

"Stand over there where we can see you." Agent Rose pointed to the wall.

They cooperated again, moving toward the side of the building. Agent Rose prayed that's how everything would go.

Agent Rashid Usman stayed outside to keep an eye on the guards while the others entered the mansion with their guns drawn. Agent Rose still expected trouble.

When she walked through the kitchen, two women wearing maid's uniforms stopped preparing a meal and set their hands on the granite counters, avoiding eye contact.

"Where is Salazar?" Agent Louis asked.

Neither woman answered.

"Is he in the house?" he asked again.

Again, no response.

Agent Rose spoke next. "Outside?"

A maid dipped her chin in a gesture that could have easily gone unnoticed if Rose wasn't watching carefully.

"Go somewhere safe and wait," Agent Rose told them, still wary things could suddenly get wild.

The women hurried from the kitchen.

Agent Rose and Agent Louis walked through the mansion toward the back of the house. Rose was keenly aware that if they let their guards down for the slightest second, their next breath could be their last.

In a center room, on a giant television screen, a lifelike character in a leather jacket silently sprayed bullets at a flying zombie who leapt out from behind a dumpster. A lanky teen sat on the modern sectional sofa with his feet up on a distressed-wood coffee table. Wearing headphones, he stared at the screen without blinking. His index fingers and thumbs moved feverishly over the buttons of a gamepad. He didn't notice the agents enter the room.

Agent Rose stepped right in front of him. "Who are you?" she asked.

"What the hell! Get out of the way!" He jumped to his feet and edged around her, fingers still moving over the gamepad at a frantic pace. With the headphones on, his voice was so much louder than necessary.

Agent Louis snatched them off the kid's head and said, "FBI. What are you doing here?"

"Nothing. Visiting."

"This isn't a place for a kid to be hanging out," Agent Louis said.

The teen's face was smug as he shot back, "I'm not a kid. I'm an employee."

"Find another job," Agent Rose said. "I hear they're hiring at McDonalds. Get out of here and don't come back."

The teen took a last look at the screen, where his avatar lay in a crumpled, dead heap. He shrugged, unplugged the gamepad, and took it with him as he left the room.

The agents continued through the house and out the back door. The backyard extended for acres into manicured gardens and what looked like a vineyard with trellises. To one side of a large terrace, Eduardo Salazar smoked a cigar in a hot tub between two beautiful women. The tub's jets bubbled noisily.

The women looked uncertain.

"Get out and stand against the wall," Agent Louis said.

The women hurried out of the hot tub wearing tiny bikinis. Definitely not hiding weapons anywhere. They grabbed towels hanging nearby and stood against the wall, already shivering in the cold air.

"Eduardo Salazar, you're under arrest for money laundering, drug trafficking, and crimes against the public trust," Agent Louis said.

Salazar leaned back against the hot tub and continued puffing on his cigar. "This is a King of Denmark. I'm sure you understand that it must not go to waste, and I intend to finish it before I join you."

"Put the cigar down and get your ass out of there," Rose said, holding up handcuffs.

"Those won't be necessary. I have no intention of letting things get ugly here," Salazar said.

They threw him a towel. He held it in one hand as he stubbed out his cigar in a nearby ashtray then tossed it into the bushes. Dripping wet, he walked across the patio appearing to be immune to the cold.

"Get him some clothes," Rose told one of the women, who rushed out of sight. Rose turned off the hot tub. The jets ceased running and silenced.

When his clothes arrived, Salazar pulled off his bathing suit and got dressed in front of them. He seemed to enjoy exposing himself to Agent Rose.

Agent Louis handcuffed him and led him through the house.

"Have my attorney figure out where they're taking me and meet me there," Salazar said calmly to one of his men as the FBI escorted him outside. "And tell the chef I want prime rib tonight."

Rose was grateful no gunfire led up to the arrest, but it angered her to see Salazar so cool and collected. As if his arrest was a mere annoyance, an interruption of his fancy cigar and a quick trip away from his mansion before his lawyer would probably drive him back later in the day. She hoped the prosecutors working on the case had what they needed to keep him behind bars. It was personal for her. Not only was the cartel responsible for drugs and violence and death and fear…but if the hitmen he'd sent to take out the Redmonds had done their jobs, she and Agent Louis would be in caskets at their own funerals right now.

An agent tucked Salazar in the back of an FBI vehicle and drove off, leaving Agents Rose and Louis and two other Feds behind to search the rest of the house.

"There's enough art here to start a museum," Agent Rose said, rolling up a large rug to search for a hidden tunnel or storage area.

Agent Louis found the door to the basement. "Let's head down here first."

Rose flipped her headlamp on and headed down the stairs with caution, her gun held in front of her, still ready to fire on anyone who might try to surprise them.

They cleared the dank basement and made sure there were no secret tunnels. Agent Louis turned on the single overhead bulb. It helped little. He aimed his headlamp at the walls. "What's this over here?" He moved his light beam over the faint scrawlings.

"I think it's Arabic. We need to get Agent Usman down here." Rose spoke into her walkie. "Rashid, we need your linguistic skills in the dungeon. It's the door in the center of that main room with the fireplace."

A minute later, Agent Usman, who could read, write, and speak five Arabic languages, clomped down the stairs. "What did you find?"

The agents pointed to the writing. "You tell us."

THE GROOM WENT MISSING

Agent Usman peered through his glasses. "It's Arabic. And at the end, it says, Scott loves Bales, forever. Scott was the doctor who said he was captive here, right? The one you two escorted to D.C.?"

"Yes," Rose answered. "What else does it say?"

"The guy wrote about everything that happened while he was here. Names. Dates. Everything. If they had any idea what it said, they would have made the effort to wash the walls." Agent Usman took out his phone and started taking pictures. "The DA is going to love this. The cartel is busted."

***

Victoria poured herself a glass of wine and joined Ned on the back patio where he sat by the fire pit, peeling the label off his beer.

"Hey," he said.

"Hey."

"You know, I still haven't heard directly from Scott and Bailey. Or Jules. Not since she told me about Redmond Galleries being audited." He studied Victoria's face, searching for answers. "No one has. It's like Scott came back and then his whole family disappeared. What happened?"

Victoria shook her head.

"Scott missing his wedding is linked to that audit of Redmond Galleries and what happened to you—the broken nose and stitches—isn't it?" Ned stared out at the mountain tops, then back to Victoria. "Do you know where they are?"

"No. Even I don't."

"Are they alive? Can you tell me that much?"

"They're okay. They're safe. That's all I can say. But you might never see them again. I can imagine how maddening this is for you, but you have to accept that's all I can tell you." If their

269

criminal activities came out during the trial, then Ned and everyone else would know more.

"Scott was my best friend. They were like family to me. What the hell?" Ned leaned forward and dropped his head into his hands.

Victoria watched him quietly, giving him time to process the news. Finally, he looked up again.

"I want to apologize," she said. "I'm sorry I didn't believe you at first, when you were so certain something happened to Scott. It's now obvious that it did. It's just, I've seen so much of people behaving badly, selfishly, and combined with the evidence, that's where I went with this. I was wrong."

"I'm glad you can admit when you're wrong. And I sure wish I knew what made you realize you're wrong now."

She offered him a sad smile before taking a sip of her wine. "You were right on with your best man speech. Scott really is all the things that you said."

Ned took a deep breath and rotated his beer bottle around in his hands. Victoria admired his patience and self-restraint. In fact, it amazed her. He needed to know what happened. He also understood and accepted she couldn't tell him.

"That came for us today." He tilted his head toward a large box leaning against the wall.

"For us?"

"Yes. Delivered to the gate earlier today."

She walked to the box and slid a framed picture from the open end. The backing faced her. She turned it around to see the front. A variety of colors, but primarily blue, splashed across the canvas, each shaped like torn scraps of paper. She'd seen an image of it on Ned's phone. "This is the painting the Redmonds gave Scott and Bailey for their wedding present, isn't it?"

"Yep. It came with a note thanking us for our help and friendship. It said you might not be allowed to accept it, but I could."

Victoria didn't know what to think or say about the painting and she wasn't sure if they could keep it or not. Instead, she wanted to tell him that just before the impact in the car crash, it was he who had flashed into her mind. Well...him and the dogs. But she couldn't tell him about the crash or the shootout that followed. And even if she could, she wouldn't. It was an unusual occurrence, something that may never happen again, and she didn't want him worrying about her every time she went to work. He'd been so concerned about her injuries. And yet he'd respected her silence on the matter.

Again...amazing.

She hated keeping secrets from him. She wanted...no, she needed him to know how much he meant to her. "Are we okay?" she asked. If they weren't, she wanted them to get there.

Ned tilted his head. "We're okay. That's not something you need to worry about. Couples can argue and disagree. They can even disappoint and hurt each other. That's life. We forgive. We learn. When we move on, we're a little more bonded because of the trouble. Don't you think?"

She moved next to him and took his hand. "I like that way of looking at it. And I like us being more bonded. I like it a lot. It's a good thing."

"It is. But no more getaways for a while, okay? Does that sound good?"

Victoria made a face. "Um...actually...define 'a while.' Because my brother and Minka pushed their wedding date up. May 10th in Colorado. He called and asked me to be a bridesmaid. I was hoping you would be my date."

Ned smiled, shook his head, and laughed. "Yes. You better not be asking anyone else to be your date. It's going to be great just as long as it's nothing like the last wedding."

"It won't be. I'll personally provide Alex with an armed escort to the ceremony, if that's what it takes."

Ned got up. He brushed her hair away from her face, then took her into his arms. His kiss was sweet and intense. After a short while, just as she was melting into his embrace and forgetting all else, he straightened. Still holding her, he stared into her eyes. "I haven't said it yet, but I've definitely been thinking about it for a long while. A very long while." He leaned closer until mere inches separated them. "I love you, Victoria."

His words warmed her heart. She didn't expect they would have such an effect on her, but they did. She loved hearing them. She wanted to hear them again and again. And it felt right saying it back to him. "I love you too, Ned."

THE END

Want to read about Victoria's next investigation? The following is an excerpt from *Vanished on Vacation.*

VANISHED ON VACATION EXCERPT

PROLOGUE

Under the night sky, the vast ocean appeared inky black at every depth.

The perfect place to hide a body.

But they didn't always stay hidden.

The mutilated corpse floated face down in the water, hands secured together in back with yellow nylon rope, long hair twisting with seaweed tendrils in the rolling waves. A slight pull back to the horizon followed each movement toward shore. With practiced patience, the current's rhythm persisted. In no rush but determined to deliver the body home.

CHAPTER 1

    The first two days of the vacation passed in a blur of sun, sand, frozen tropical drinks, and dancing into the early morning hours. With only one night remaining, Avery Jennings planned to relish every minute. Tomorrow morning, she and her friends had to wake up crazy early to catch the first flight back to Virginia. They'd be hungover but sun-kissed and ready to embrace the final weeks of their college senior year.

    Wearing her workout clothes, Avery tied up her shoelaces, tucked her water bottle into her bag, and headed for the door. Before she got there, it swung open and her friend Brie burst inside, waving a piece of paper through the air then holding it against her bikini top. "I'm negative! Yes!" Brie shouted.

    Of the three friends, Brie had been the most anxious about testing positive for Covid and getting stuck in Mexico. She had two job interviews lined up for the following week and didn't want to miss them.

    "Whew. I can finally relax now that I've got this." Brie slapped the paper down on the desk. "I love it here, but…you know…I have to get home. And if I don't have Covid, then none of us should."

    Brie took out her phone and typed away. A second later, a new text popped up in the *Azure Cove Babes* group chat on

Avery's phone. It said, *Negative Covid Test!* followed by heart and smiley face emojis.

"I'm totally going to party now," Brie said, opening the closet and removing a silk pouch from under a pile of folded clothes. She uncinched the pouch and shook out colored pills. Some mint green, some white. "Want one?"

"No, thanks." Avery wasn't even tempted. "Where did you get your test result?"

"At the registration counter. We need the paper to get through Customs. I tried to get all of ours when I was there. They wouldn't let me. Confidentiality and all that."

As much as Avery wanted the reassurance her negative test result would bring, the reception desk was in the opposite direction from the exercise area where they held the group classes. "I'll get mine after Zumba," Avery said before waving goodbye to Brie.

Walking across the beautiful resort on a path lined by lush flowers and palm trees, Avery cringed as she thought about her recent nasal swab. It had been unnecessarily brutal. She'd taken countless tests by now. Random selection tests throughout the school year, and almost every time one of her good friends had tested positive. Another test when she was so sick, she couldn't get out of bed for two days, which ended up only being the flu. Yet none of those compared to her experience yesterday in the resort's health office. The woman administering it stuck the swab so far up Avery's nose, she was certain it pierced her brain. If that wasn't bad enough, the woman twirled the swab around for what seemed like forever. It was almost as if she was desperate to find a trace of the virus and keep people from leaving. Avery stumbled out of the health office with tears in her eyes. Thank God that was behind her.

As she neared the water sports pavilion, the launch area for the sailboats, paddle boards, and kayaks, she slowed to a stroll. The young men who worked at the resort were handsome and charming and they knew it, but none of them caught her attention like Henri, a hottie from France with piercing blue eyes who worked at the pavilion. When he flashed his sweet and seemingly shy smile, Avery almost forgot about her no-random-hookups rule. On her second paddleboard excursion, Henri had carried her board down to the water and given her some pointers, totally flirting with her. Flirting was okay. And maybe it wouldn't hurt to kiss him later that night.

Under a huge gazebo next to the paddleboards, the Australian woman with long blonde hair and an impossibly tight, tan body—Avery couldn't remember her name—was handing out life jackets to a pale-skinned couple.

Avery's gaze moved to the sailboats by the water. They looked picture perfect against the blue sky with *Azure Cove* stitched into their brightly colored sails. There was no sign of Henri there, and she hadn't seen him earlier in the day either. Perhaps Sunday was his day off. Huge bummer.

Avery pushed aside her disappointment and continued to the outdoor exercise area where she joined other women in sports bras, tiny shorts, and even bikinis, and a guy wearing a hoodie, despite the heat. Some of their faces were now familiar, including Teresa, who attended the exercise class every day. Teresa stood dead center in the front, only a few feet away from the instructor, and kept up with the dance moves well, considering she had to be at least seventy-five years old and didn't weigh much more than her age. Maybe she'd been a dancer when she was younger. As much as Avery admired the woman, Teresa also acted like she owned the place and could boss everyone around. With this being Avery's last day, she didn't want any more trouble from anyone. She made a point of finding a spot on the floor as far from Teresa as possible.

For the next forty-five minutes, Avery danced along to energizing music, following Nicole, an instructor from Brazil whose hips could move in ways most people's, including Avery's, never would. The fun outdoor class was exactly what she needed to sweat the alcohol out of her system and detox before they started drinking again.

When the class ended, Avery dabbed her face with a towel, swigged from her water bottle, and headed back to her room thinking about how to make the most of the evening. She still had to try the Dirty Monkey cocktail Haley raved about, bananas and chocolate and three different liquors, and the Caribbean Rum Punch Brie swore was her favorite. But first a shower, maybe a quick power nap, and then dinner.

A resort employee wearing the light blue uniform shirt walked toward her on the path. Impressive muscles bulged from his arms and under his tight shirt. He stared at her for longer than normal.

"Hey." She offered a smile. The guests didn't have to wear their masks outside, but the staff wore them everywhere. Even with masks, a slight crinkling of the skin beside the eyes usually indicated a smile. If this man had smiled back at her, it didn't show. Feeling a little uncomfortable, Avery looked away.

"Avery Jennings?" the man asked.

"Yes."

He stopped in front of her, blocking the path. "I was looking for you."

"Why? What's wrong?"

"Uh, sorry to tell you this. Your Covid test came back positive."

Avery felt blood drain from her face. "Are you serious?"

"Yes. It could be a false positive. We'll do another test for you."

"I...yeah, let me take another test. Because I'm vaccinated and boosted. And my friend, one of the girls I'm with, she already got her test result back and it was negative."

v

"We always retest. But first you'll need to get your belongings. If the second test comes back positive, you'll have to go to our quarantine area."

Avery wiped away a single tear as they walked to her room. False negatives weren't uncommon, but false positives were rare. She didn't have any Covid symptoms—no cough, runny nose, sore throat, nor fever—but she suddenly felt sick to her stomach. She'd known this might happen and she'd mentally prepared for it, but it still rocked her world and it scared her that she was no longer in control of her plans or her life. She might be stuck in Mexico while her friends got to go home.

As she followed the employee back to her room, she sent a message on the group text. *OMG! Positive test!* followed by a long line of crying face emojis.

CHAPTER 2

Working on a fishing trawler in the Pacific for a few months had sounded a lot cooler than it was in real life. After only two days toiling and sweating like crazy on the bare-bones ship, Trevor's whole body ached. He had thought he was tough and the muscles he was sure to develop would look great under deeply tanned skin, proof of his awesome experience. Instead, he'd gotten the worst sunburn of his life. His mother hadn't helped one bit when they finally had cell service and he called her. She reminded him his grandfather had died from skin cancer after having lots of disgusting lesions removed from his face and shoulders.

The captain and the other crew members had a good laugh about the zinc oxide Trevor slathered over his peeling nose. He didn't care. He was going to quit this awful job as soon as they returned to shore. This filthy drudgery was not for him. McDonalds and Wendy's seemed more appealing now. They had air-conditioning and scheduled breaks.

With a cigarette hanging from one side of his mouth, and the sun still baking his skin, Trevor cranked the winch around. The heavy fishing net rose out of the ocean with a shrieking grind of metal. Sargassum, a brown seaweed, dangled from every haul, and this one was no exception. Trevor could also count on a surprise or two. Yesterday he'd reeled in a squid. It wasn't Squid-versus-

Godzilla sized, but it was freaky enough to provide a few much-needed minutes of entertainment on the ship.

Trevor scanned the haul. Within the confines of the slimy ropes, brown and silver fish thrashed around a red piece of something large. Really large.

He guided the net into place and pressed a button to release its contents over a giant trough.

The slithering fish tumbled out. And with them...a girl.

Trevor froze.

The girl wore a red shirt and nothing else. The shirt was twisted around her torso, exposing one breast. She looked like she could have been Trevor's age, though he wasn't sure how he knew that. Her body was crumpled into a grotesque form beneath the writhing fish. She was definitely dead. But that wasn't the worst of it. Her hands were tied together. And something wasn't right with her face. Her ear...

Trevor had just enough time to shout for the ship's captain before vomiting on the deck.

CHAPTER 3

On Monday afternoon, FBI Special Agent Victoria Heslin sat on her back patio with her boyfriend, veterinarian Ned Patterson, and a glass of chardonnay. The glow from the flames in the firepit illuminated his face as he looked out over her expansive property at the long-range mountain views. Ned had the lean build of someone who ran, biked, and swam as often as possible for the sheer joy of it, and Victoria couldn't help but appreciate that. She'd never been preoccupied with looks, her own or anyone else's, but having a boyfriend with granite muscles and not an ounce of body fat made her pay slightly more attention to her own upkeep, lest people think Ned was only interested in her for her inheritance. Thinking about it made her laugh because she knew it couldn't be farther from the truth. She and Ned had too much in common. Nonetheless, Victoria had applied a little gloss to her lips and brushed her hair when she got home from work.

Three of Victoria's greyhounds stood close by, between the heat lamps, their full attention devoted to a platter of cheese and crackers.

"Not for you," she told them as she put her feet up on the ottoman and leaned back against her chair.

"I'm glad you could leave work early," Ned said. "There's something I want to talk to you about."

"Oh. What's that?" She took the first sip of her wine and gave Ned her full attention.

"You."

"What about me?"

"I don't know what happened recently, you know with your nose and your stitched side, since you can't or don't want to tell me—which is fine, I get it—but when I think about you putting yourself in danger...it makes me sick, Victoria. I can't help it. Is there any way you can...you know, not be involved with cases that risk your life?"

"Because you don't think a woman with two black eyes and a broken nose is attractive?" Victoria joked, smiling at him, though she fully understood that's not what he meant. He'd worried more about her job ever since she came home banged up a few weeks ago, the consequences of a shootout that occurred while delivering witnesses from one safe house in Boston to another in D.C. She didn't want Ned to worry, but it was also nice that he cared so much.

Her phone vibrated on the stone edge of the firepit. She hesitated before leaning forward and grabbing it. Murphy's name lit up on the screen. "It's my boss. I better take this." She went inside as she swiped the screen to answer the call. "Hi, Murphy."

"Hey," the FBI Special Agent in Charge answered. "Where are you?"

"In my kitchen. Why? What's up?" she asked, looking around her sparsely furnished home. She was still feeling a little light-hearted because she was home with Ned, though she sensed both her mood and her situation were about to change.

"A twenty-two-year-old woman is missing. Avery Jennings. She was on vacation in Mexico with friends. She tested positive for Covid-19 yesterday, the day before she was supposed to return, which meant she couldn't come back to the States. An employee said he was taking her for another test and possibly to a quarantine area. No one has heard from her since."

"She's only been out of communication for one day?" Victoria asked, thinking aloud.

"Yes. The resort can't find her on their property. She's not responding to any calls or texts, which isn't like her."

"Still, it's only been a day?"

"Yes. Only a day since anyone heard from her," Murphy said. "But there some suspicious circumstances involved. And Avery is Payton's niece."

"Our Payton?" Of course it was their Payton. Same last name. Payton Jennings was the head of the FBI's Financial Crimes Department. She often talked about her niece, Avery, and had recently visited her at the University of Virginia.

"What are the suspicious circumstances?" Victoria asked.

"I'll let Payton fill you in from the beginning, but understandably, she doesn't want to sit idle while more time passes. Anyway, I know the Police Chief there. We worked an international case together and kept in touch. He's going to have a team look for her, and he's invited us to assist in the investigation."

"Oh, okay."

"I've got you booked on a flight to Mexico tonight. You'll arrive in the morning. I'll alert the FBI field office in Mexico and the U.S. Embassy that you're coming."

"Do I need to take a Covid test to get in?" Victoria asked, unsure of the protocol for different countries because policies were constantly changing.

"No. You only need the negative test to get back home. Payton specifically asked me to send you. She's at her brother's house in Virginia right now. My assistant sent you that address, along with your flight information. Can you get over there as soon as possible so you can meet with the family before your flight?"

"Yes. I'll go now. Talk to you soon."

If something had happened to Avery, Victoria knew every minute would matter. The first forty-eight hours of a missing persons investigation were the most critical. With each passing hour, the chances of finding that person decreased.

Victoria checked her email for the Jennings' address, called an Uber, and looked up the weather in Mexico. She grabbed the bag she kept packed for short notice travel and exchanged a heavier-weight suit for a lightweight one. After opening her closet, she changed out of jeans into black pants with a silk t-shirt, an outfit from a design service that sent her a box of professional clothes every few months.

Back in the kitchen, Victoria got out the laminated sheets that listed instructions for watching her animals: their feeding schedules, health issues, medicines, and individual quirks. No sooner had she set them on the counter, she picked them up again. Ned knew what the dogs needed as well as she did by now.

When Victoria returned to the patio carrying her bag, Ned was still nursing his beer. He watched her walk toward him.

"Sorry about the super short notice, but I've got to go," she said, pulling her blonde hair back into a ponytail.

"What did Murphy tell you?" Ned asked.

"Payton's niece is missing in Mexico. She just disappeared from her resort. That's pretty much all I know. I'm not sure when I'll be back, though it shouldn't be more than a few days. Can you take care of the animals, or should I schedule one of the vet techs?"

"I can stay. I'm working three days at the clinic this week. I'll schedule someone to come by if I'm not home by dinner on those days."

"Thank you so much." Victoria really didn't know how she could continue her job without his help. She didn't trust just anyone to properly care for her animals. Leaning down, she planted a kiss on his lips.

"Hold on," Ned said, rising from his seat. "That's not how we say goodbye."

He pulled her into his arms. She felt his strength and something fiercely protective as he kissed her deeply. When they finally separated, he nuzzled her neck for a few more seconds and said, "That's more like it. I love you."

"I love you, too."

That was a very new thing for them—saying I love you. She enjoyed the feelings it gave her. Warm. Hopeful. A little bit lightheaded. All her life, she'd preferred animals to most people, so Ned establishing a firm place deep inside her heart was no small feat.

She smiled up at him. "Don't worry about me. I can take care of myself. Okay?"

"I know you can. And if you want, I won't tell you I'm worried, but I can't stop it from happening. Just send me updates when you can so I know you're okay."

"I will." She kissed him again.

"Because…I don't know what your dogs would do without you." His tone made clear he wasn't just talking about the dogs. "I hope you find Payton's niece."

Victoria said goodbye to each of her dogs, stroking necks and ears, before heading down her driveway to wait for her ride outside the tall iron gate.

When her Uber appeared, she called Payton. The call went straight to voicemail. She was probably making a slew of calls trying to find out what happened to Avery.

Victoria left Payton a message. "It's Victoria. I'm so sorry Avery is missing. Murphy gave me your brother's address. I'll be there in twenty minutes, and I'll head to Mexico later tonight. See you soon."

CHAPTER 4

A horn blared behind Tom Jennings as he swerved into the adjacent lane with mere inches to spare, racing to get home. He wasn't one of those annoying drivers who normally wove in between cars, switching lanes constantly to gain a few extra seconds. Today was different. He wished he'd stayed home and hadn't gone to his office. Faced with impossible decisions, he'd certainly been avoiding it lately. He'd lost investments, slowly at first and then in a cataclysmic avalanche-like fall. He'd finally mustered the courage to tell Jennifer. There was no avoiding that now. The problem wasn't going away. He'd planned to tell her tonight. But that plan changed with Avery's disappearance, which had quickly thrown his other problems into perspective. Hearing from their daughter, making sure she was safe, became priority one. Everything else paled in comparison. They needed to find their daughter, their only child, and get her back to Virginia.

"I just called the resort again and talked to the manager. I told them we still haven't heard from her," Tom said to his sister, speaking through the Tesla's Bluetooth. "They're checking all the rooms again. Supposedly, they're checking everywhere."

"Good," Payton said. "I'm praying she's there, that there's been a misunderstanding and she's just sleeping through all of this."

"But you and I both know that's not Avery," he said. "She's not that...clueless."

"I know. Anyway, the FBI is getting involved. They're sending someone to Mexico tonight. A friend of mine. Victoria Heslin."

"I can't believe this is happening." Tom stared through his windshield, barely registering the traffic. "Are you with Jennifer?"

"Yes. I got to your house about ten minutes ago."

Tom was more worried about Avery than anyone or anything else, but that didn't stop him from being concerned about how his wife was handling the situation. It was fair to say Jennifer micromanaged their lives down to the last details whenever she could. She didn't cope well when events strayed from her own carefully made plans and what most people would consider a perfect life. Her dream house and surrounding weed-free yard. A rewarding job with colleagues who were also friends. Vacations. New cars. And most of all, the child they always wanted. Avery. She turned out to be healthy, intelligent, and a pleasure to be around even through her teen years.

"Is she...how is she?" he asked.

"She's doing all right, considering." Payton lowered her voice, making Tom think his wife must be nearby. "She's anxious for you to get home."

Tom flicked his blinker on as he cut back into the adjacent lane and accelerated. "I'm almost there. I'll see you soon. Thank God you can help us figure this out. Really, thank you, Payton."

"Of course. You know I love Avery just as much as you and Jennifer. It's going to be all right, Tom. I just know it. It has to be. Drive safe and I'll see you soon."

Questions raced through Tom's mind as he maneuvered through the streets in a panicked daze. Later he wouldn't be able to recall making the drive home at all. Could Avery really be in danger? Or was a reasonable explanation lurking somewhere close, about to come to light and wipe out what was quickly turning into any parent's worst nightmare? The weight of guilt added to his mounting fear. If someone had taken Avery—the thought sent a dizzying wave of terror coursing through him—it was his fault. If not for him, she wouldn't have been there. Jennifer hadn't wanted her to go.

"Why can't they go to somewhere nice in Florida?" Jennifer had asked. "Then they wouldn't have to deal with Covid tests to get home. People are getting stuck in foreign countries because they're testing positive before they can leave. It's her last semester of college. I don't want her to miss any of it. And what if she got sick and needed medical help there? I really don't think she should go, Tom. I don't want her to go. I'm saying no."

Jennifer tended to focus on worst-case scenarios and overanalyze things. It often fell to Tom to tell her not to worry. Everything would be okay.

"She should go with her friends and have a great time," he'd said. What he didn't tell Jennifer was that there would be no vacations like that or any others in their future. Not for a long time. Not unless his business made a miraculous recovery.

Jennifer shook her head. "I don't want her to go."

But Tom persisted, running through a checklist of reasons Avery shouldn't miss out on the vacation. "Brie's father is paying for the entire trip. The girls are all vaccinated and boosted. They're young and healthy. She's worked hard. She's already got a great job. She deserves it. It will be fine."

Now it appeared he'd been wrong.

There had to be a misunderstanding. Avery would show up. She had to. Because these things did not happen.

But I'd also never imagined my business could face bankruptcy.

Tom let go of the steering wheel and pressed a hand over his chest, feeling the sharp thump of his heart. He was on an emotional roller coaster and the simple act of pulling air into his lungs seemed a challenge.

Thank goodness for his sister and her FBI connections. Payton would help them navigate the unimaginable.

End of *Vanished on Vacation* excerpt.

ABOUT THE AUTHOR

USA Today bestselling author Jenifer Ruff writes mysteries and medical thrillers in three series: The Agent Victoria Heslin Series, The Brooke Walton Series, and The FBI & CDC Thriller Series.

Jenifer grew up in Massachusetts, has a biology degree from Mount Holyoke College and a Master's in Public Health and Epidemiology from Yale University. Before she discovered her love of writing, she worked in management consulting for PriceWaterhouseCoopers and IBM Business Consulting.

Jenifer lives in Charlotte, NC with her family and a pack of greyhounds. If she's not writing, she's probably out exploring trails with her dogs.

Sign up for her Reader's Newsletter at Jenruff.com and never miss a new release.

NOTE FROM THE AUTHOR

Thank you for reading *The Groom Went Missing* and joining Victoria Heslin on another investigation. I'm so grateful each time someone finds and reads one of my books. If you enjoyed it, please leave a review someplace such as Goodreads, BookBub, Amazon, or similar sites, so I know I'm doing something that works, and so others might discover it as well. Thank you again.

Sincerely,

Jenifer

BOOKS BY JENIFER RUFF

The Agent Victoria Heslin Series
The Numbers Killer
Pretty Little Girls
When They Find Us
Ripple Of Doubt
The Groom Went Missing
Vanished On Vacation
The Atonement Murders

The FBI & CDC Thriller Series
Only Wrong Once
Only One Cure
Only One Wave: The Tsunami Effect

The Brooke Walton Series
Everett
Rothaker
The Intern

Suspense
Lauren's Secret

Made in the USA
Columbia, SC
28 September 2023

23531577R00178